PRAISE FOR THE DCI RYAN MYSTERIES

What newspapers say

"She keeps company with the best mystery writers" – *The Times*

"LJ Ross is the queen of Kindle" – *Sunday Telegraph*

"*Holy Island* is a blockbuster" – *Daily Express*

"A literary phenomenon" – *Evening Chronicle*

"A pacey, enthralling read" – *Independent*

What readers say

"I couldn't put it down. I think the full series will cause a divorce, but it will be worth it."

"I gave this book 5 stars because there's no option for 100."

"Thank you, LJ Ross, for the best two hours of my life."

"This book has more twists than a demented corkscrew."

"Another masterpiece in the series. The DCI Ryan mysteries are superb, with very realistic characters and wonderful plots. They are a joy to read!"

Also by LJ Ross

THE DCI RYAN MYSTERIES

1. *Holy Island*
2. *Sycamore Gap*
3. *Heavenfield*
4. *Angel*
5. *High Force*
6. *Cragside*
7. *Dark Skies*
8. *Seven Bridges*
9. *The Hermitage*
10. *Longstone*
11. *The Infirmary (Prequel)*
12. *The Moor*
13. *Penshaw*
14. *Borderlands*
15. *Ryan's Christmas*
16. *The Shrine*
17. *Cuthbert's Way*
18. *The Rock*
19. *Bamburgh*
20. *Lady's Well*
21. *Death Rocks*
22. *Poison Garden*
23. *Belsay*
24. *Berwick*

THE ALEXANDER GREGORY THRILLERS

1. *Impostor*
2. *Hysteria*
3. *Bedlam*
4. *Mania*
5. *Panic*
6. *Amnesia*
7. *Obsession*

THE SUMMER SUSPENSE MYSTERIES

1. *The Cove*
2. *The Creek*
3. *The Bay*
4. *The Haven*

LADY'S WELL

A DCI RYAN MYSTERY

LADY'S WELL

A DCI RYAN MYSTERY

LJ ROSS

PENGUIN BOOKS

PENGUIN BOOKS

UK | USA | Canada | Ireland | Australia
India | New Zealand | South Africa

Penguin Books is part of the Penguin Random House group of companies
whose addresses can be found at global.penguinrandomhouse.com

Penguin Random House UK,
One Embassy Gardens, 8 Viaduct Gardens, London SW11 7BW

penguin.co.uk

First published by LJ Ross 2023
Published in Penguin Books 2026
001

Copyright © LJ Ross, 2023
Cover artwork and map by Andrew Davidson
Cover layout by Riverside Publishing Solutions Limited

The moral right of the author has been asserted

Penguin Random House values and supports copyright. Copyright fuels creativity, encourages diverse voices, promotes freedom of expression and supports a vibrant culture. Thank you for purchasing an authorised edition of this book and for respecting intellectual property laws by not reproducing, scanning or distributing any part of it by any means without permission. You are supporting authors and enabling Penguin Random House to continue to publish books for everyone. No part of this book may be used or reproduced in any manner for the purpose of training artificial intelligence technologies or systems. In accordance with Article 4(3) of the DSM Directive 2019/790, Penguin Random House expressly reserves this work from the text and data mining exception.

Typeset by Riverside Publishing Solutions Limited

Printed and bound in Great Britain by Clays Ltd, Elcograf S.p.A.

The authorised representative in the EEA is Penguin Random House Ireland,
Morrison Chambers, 32 Nassau Street, Dublin D02 YH68

A CIP catalogue record for this book is available from the British Library

ISBN: 978–1–804–96034–9

Penguin Random House is committed to a sustainable future
for our business, our readers and our planet. This book is made
from Forest Stewardship Council® certified paper.

On Hallowmas Eve, ere ye boune to rest,
Ever beware that your couch be blest;
Sign it with cross and sain it with bread,
Sing the Ave and the Creed.
For on Hallowmas Eve, the Night Hag shall ride
And all her nine-fold sweeping on by Her side,
Whether the wind sing lowly or loud,
Stealing through moonshine or swathed in cloud.
He that dare sit in St. Swithin's Chair,
When the Night Hag wings the troubled air,
Questions three, when he speaks the spell,
He must ask and She must tell.

—Sir Walter Scott

PROLOGUE

Holystone village, Northumberland

Twenty years ago

The woman lay on a bed of autumn leaves, her spine shattered beyond repair.

"This was your fault."

She heard their voice as if through water; dim and distorted, the words garbled. They continued to talk, muttering as they paced around her body, and the physical pain began to recede. Her conscious mind went with it, floating from her body to enter that 'Otherworld' she'd heard people speak of.

Was this it? she wondered. *Was this death?*

"Look at me while I'm talking to you."

The blow to her head had caused an enormous clot to form at the base of her skull, so she couldn't have moved nor controlled the direction of her gaze, even if she'd wanted to. All she could do was emit a long, guttural moan.

"You never had any respect for me. Well, look where you are now! Nothing but dirt at my feet."

She thought she saw stars through the branches overhead. When another brutal kick was administered to her ribcage, she felt nothing at all.

"You've always been *selfish*, and *self-centred*."

More kicks, more harsh panting from the exertion.

"Nobody will miss you. D'you know that? *Nobody*."

Through the fog, a vision of her son materialised, though she knew it couldn't be real—merely a trick of the mind. She smiled at the image of the boy he'd once been, with eyes the same as her own. Tears began to fall down her cheeks as she lay in the fold of the earth, where once she'd played as a child and walked with her love, hand in hand. Her fingertips brushed the soil and, as the last vestiges of life drained from her body, she thought of Nick again, kicking up the leaves in his blue wellie boots many years before.

I love you, Mummy.

I love you, too, sweetheart.

It was only ten minutes later, once the mindless, visceral anger was spent, that they realised she was dead.

CHAPTER 1

Lady's Well, near Holystone village

Hallowe'en—twenty years later

Day moved swiftly towards night, and the leaves that once burned golden brown began to wither. No longer a warm canopy, but a menacing cloak in the gathering darkness, at the centre of which was an ancient pool. Its waters were perfectly still as the shadows crept closer, long fingers reaching towards the people gathered beside it.

"Blessed Samhain to all," Sabrina said, as she moved around her small congregation. "We are the sum of all that has come before us. The fires of our ancestors burn brightly within us."

Blessed be, came the chorus.

She held a torch aloft and walked around the circumference of a circle, lighting four smaller torches staked into the ground and positioned at the cardinal points for north, south, east and west, each one separated by a scattering of pine branches and flowers.

"We will carry the memories of loved ones who've passed from this world into the Otherworld through the long months of darkness. For, in the darkness, the world will replenish," she murmured. "Be not afraid of death, for it heralds new life."

All the same, she lit several pumpkins, their shells carved into ghoulish effigies to ward off unwelcome spirits of the dead, who could more easily cross back into the world of the living on that special night of the year.

Sabrina blessed the circle just as the last rays of sunlight burnished her head with a bright halo of light, then reached for a bowl filled with water from the well. She held it in one hand, drawing out a small ornamental dagger with the other, the tip of which she touched to the surface of the water.

"I consecrate and cleanse this water that it may be purified and fit to dwell within the sacred circle," she said. "In the name of the Mother Goddess and the Father God, I consecrate this water."

She touched the dagger tip to some salt she'd brought in a Tupperware dish.

"I bless this salt that it may be fit to dwell within the sacred circle," she said. "In the name of the Mother Goddess and the Father God, I consecrate this salt."

She turned to face north, then walked around the circle once again, visualising her energy stretching across it like a forcefield.

"Here is the boundary of the circle," she declared. "Naught but love shall enter in. Naught but love shall emerge from within. Charge this by your powers, Old Ones!"

By the time the circle was sealed, and the brave were seated comfortably within its hallowed ground, the temperature in the clearing had dropped and the sun was little more than a thin, fiery line just visible through the surrounding trees.

"For centuries, these waters have healed the sick," she began again. "The spring was named 'Lady's Well' after the Virgin Mary, from the Christian faith, but we of the Old Ways know that the powerful source of this water was gifted by the Mother Goddess herself, to quench the thirst of every living thing in these parts and heal that which may need healing. For the Mother sees everything through the water—including all that we *cannot* see."

She gestured for a young woman from the village to step forward. "Helen, of Holystone village," she said. "What do you seek, on this Samhain night?"

A woman of around thirty moved forward and tried to find her voice. "I seek to heal my heart," she managed. "My husband has left me for another woman and now she's pregnant. I was never…never able to have a baby. I am broken in heart and in mind."

The older woman felt a small stab of pity. The secular part of herself was already aware of what had happened—it was the talk of the village that young Grant Newman had been carrying on with some fancy woman from the city and had upped and left his wife of two years to start again. He'd found Helen's country ways too parochial for his newfound tastes and had shattered her modest dreams of a home and family.

"That is indeed hard to bear," she said, and took the woman's hand. "But you have *much* living yet to do, and whatever has happened is for the best. It is the wish of the Mother and the Father—"

Helen began shaking her head from side to side, unwilling and unable to stomach any more well-intentioned advice. "I can't *sleep*," she said, and set down a bag of coins as an offering on the alter with a heavy hand. "I can't *eat*. All I think about is the two of them together, while I'm sure they don't think of *me* at all." Her lip wobbled, and she tried to stem the flow of bitter tears. "I can't live this way," she said, half to herself. "I don't want him to be happy with *her*. I want him to remember he was happy with *me*. I want him to *suffer*. I beg the Mother and Father to help me."

Frowning, Sabrina held her hand a little tighter. "That is the path of darkness," she cautioned. "And it is not the path we follow."

Something inside her shivered.

"We must not look outwardly, but inwardly," she said. "We must look to ourselves, Helen. Do not sully your mind with thoughts of revenge; cast out his betrayal and make space for better things."

She held up the bowl of water.

"Look into the water and see yourself through the Mother's eyes," she murmured. "You are perfect, just as you are, for you are built by Her creation and form part of the wondrous blessings that surround us. Let the lightness of your soul shine through the darkness and be whole again. Blessed be, Helen."

Blessed be, the chorus of voices said.

She dipped her hand into the water and blessed the woman, murmuring words of healing. Then, she rose to her feet and turned north, drawing herself in, feeling the cosmic energy course through her body once more.

"On this night, when we bid farewell to the light and welcome in the darkness until Yuletide, the veil between this world and the next is at its thinnest."

She paused, allowing her words to echo on the quiet air, accompanied only by the soft crackle of burning wood and the distant call of a night bird.

"All around us, the spirits walk," she said, with a smile. "In this world and in the Otherworld, there are forces of Good and Evil."

A sudden gust of wind charged the air, whipping up the leaves from the ground as if to punctuate her words. The torchlight flickered, and those within the circle looked all around, unnerved and curious in equal part.

"Let us look into the mirror, through the eye of the Goddess, and see what she can tell us."

Sabrina believed she'd been blessed with Second Sight and stepped outside the protective circle to walk to the very edge of the well, where she knelt and watched her own flickering reflection against the inky black water.

"I see love," she called out to Helen. "There is *love* in your future, a far greater and more powerful love than before."

Helen wanted to believe it.

She wanted to believe it so badly.

"What else?" she dared ask. "What's his name?"

"That will never be known, unless your heart is healed and open to finding and discovering the new love the Mother will create," came the reply. "Remember, from decay comes renewal and rebirth. Old wounds and hurts must be healed."

Helen found herself nodding. "Can you—can you see my grandmother? What does she say?"

"Edith is with you always, not just on this night," the woman replied, and raised her hands high. "Let us see if her spirit will join us."

She cast her hands aloft, then sank them into the cold water of the well. "Edith! We are—"

Her voice trailed off as she withdrew her hands from the water. She studied them, not quite understanding what she was seeing.

"We—we—" she began again, before the words caught in her throat.

The water was red.

Blood red.

She turned back to the circle. "The water is red!" she cried and held her hands out for them to see the stain against her skin. "There are dark forces at play—go home to your families and make sure they're safe!"

Galvanised, the small gathering scattered through the clearing until only she remained.

Then, she turned and reached inside the skirts of her long dress to retrieve a pouch filled with pound coins, which she threw into the well, one by one.

"Blessed Samhain," she said.

CHAPTER 2

Frederick Humble's character was no match for his name.

Known variously as 'Humbug', 'Ebenezer', or—rather less charitably—'Fat Freddie', on account of his general greed in all things, Fred had reached a time in life when he neither thought about nor cared what his neighbours said about him. Indeed, it was a matter of debate whether he'd *ever* cared. Certainly, he never sought out their company, and he avoided unnecessary social interactions whenever possible, especially since his wife had left him twenty years ago. Back then, he'd taken the wise decision to hunker down and speak only when necessary, closing his ears to the gossip which had inevitably run around the houses from one blabbermouth to the next.

Idiots, the lot of 'em.

When they were first married, Fred had moved to Holystone on account of Diane, because she'd claimed to be a homebird who missed her family. He'd never liked the place, with its smattering of stone cottages and quiet ways—much too quiet for his taste—but he'd tried to make the best of it, for her sake, and because she'd inherited a cottage, which meant he didn't have to work so hard. Now, even though Diane was no longer with him, he found he was still stuck there and was likely to remain so for the rest of his miserable life.

Sighing at the prospect, Fred stomped through to the kitchen and threw open a cupboard, where he kept the bottles of beer that he brewed himself in the shed the end of his garden. Unscrewing one of them, he took a long, satisfying gulp and then made his way through to the tiny living room of his terraced cottage, which sat at the end of the row and enjoyed a corner plot with far-reaching views over the countryside from the back, and of the main street, such as it was, from the front.

His arse had barely touched the worn threads of an easy chair, when there came a knock at the door.

"Bloody kids," he muttered, and heaved himself up again. "Should know well enough, by now, they'll get no sweets from me!"

Full of righteous indignation, Fred ignored the sharp pain shooting through his bad knee, and hobbled towards the front door.

"You can all just—!"

The words died on his lips, for it wasn't a motley collection of children dressed as polyester vampires waiting for him on the doorstep, but an attractive woman of around fifty with a pleasant smile already plastered on her face.

"Hello there," she began, stretching her smile a bit wider. "I'm sorry to bother you, Mr Humble, but I'm

Christine—you remember? Christine Harvey? I'm your new neighbour—"

His frown grew deeper.

Neighbour?

Oh, aye. He remembered her callin' round a few weeks ago, basket in hand full of cakes and all sorts, to bribe him to do her bidding, no doubt. The cakes had been good, but now came the reckoning, and he was in no mood for it.

"What d'you want?" he barked.

Christine swallowed. "Well, I'm glad you asked," she said, as cheerfully as she could. "You see, *the thing is*, I've been noticing the most dreadful smell over the past few weeks since I moved in, and it isn't getting any better. I thought it might have been the beer containers, but it's more than that—"

He ignored the subtle dig about his brewery operation and waited, frowning heavily while she squirmed on his doormat.

"It must be coming from the septic tank," she blurted out. "I know that we share a tank but it's at the bottom of your garden or, at least, that's what the plans seem to suggest. Now, I'm very willing to chip in to have it emptied…"

She trailed off, hoping he'd do the decent thing and lean into the discussion, to save her having to spell out the unpalatable truth—which was, of course, that their accumulated faeces stank to high heaven, and they needed to do something about it, pronto.

"I've been here for nigh on forty years, and I've never needed to empty any tank," he growled. "Now you're turnin' up, wantin' money for nothin'. Well, you can just turn straight back round again, because there's no need to go messin' with things that've worked well enough for more'n half a century."

On which note, he began to close the door in her outraged face.

However, Christine hadn't been a schoolteacher for the best part of thirty years without learning a thing or two about how to handle difficult characters.

"That's not quite true," she said, nudging a forearm against the wooden door to hold it open a while longer. "The tank is old, and probably needs replacing. We've got a duty not to be a nuisance—"

"That's rich, comin' from *you*," he threw at her. "It isn't *me* goin' round knockin' on people's doors at all hours, disturbin' the peace. I'm mindin' me own business here—or tryin' to!"

Christine took a long, fortifying breath. "Look, it's smelly and unpleasant, and puts me off wanting to spend time in the garden," she said, and there was a wobble to her voice she couldn't quite conceal. It had been difficult leaving their old home, and it was only the prospect of clean country living that had made things easier to bear. Now, even that happy thought was in jeopardy.

"Please, Mr Humble," she said softly. "We need mutual agreement before I can go ahead and ask somebody to empty it. I'm prepared to help pay for your share, if finance is an issue—"

As soon as the words were spoken, she regretted them.

"Oh, aye, that's about right!" he jeered. "You come up here, buyin' property for inflated prices, stealin' chances from young, hardworkin' folk, then you've got the nerve to try and throw your money about? Well, you can take your cash and shove it!"

With that, he thrust her aside and slammed the door shut, leaving Christine shaking in the murky twilight. She was debating the merits of raising her fist to bang on the door again, when there came the sound of running footsteps at her back. Turning to peer through the gloom, she saw a small group of people tearing along the street as though the very hounds of hell were yapping at their heels. She called out, but nobody stopped, each of them eager to return to the safety of hearth and home. A bit unsettled, Christine was in two minds about whether to try again with her neighbour or return home and lock her door, when she spotted a solitary figure she recognised as Lynn Gibbins, landlady of the only pub in the village.

"Lynn? *Lynn!*"

The woman paused beneath the fizzing light of a streetlamp, her eyes wide and frightened.

"Is everything all right?" Christine demanded. "You look as though you'd seen a ghost—"

"It's the—the water," Lynn whispered, wrapping her arms around herself.

Christine frowned. "The water? What about it?"

"It's *red*," Lynn told her. "The water at Lady's Well is running red. It's a bad omen."

Christine had heard that some members of the community still followed the old Pagan ways, believing in a religion that was far older than her own, and she hadn't given it a second thought. Above all else, she believed in the maxim 'live and let live', so it made no difference to her whether some of her neighbours thought of themselves as Pagan, Wiccan or whatever else, but she wasn't a woman who set much stock in different worlds, second sights—or bad omens, come to that.

However, one thing she *did* know was that the water from Lady's Well came from a natural spring—the same spring that provided drinking water to the entire village.

"Red?" She made a small sound of disbelief. "It's probably just a trick of the light, or kids playing games."

Lynn shook her head, her eyes flicking this way and that, and she pulled something from her pocket which she thrust into the other woman's hand.

"Keep this with you," she said urgently. "It'll keep you safe."

"Safe?" Christine laughed, and looked down at the little wooden talisman. "There's nothing to be scared of—I'll put a call through to the Environment Agency or Northumbrian Water, and they'll come and sort it out."

Lynn gave her a sad smile. "You don't *understand*, do you?" she said, and took a step closer, so their faces were only a breath apart. "Blood in the water, and blood on the moon."

She pointed a tremulous finger towards the sky, and Christine looked up to find that the moon *did* seem to have a reddish halo that night.

"Somebody will die, if they haven't already," Lynn whispered. "There are forces at work here—forces outside our control." She clutched the lapels of her long coat together, as the wind rocked them both. "Stay inside," she advised. "Lock your doors."

Without another word, Lynn turned and ran towards the pub further down the street, whose windows glowed like watchful eyes. After a moment, Christine turned to face Fred Humble's door and found herself paralysed by a fear which had worked its way beneath her skin, niggling at the corners of her mind so that she felt suddenly cold, and very alone.

Another gust of wind brushed the back of her neck, and she spun around.

The street was empty.

"Evil spirits?" she muttered. "I must be losing my mind."

With a final glance towards Fred Humble's door, she hurried back to her own, which she shut firmly behind her.

CHAPTER 3

Detective Chief Inspector Maxwell Finley-Ryan could think of at least a hundred other things he'd rather be doing than driving through the winding country roads of Northumberland in the dead of night, with only a flask of coffee and Uncle Fester for company.

"I can't believe you didn't change out of that costume," he said. "And you could at least have washed off the make-up. It's enough to give me nightmares."

His sergeant and, as it happened, his very good friend, turned to him with as much dignity as he could muster for a man in a bald cap and a long grey habit.

"You said it was an *'emergency'*," Frank Phillips pointed out. "For all I know, there could've been an axe murderer on the loose."

"If there is, he'll take one look at you and run for the hills," Ryan muttered, turning briefly to cast an eye over his friend's apparel. "I swear, you spend half of your waking hours in fancy dress. I used to think the ties were bad enough—"

Phillips made a small sound of outrage. "I get a lot of compliments on my ties, I'll have you know."

"Your daughter doesn't count—she's only thirteen, and doesn't know any better."

Phillips turned away to hide his smile. "They're *fashionable*," he argued, loftily. "I wouldn't expect you to understand."

"They're creepy and kookie, is what they are," Ryan said. "Not to mention mysterious and spooky."

Phillips let out a rumble of laughter, and clicked both of his fingers in time to the old *Addams Family* melody.

"Christmas is comin'," he said, after a moment. "I know just the thing I'll be gettin' you."

"What's that? A blindfold?"

"A slap round the chops, if you divn't watch it." Phillips chuckled.

Ryan slowed the car, looking for a sign—*any* sign— that would tell him they weren't simply lost in the depths of the Northumbrian countryside. What might have been an easy journey in the daylight was infinitely less so in the blanket darkness of an October night, and, after a while, one field and hillside began to look very much like the next.

"I knew I'd come off the A1 too soon," he muttered.

Both men peered through the windscreen, then gave a long sigh.

"We could look at a map," Ryan suggested. "If there's no signal on the GPS, maybe we'll come across a house where we can stop and ask for directions."

Phillips turned to him with a look caught somewhere between male indignation and paternal disappointment.

"That's enough of *that* kind of talk," he told him, jabbing a finger against Ryan's chest. "There's no need to be thinkin' of lookin' at maps or askin' for directions. We're men, lad. *Blokes*. Hunter-gatherers. Leaders of the pack. We're—"

"Lost," Ryan told him, succinctly.

"Temporarily," Phillips said, waving it away with one broad hand.

Just then, a dark van materialised, its headlights blinding them in the rear-view mirror before it drew up alongside them on the deserted road. Ryan lowered his window to greet its driver, a man he recognised instantly as being Tom Faulkner, their most experienced Crime Scene Investigator attached to the Northumbria Criminal Investigation Department.

"Fancy meeting you here! You're not lost, are you?" he called out.

"As a matter of fact—" Ryan began.

"Just takin' in the views," Phillips interjected, and the other two looked around in confusion, for they could barely see beyond the tips of the hedgerows lining either side of the road.

"I see," Faulkner said, with a smirk. "Well, as it happens, I used to see a lass from Holystone for a while, so I know how to get to the village from here. If you've finished *admiring the scenery*, you can follow me, if you like."

Phillips folded his arms and Ryan nodded gratefully, winding his window back up to stem the gust of cold night air that whipped through the car's interior. Once they'd moved off again, trailing behind the glowing red taillights of Faulkner's van, Phillips gave it a moment or two and then cleared his throat.

"So, tell us a bit about the bloke we're up here to see," he said, linking his fingers across his paunch as he settled in to talk shop.

"Man by the name of Frederick Humble," Ryan told him, and slowed as they approached a tight bend in the road. "Aged sixty-eight, resident of the village for almost forty years. Apparently, his son found him dead at home, less than an hour ago."

Phillips nodded, sombrely.

"Coincides with all the reports of water poisonin' that've been comin' in," he remarked. "Wonder if the auld codger's fallen foul of a bad Hallowe'en prank? Kids these days, an' all that…"

Ryan said nothing, for it struck him suddenly that, as a man in his fifties, Frank Phillips wasn't all that many years behind the unfortunate soul they were called in to see. He'd *never* have called his sergeant an 'auld codger', being as he was a vital man and full of life—not to mention being full of the blarney. All the same, nobody was immune to the unstoppable hand of time, and he knew there would come a day when Frank would be forced to slow down. It was a sobering thought, and one he wasn't ready to delve into; he could only hope that day was a long way off yet.

"I guess we'll have to wait and see," he said, distractedly.

"Aye, the tox report will give us a good steer," Phillips agreed. "I just hope there aren't any other nasty surprises waitin' for us when we finally get to the village. Speakin' of which...where the bleedin' heck is this place, anyhow? Feels like we're on the road to Brigadoon."

Ryan smiled to himself, soaking up their easy camaraderie and thinking of all the years he'd taken it for granted. He was almost moved to say something; perhaps a heartfelt word about their friendship and what it meant to him, when Phillips' voice broke the silence once more.

"Now I wish I *had* changed out of this gear," he grumbled, wriggling in his seat as he tugged at the rough material of his costume. "Although, I s'pose it could be worse. At least I'm not dressed as a French maid, or owt like that."

Ryan tried valiantly to block the image from his mind's eye, and failed.

"Thank God for small mercies," he muttered.

By the time their modest convoy arrived at the village of Holystone, what was usually a quaint little hidden gem had been reduced to an unholy spectacle, filled with ambulance and police personnel and, more concerning to Ryan's eye, several press vehicles brimming with local hacks who'd caught the scent of a juicy Hallowe'en story.

"It's a circus," he snarled.

Phillips could only agree. "How do they always manage to get up here before us?" he wondered aloud, although they both knew that the Control Room at Northumbria CID could always boast a reliable leak.

Executing a hasty parking manoeuvre, Ryan unfolded himself from the car and proceeded to make his way directly towards a gaggle of police staff who appeared to be enjoying themselves immensely, standing around sipping takeaway cups of steaming coffee while nibbling leftover sweets and laughing at something or other, entirely unaware of the danger approaching them on swift, striding feet.

"Poor buggers," Phillips said to himself, as he made his way around to Ryan's boot and began rummaging around for a spare jacket. "They'll be in for a tannin' now."

"*You!*" Ryan's voice sliced through the night air like a whip, and several coffee cups toppled as the first responders came to attention, their faces a picture of comic horror at the sight of their senior officer—and not just *any* senior officer, either. This one had a short temper, and a reputation for not suffering fools gladly.

"*M—me?*" One such fool pointed a finger at himself.

"Are you the first attending officer?" Ryan demanded, raking his eyes over the others with professional contempt.

"It was me and Elliott, sir. PC Elliott and myself, that is. Together. The two of us."

Ryan's cool blue gaze flicked to a young man of twenty or so, who was doing his best to dispose of a bag of foil-wrapped chocolates in the shape of eyeballs.

"And you are?"

"PC Waddell, sir. From the Berwick office."

"I see," Ryan purred. "Waddell and Elliott, from the Berwick office. What about the rest of you?"

Several nervous voices spoke at once, and he held up a hand.

"Unless you're liaising with the emergency services, taking preliminary statements or otherwise making yourself *useful*, I couldn't give a flying fart which office you've come from."

They nodded, vigorously.

"As for the two of *you*," he said, turning back to the first responders in a voice that was deceptively quiet. "Let me ask you a simple question, Waddell."

The young man nodded eagerly. *Too* eagerly.

"Where exactly is the 'scene'?" Ryan spread his arms to encompass their surroundings. "I can see four ambulances attending different addresses, numerous paramedics and villagers milling around panicking, not to mention God knows how many roaming journalists. So, I ask you again: *where is the scene*?"

"Sir—I—I'm sorry, we should have—"

"Made it secure?" Ryan finished for him. "Posted a sentry at the door, to log all those entering or leaving? Too *right*. This entire area is a free-for-all. What do you have to say for yourself?"

Wisely, those not in the firing line beat a hasty retreat, while the two remaining officers prayed for deliverance.

Ryan took their silence as an admission. "Do you mean to tell me, while you've been standing here chattering like a bunch of bloody magpies, not a *single* person in uniform has been guarding Fred Humble's door? Where's your logbook?"

"I—I—um, I made a note of the names on my phone—"

Ryan swore volubly, and, from his vantage point several feet away, Phillips could almost see the air above their heads turn blue. Having taken the time to remove the worst of his face paint, and sheath himself in one of Ryan's spare overcoats which was, he had to admit, a trifle snug around the belly and long in the hip, he made his way across the street to catch the tail end of it.

"...and think yourselves lucky I'm not booting your sorry arses back to Basic Training! Now, bugger off, before I change my mind!"

"Aye, and you can hand over those chocolates, n'all! What d'you think you're on? Your granny's yacht?" Phillips tagged on, confiscating the bags of confectionary with a stern look of disapproval before they scarpered like rats.

After a couple of seconds, he popped one of the eyeballs into his mouth. "What?" he said, catching Ryan's eye. "Waste not, want not…" He offered the bag to his friend, who shook his head, and decided not to mention that his granny had indeed had a yacht—it was neither here nor there.

"I'll wait until I've looked in the dead man's eyes, before stuffing my face with sugar."

Phillips swallowed with an audible *gulp*. "Well, now you've done it," he complained, pocketing the chocolate for later. "Y'nah I can't stand seein' their *eyes*."

Ryan schooled his features into a serious expression.

"There's only one thing worse than seeing the eyes on a recently deceased pensioner, and that's seeing the cold, dead eyes of your *wife* when she finds out you've fallen off the diet wagon again."

Phillips' blood ran cold at the thought of Detective Inspector Denise MacKenzie getting wind of his recent transgression.

"Who'd tell her?" he crooned. "Certainly not my *best mate*, who knows that I'd be forced to retaliate…" Phillips wiggled his bushy eyebrows.

"All right, *all right*," Ryan said, with a laugh. "Your secret's safe with me, baldie."

Phillips slapped a hand to his head, realising he was still wearing a shiny plastic bald cap, and tugged it off with a muttered expletive.

Then, as the force of the night air hit his own thinning scalp, immediately put it back on again.

"Howay, let's get inside," he said. "It's Baltic out here!"

Ryan watched him scurry towards Fred Humble's cottage and reflected that, in all the years they'd worked together, he'd never seen his sergeant so eager to see a fresh corpse.

CHAPTER 4

Fred Humble looked anything but 'fresh'.

He lay sprawled in his easy chair, legs extended on a footrest, arms thrown wide in a grotesque cruciform position. A bottle of beer had fallen onto the carpeted floor beneath his right hand, and an unpleasant odour of stale, drying alcohol mingled with the subtle scent of early decay, which made for a heady combination.

"Well, I've gotta say, all things considered…I've seen worse."

Ryan and Faulkner turned to look at Phillips, who made his blunt statement from the doorway, several feet away from the body.

"That's a great comfort to us all," Ryan said. "Any other insights, sergeant?"

Phillips cocked his head, and sniffed thoughtfully—if such a thing was possible.

"If y'ask me, the bloke looks like he had a heart attack," he said. "Can't see any wounds, or owt like that." He shrugged. "If you're gonna pop your clogs, you might as well do it in a comfy chair with a bottle o' beer in your hand and the telly remote in the other."

The plain truth of it drew a reluctant smile from Ryan, who cast his eye around the room, with its orange and brown eighties décor and generally faded air, then back at the man who had been Fred Humble. There were indeed no obvious signs of aggression, nor any indication of defence wounds. Taking a step forward, he lifted one of the man's stiff hands to peer beneath his yellowed fingernails and found none of them torn or bloodied, which might have indicated a struggle. However, he knew from long experience that not everything was visible to the naked eye.

He turned to Faulkner, who'd begun the process of snapping a series of photographs from every angle, shuffling this way and that with a rustle of his polypropylene suit.

"Anything jump out at you, Tom—aside from Uncle Fester, here?"

Faulkner lowered his camera to crouch down beside the fallen beer bottle. "I'll take a sample from the carpet and the bottle," he said, voice muffled by the mask he wore. "Just in case there was anything in the beer."

"I'd like all drinking vessels to be checked for contaminants," Ryan put in.

Faulkner nodded. "Will do, but, to be honest, there are no obvious physical indicators of poisoning...usually, the veins are distended and there are self-inflicted wounds around the neck, swollen glands—" He scratched the top of his head, which was covered in a hairnet and plastic hood. "Jeff will be able to give you a more accurate report, of course."

Ryan nodded, thinking of Doctor Jeffrey Pinter, the police pathologist who would perform a post-mortem just as soon as the body could be transferred to the mortuary. All things considered, Phillips' idea that Humble might have suffered a heart attack was a reasonable hypothesis, and most Senior Investigating Officers would probably conclude there were no suspicious circumstances surrounding the man's death.

And yet...

"Something doesn't feel right," he said, and moved carefully around the room, eyes sharp for any sign of third-party interference. "How many people have been affected by the water contamination, Frank?"

Phillips sucked in a breath, then blew it out again. "Number's still risin'," he said. "Accordin' to PC Waddell, they've had a dozen confirmed cases, which is a sizeable amount considerin' there can't be more than fifty people resident in the village."

"What symptoms are being reported?" Ryan asked him.

"We'll need to have a word with the medics but, from what we can tell, there's been quite a range, dependin' on how much water people had drunk. It's had them bent over double with stomach cramps, uncontrollable shakes, headaches, vomiting...not to mention the runs."

The runs?

Ryan used his common sense and came to the obvious conclusion.

He meant diarrhoea.

"Any of them been affected badly?"

"Well, I wouldn't like to say," Phillips replied, pulling an expressive face. "I'm sure one or two might've been caught short—"

Ryan almost slapped a palm to his own face. "I meant, have any of them been hospitalised!"

"*Oh*," Phillips grinned. "Well, if you're talkin' about folk who've needed more than a roll o' toilet paper and a prayer, then I think one or two of the older ones have been taken down to the hospital in Alnwick for fluids and observation. Don't know how many others might've joined them, since we've been in here."

"Nobody reporting cardiac or other side effects?"

Phillips shook his head. "Not so far, but it's still early doors."

Ryan nodded, and continued to scan the room until his eye fell on an old wooden photograph frame resting on the mantel. It featured the faded image of a lovely young woman wearing clothing from the seventies or eighties, and what his mother might have called a 'Farrah Fawcett' hairdo.

"His wife, d'you reckon?" Phillips asked, following his gaze.

Ryan nodded. "Probably," he said, and turned to check the old man's ring finger, which bore no slim band of gold, but a faint groove where one might have been, long ago. "Perhaps they're divorced."

"Funny for him to keep her picture up, if they are," Phillips remarked. "But then, there's nowt as queer as folk."

Ryan tended to agree and, without another word, turned to make his way back through the hallway and into the tiny kitchen at the rear of Humble's cottage. He inspected the back door, which he found to be securely locked from the inside, then made directly for the sink. With gloved fingers, he turned on the tap, which spluttered into life and began pumping out red-coloured water.

"Find anythin'?" Phillips joined him on the grubby linoleum floor, his shoe coverings clinging slightly to its unwashed surface, and looked around the small space.

"I've just checked the tap," Ryan said. "It's running red in here, but I want to know if the red water has been drawn down into the plumbing in other areas of the house. Would you mind checking the taps in the bathrooms?"

A minute later, he heard the creak of Phillips' footsteps on the stairs and the floorboards overhead, then the distant sound of running water.

"Aye, it's runnin' red up here, n'all!" came the cry.

Ryan was considering the implications of that, when Phillips came back into the poky kitchen and planted his feet. "Dunno if you heard me, but the taps are runnin' red upstairs, too."

"Frank, even Fred Humble heard you."

Phillips grinned. "Well? What do you make of it? I s'pose there must've been plenty of the red dye, or whatever was used, otherwise it might have been a bit more flushed out by now, eh?"

Ryan nodded slowly. "We'll ask Faulkner's team to check the pipes," he decided.

Phillips didn't bother to remark about the added costs or time; he knew his partner to be a thorough man with a nose like a bloodhound. If Ryan thought the death of Fred Humble warranted the extra manpower and resources, he would not be the one to argue.

"By, it's grim in here, like," he said, taking in the overflowing bin in the corner of the room, the unwashed countertops and general odour of over-ripe fruit and vegetables. "Pity we can't crack open a window."

Ryan began opening the kitchen cabinets. "The first report of red water was made at seven-thirty or so," he said. "The window of opportunity when person or persons unknown could have contaminated the water will depend on *where* the contaminant entered the waterworks, and how long it would have likely taken to reach the village and make its way into people's taps."

Phillips nodded. "We can have a word with the lass from the Environment Agency. Still, the water might not have anythin' to do with why Fred's no longer in the land of the livin'."

Ryan said nothing, and continued to inspect the cupboards.

"What're you lookin' for?"

"I don't know, Frank."

Phillips rolled his eyes. "Y'nah what your problem is, son? You're too cynical," he pronounced, before Ryan could formulate any answer to what had, in any case, been a rhetorical question. "It's not *always* murder or manslaughter. Sometimes, folk just keel over and die."

Ryan laughed. "It's a constant education, working with you," he said.

"You're welcome," Phillips replied, and gave a huge, jaw-cracking yawn. "Any time you want my advice on anythin' else—like dancin' or the art of love—I'm here for you, lad."

Ryan shook his head and opened the last cupboard. Inside, he found shelves stacked with bottles of beer, lined up in neat rows. "Come and look at this."

Phillips moved across to follow his line of sight.

"Looks like Fred was a connoisseur," he said, with a touch of admiration. "No labels on them, mind."

"I wonder if he brewed them himself."

Phillips looked around the kitchen, then back at his friend.

"If he did, he didn't do it in here. There's barely room to swing a cat."

After a moment's thought, Ryan moved to the back door, turned the key that remained inside the lock, and opened it. Cold air rushed inside the stuffy room, and with it came the faintest stench of hops.

"There's our answer," he said, closing the door again. "There must be a shed or something in his garden. You can smell it from here."

"I bet that made him popular with the neighbours," Phillips joked.

Ryan's eye caught on a wicker basket thrown in the corner beside the bin. Crouching down, he picked it up and found a card inside, written in a neat hand.

"We can ask them," he said, tapping the card before sliding it into a plastic evidence bag.

A while later, after they'd taken a thorough turn around Fred Humble's cottage and rifled through the shabby remains of what had once been a man's life, they stepped back outside and breathed deeply of the chilly night air.

"No sign of vomiting or diarrhoea, except the usual... er, *evacuation* which we see with most bodies," Phillips pronounced. "No signs of attack, no sign of any break-in, either. You can't be thinkin' this one's suspicious just because it's Hallowe'en."

Ryan shook his head, and peeled off his nitrile gloves, which he dropped into a small evidence bin laid out by Faulkner for that purpose.

"I don't think it's suspicious because it happens to be Hallowe'en," he said. "I think it's suspicious because Fred Humble died on the same night there was an unprecedented case of water poisoning in his village."

Understanding dawned upon Phillips.

"Because you don't believe in—"

"Coincidences," Ryan finished for him, and gave his friend a manly slap between the shoulder blades. "You're damn right, I don't."

CHAPTER 5

Detective Constable Melanie Yates didn't believe in coincidences either.

For instance, it was surely no coincidence that she'd seen the same white, '21 plate Volvo sitting across the road from their house the previous evening, as was sitting there, right now. She happened to know that their neighbours owned a dark blue Mazda SUV, which was parked a little further along the narrow street of smart, terraced houses. Which begged the question: who owned the Volvo, and why were they just sitting there?

She noted the time and scribbled it down in a notebook she'd taken to keeping in her pocket.

"Mel?"

She jumped at the sound of Jack's voice.

"What are you looking at?" he asked, coming to stand beside her at the bedroom window.

"Keep out of sight," she hissed, dragging him to the side. "They'll see you."

"Who's *they*?"

Melanie opened her mouth and then shut it again, unable to find the words.

"Are you hiding from the kids?" he guessed, thinking of the packs of children who'd been out 'trick or treating' that evening. "I think they've all gone home, now, love. It's getting late."

She nodded, mutely.

"They never *actually* do a trick, you know," he tagged on, stealing his arm around her shoulders to draw her against him.

Tell him, her inner voice whispered. *Tell him about the car.*

It was on the tip of her tongue to do just that when, at that very moment, she watched the driver of the Volvo exit the vehicle, rubbing eyes that looked worn with tiredness and, if she wasn't much mistaken, ravaged by tears. They carried a small overnight bag which they slung over their shoulder while they made the short journey to one of the painted front doors of the houses on the opposite side of the street. After a brief knock, it opened, and Melanie's neighbour appeared, arms outstretched to receive their friend.

Watching the exchange, her fingers grew limp on the notebook she'd been gripping, and it fell to the floor.

"What's this?" Jack bent down to retrieve it, and his eye caught on the scribbled columns of dates and times, plus a myriad of other general observations about their neighbours' comings-and-goings. "Mel?"

She turned away, too embarrassed to face him. "Just put it on the table," she muttered.

He stood there for long seconds, caught between a desire to comfort and an even stronger desire to know the inner workings of her mind. The previous spring, Melanie had finally brought her sister's killer to justice, ending fifteen long years of purgatory, in which she and her family had waited for answers they thought might never come. In the end, Fate had taken pity upon them, but ending Andrew Forbes' long run as one of the nation's most prolific serial killers had not come without a cost; Melanie had almost lost her life and, as Jack was beginning to appreciate, she remained a long way off regaining the person she'd once been. He tucked the notebook into his back pocket, out of sight, and decided to prioritise comfort over understanding, at least for the present.

"Mel," he said, and laid a gentle hand on her arm. "Why don't we sit down for a while?"

Some days, she would fly into a rage. Today, it seemed the idea suited her. "Okay," she said, in a flat tone.

He led her to the sofa, where their cat lay stretched out, paws akimbo, for all the world like a human nursing a hangover.

"Move over a bit," Jack said, and laughed when the animal merely opened one amber-coloured eye and yawned.

Taking matters into his own hands, he scooped up the cat in one arm and guided Melanie down with the other, niftily plonking the furball onto her lap so that she'd feel less inclined to hurry off. As he'd hoped, she began to stroke the cat, who made itself comfortable and promptly fell asleep again.

"I don't want to talk," Melanie said, straight off the bat.

Jack sat down beside her and took a deep breath, thinking there was so much to say, he didn't even know where to begin. He tried to imagine what Ryan or Phillips might advise him to do, were they in his situation. Both were men he respected; both had seen their share of hardship and worry for those they loved. Unfortunately, he had a feeling their advice would be to follow his heart and be patient.

Easy to say, far less easy to do.

"You don't have to talk, if you don't want to," he said carefully. "But I'm here if you do."

The words hung on the air for a long time, and he began to think he'd said the wrong thing.

"I can't..." She swallowed. "I can't seem to stop thinking there's danger all around us. I see it everywhere, in every strange face, strange car...I don't know how to stop imagining the worst."

She could hardly be blamed for developing a certain paranoia, he thought, especially after all she'd been through. When the truth came to light about Forbes' murders, all it had taught her was never to trust those around you, no matter who they happened to be.

All the same, she needed to trust someone, and he hoped she could start by trusting *him*.

"You have to remember, the people we deal with represent the minority," he said, unconsciously echoing

Phillips' words, earlier that evening. "Not everyone is a killer, Mel. Not everyone will hurt you."

"They look the same as everyone else," she muttered.

Jack could find no answer to that, because, of course, she was right. They didn't have horns or breathe fire. They tended to be very ordinary-looking people, who led extraordinarily savage lives.

"You have to find a way to carry on," he said softly. "You can't keep spying on our neighbours through windows or keeping track of the times I leave for work and come home again."

Jack blinked away unexpected tears, for the grim reality hit him like a fist to the face—Melanie didn't trust him, because she trusted *nobody*.

"I'm not the same as that man," he said. "You don't need to monitor my movements or anyone else's. I'm not leading a double life. Few people are."

The fact she could even *think* of him as anything other than the man who loved her was galling, but he tried to remember it was a function of the post-traumatic stress she was suffering. All the same, it hurt like hell.

"I can't seem to stop," she confessed, and her breathing began to hitch as she battled tears. "It's a compulsion. I need to know what the people around me are doing."

"I don't mind if you track my phone," he said, a bit wearily. "You can call me any time and I'll answer if I can. But, Mel, I need you to tell me that you don't seriously think I could be anything other than who I am. At least tell me that."

She looked at him then, into his open, mid-brown eyes that searched for reassurance, and wished she could say the words he wanted to hear. In her rational mind, she knew Detective Constable Jack Lowerson was a good man and an upstanding officer of the law, just as she knew it was the same with her other colleagues in Northumbria CID. Likewise, if she cast her mind back to life before the previous spring, she would never have wondered what time her neighbours came and went in their own homes, nor worried about new cars parking on the street, which they were perfectly free to do. She would have been able to walk to the supermarket or the corner shop without a creeping sense of being watched or followed, and she wouldn't have seen the ghost of *his* face in every passing window. The wider world had become a terrifying place, one she could no longer trust, and she'd retreated inward, making their home her sanctuary and a place she could control. Unfortunately, she was beginning to think she was no longer safe inside its four walls, because the truth was that there was nowhere in the world she could run to, nowhere big or small enough to hide from the workings of her own mind. For, there, in a deep, dark corner, Andrew Forbes was not dead and buried but very much alive and well, twisting his evil knife through her very core.

"I can't tell you that," she whispered finally. "I want to be able to, Jack, but I can't. I've been trying to fight this—"

Fight him.

"—But, if anything, the paranoia is getting worse."

Jack frowned, thinking of the weekly therapy sessions she'd stopped attending. "I thought you said you were feeling better, and that's why you didn't need to see Doctor Harris?"

"I lied," she admitted. "The sessions weren't helping, Jack. I feel like nobody understands."

"I'm trying to—"

"But you can't!" she burst out. "How could you? You haven't lost someone you love…"

"Haven't I?" he said softly, but she didn't hear him.

"I thought taking some time off work would help," she carried on. "Instead, every day is just like the next, and I feel trapped inside these four walls."

"Are you saying you'd like to try coming back to work?"

It had been more than six months, he thought. Perhaps Melanie needed to get back on the proverbial horse and distract herself from thoughts of the past.

"Maybe," she said. "I'll have a word with Ryan."

She sat up then, and moved off to find her laptop, intending to send an email to her boss and set up a meeting. The cat padded across to Jack and nudged his hand.

"I know," he murmured. "I'm worried too."

CHAPTER 6

While Melanie and Jack grappled with demons of the mind, Ryan and Phillips faced another kind of demon entirely, in the form of Mia Humble. At the tender age of four and a half—don't forget the half!—it was long past her bedtime. Unfortunately, as both her mother and father had taken ill at varying stages of the evening and, with the added excitement and physiological impact of excess sugar consumption, sleep had been evasive and so it was she who stood on the threshold of her parents' doorway, still dressed in her black and red devil costume.

"Are you trick or treating?" she asked.

The two men looked at one another, then back at the girl.

"Ah…no, pet," Phillips replied, recovering quickly. "Actually, we were wonderin' if we could have a word with your Mam or Dad?"

She sucked in a breath and then turned to bellow over her shoulder, in the kind of high-pitched tone that shredded nerves and eardrums.

"*Mammy! Daddy!* There's two strange men at the door!"

They looked at one another again, not feeling overly confident about that description.

"We're from the police—" Ryan started to say, and held out his warrant card for her to look at.

"*Mammy!* Now, he wants to give me something!"

Ryan snatched the card back, and rolled his eyes.

"What—?" In response to this troubling report from his young daughter, a man in his early forties hurried down the hallway from the kitchen, looking pale-faced and exhausted.

"Mia, what have I told you about not opening the door?" he said. "Go on back and find your mam—she's in the living room."

With one last suspicious glance in their direction, the little girl bounded off.

"Well?" her father asked. "What's all this about?"

He narrowed his eyes and, at over six feet of pure 'outdoor muscle', neither Ryan nor Phillips would have wanted to cross him.

"Nicholas Humble?" Ryan asked and, at the affirmative, made the necessary introductions. "I'm Detective Chief Inspector Ryan and this is Detective Sergeant Frank Phillips, from Northumbria CID. We're sorry to trouble you so late in the day, but we've come to speak with you about your father."

Nick's face turned slack, any fight seeming to drain from his body.

"Oh," he said. "I thought—ah—that is, one of your colleagues came around earlier. PC Waddell, or whatever his name was."

"Yes, I think my colleague took a preliminary statement from you," Ryan agreed, and didn't bother to mention the 'statement', such as it was, had been incomplete, poorly-drafted and riddled with spelling mistakes. "Unfortunately, we need to make a record of certain key facts, and we find it's always best to try to do that as close to the time of the incident as possible."

Nick ran a hand through his mop of ash-blond hair, and let it fall again with a shrug.

"Sure. Okay. You'd better come in," he said, and turned away, leaving them to follow along the narrow passageway towards a kitchen at the back of the house. The layout was very similar to his late father's but, where that had been dated and in need of a good scrub, they found his son's home sparkling clean and cheerfully decorated with framed photographs of Mia at varying ages, alongside family snapshots which, they noted, did not feature the girl's paternal grandfather in any capacity—nor her paternal grandmother, come to that.

Nick indicated a large breakfasting table where they should sit.

"I would offer you a cup of tea, but we've been told not to touch the water until it's been given the 'all clear,'" he said. "I have some bottled water around here, or there's orange juice?"

"Thank you, Mr Humble, but we're both fine," Ryan said, and Phillips nodded weakly, thinking he'd have argued, if he had any spit left in his parched mouth.

"Just call me, 'Nick.'"

Ryan nodded. "I want to apologise again for our visit being so late," he reiterated, having caught sight of a large plastic clock on the kitchen wall which told him the time was now quarter to eleven. "We'll make this as swift as possible."

Nick pulled up a chair and rested his forearms on the table. "Go on," he said.

"We'd like to offer you our condolences on the loss of your father," Ryan continued, watching closely for the man's response.

In this case, it was unreadable.

"Thanks."

No words of love or grief, no signs of tears or any emotion aside from tiredness, which piqued the interest of at least one detective in the room.

"We understand you were the one to find him," Ryan said. "Could you tell us about that?"

"I don't know what there is to tell," Nick said, and rubbed a hand over his tired eyes. "I had a knock on the door about the water problem, which we'd noticed for ourselves when we tried running a bath for Mia. We mostly drink coffee or tea, so we boil the water first, but, even so, Lorna and I both felt a bit peaky."

"What time did you receive the knock—and from whom?"

"Um, it must have been around seven-thirty, or maybe a bit after? It was my friend, Davie Hetherington, the farmer. His place is on the outskirts of the village, but he'd come in to see if we were all having the same problem. Said he'd felt sick and, as I say, we were starting to feel unwell ourselves."

Ryan nodded. "What did you do then?"

"We agreed to go around the houses to see if everyone was okay," Nick replied. "There are quite a few elderly residents here, so I wanted to make sure they weren't laid up too bad."

Phillips thought, if that was true, it was the kind of community spirit he and Denise would have liked to find in the area where they lived. Unfortunately, with so many houses changing hands lately, and younger families spending all hours working and whatnot, it was hard to build the kind of community who'd throw summer barbeques in the street or host parties to welcome in the New Year. He thought, not for the first time, that perhaps it was time they made the 'Big Move' they'd been talking about for so long, to somewhere in the country—near Ryan, or beside the coast… He set the thought aside, for now. "That's when you paid a visit to your father's cottage?" he asked.

Nick nodded. "I made my way along the street here, then started on the High Street," he explained, and Ryan exchanged a furtive glance with his sergeant, who mirrored the unspoken question.

Why hadn't the son gone straight to see his father?

"Methodical," Ryan said, nonchalantly. "Is there any reason why you didn't head directly to your father's home?"

Nick's eyes turned glacial. "There are vulnerable people between here and there who might have needed me," he said, and clamped his lips shut.

Ryan set it aside.

For now.

"What time would you say you arrived at your father's house?"

"It was exactly eight o'clock," he said and, pre-empting their next question, went on to explain that he had a standing alarm set up on his smartphone at eight o'clock every Sunday evening, to remind him to set out his wheelie bins for the council's rubbish collection the next day.

It happened to be a Sunday.

"How did you enter your father's home?" Ryan asked him. "Presumably, nobody answered the door?"

Nick gave him the ghost of a smile. "There was no answer," he confirmed. "It wouldn't have been the first time my father chose not to answer the door, so I was tempted to move on to the next house."

He paused to sit up and roll his shoulders.

"I don't know why I bothered to fish out a key," he muttered. "I suppose it was because there was a bit of rising panic. Davie had already found a couple of people in need of medical attention, and they're both over seventy. My father wasn't far off being in the same age bracket, so I was worried."

It was said grudgingly, but he said it, nonetheless.

"So, you let yourself in," Ryan prodded him. "What then?"

"I called out, to let him know it was me," Nick said. "There was no reply, but I could hear the telly was on in the living room."

Ryan looked up sharply at that. "The television?"

Nick looked between them, and nodded slowly. "Y-yes, the television was on," he said. "I can't remember what programme, but—"

"Did you turn it off, at any time?" Ryan looked him squarely in the eye, commanding his attention.

Nick shook his head, his face betraying a degree of confusion about why a murder detective should be so interested in whether his father had been a watcher of early evening drama.

"No, I left it on," he said. "When I walked into the living room, I saw him…" He swallowed, then began again. "I saw him lying back in his chair. It was obvious he was gone, because his eyes…his eyes were still wide open. I didn't even think about the telly, then."

"You're absolutely *sure* you didn't turn it off?"

Nick nodded again. "Absolutely sure," he said.

To his surprise, Ryan smiled beautifully. "Thank you, Mr Humble," he said. "You've been very helpful."

CHAPTER 7

Once they'd taken the time to ask a few more salient questions of Nicholas Humble and his wife, Ryan and Phillips decided to call it a night. It was almost the witching hour and, since the standing population of Holystone remained in their sick beds or in hospital under strict orders to rest, there was little opportunity to extract much in the way of valuable intelligence for the time being. Following the transfer of Fred Humble's body to the mortuary, Faulkner had bidden them both farewell—not before delivering a departing wisecrack along the lines of making sure they didn't get lost while 'admiring the scenery' on the way home, to which Phillips had replied that his boot wouldn't get lost on its way to connecting with the other man's arse, if he didn't watch himself.

Now, with the crime scene sealed and locked, and the most important forensic work complete, Ryan dismissed any remaining support personnel, some of whom would return the next morning to continue door-to-door interviews. The ambulance crews and first responders had departed, the press crews had sated themselves with enough juice to keep their producers happy, and the villagers had long since retreated to their homes. Holystone was, once again, a haven of peace and solitude, its streets no longer overflowing with rubberneckers but still and silent beneath a sky peppered with stars. Aside from the occasional eerie glow from a carved pumpkin or a night light, all other window lights had been extinguished, and the two detectives were left with an uncomfortable notion of what it might be like to be the last men standing after an apocalypse.

While they were contemplating the prospect, a shadow loomed.

"DCI Ryan?"

"BLOODY NORA!" Phillips bellowed, and his voice ricocheted around the surrounding houses, causing resting birds to squawk and flap up into the sky.

They spun around to face the approaching figure, whose ski jacket and woollen hat obscured most of his face.

"What're you tryin' to do to us?" Phillips demanded, while his heart rate made its way back to normal. "I nearly jumped out of me skin, man!"

"Sorry, I didn't mean to startle you," the man said, lowering the neck of his coat. "I don't know if you'll remember me—Marcus Atherton, from the *Daily Chronicle*? I've been waiting around, hoping to have a brief word with you both before we all turn in for the night."

Ryan might not have liked the occasional interference but, as a citizen of the world, he appreciated good investigative journalism when he saw it. He happened to know that Atherton was one of the few remaining who truly fell into that category and, moreover, he remembered the man had been pivotal in steering his comrades away from much of the easy fodder that might have been available following the sensational story of his sister's death at the hands of The Hacker. Lesser men would have printed and be damned, so Ryan gave him credit for a modicum of integrity, and it was that which prevented the immediate 'no comment' from escaping his lips.

"You know we can't comment on an ongoing investigation," he did say, because it was the truth.

Atherton decided to press on, regardless. "I understand, of course, about the specifics of your investigation—it *is* an investigation, then?"

Ryan rattled off the standard facts he'd have incorporated into a press release. "As next of kin have been informed, I can tell you that a local man who's been identified as Frederick Humble, aged sixty-eight, was found dead in his home earlier this evening. We are investigating."

Ryan began walking back towards his car and Phillips took up his cue to follow, with Atherton trotting at their heels.

"Would you say his death has any connection with the water contamination reported today?"

"No comment at this time."

"Has the issue with the water been resolved?"

"Teams are working throughout the night to make the water supply safe," Ryan told him.

Again, it was the basic truth, and something he was sure Atherton already knew.

"Water running red—*blood red*—is quite symbolic, especially on Hallowe'en night," he persisted. "Do you have any idea what kind of message person or persons unknown were trying to convey, Chief Inspector? You'll be aware of the fracking dispute, I'm sure."

Neither by word nor deed would Ryan have let on that he was entirely *unaware*, but he made a mental note to find out about it at the earliest opportunity.

"There are always local disputes over land or planning," he prevaricated. "No party or parties have taken responsibility for the water contamination, nor are we in a position to charge anyone at the present time."

Ryan pressed the button to unlock his car but, while Phillips bundled himself inside to stave off the chill, he held back a moment longer, in case Atherton should afford them any more useful titbits of information.

"Are you treating Fred Humble's death as suspicious?"

Now it came to it, Ryan thought.

"Quid pro quo," Atherton added, with a smile that told him he was aware Ryan knew nothing of any fracking dispute, and had given him that one for free.

"All right," Ryan said. "Yes, I can tell you Fred Humble's death is being treated as 'suspicious'. Nothing further."

Atherton nodded, and stepped away from the car before melting into the surrounding night, which had turned misty as fog rolled in from the nearby River Coquet.

Inside the car, Ryan cranked up the heating.

"He's got a point, y'nah," Phillips said, popping another chocolate eyeball in his mouth. "It must mean somethin', the river turnin' red."

Ryan leaned back against the headrest and closed his eyes, allowing himself a moment's respite as he mulled over the question.

"I think it's from *Exodus* or maybe *Revelation*," he said, at length. "The River Nile turned to blood, so that nobody could drink from it, as part of the plagues inflicted upon Egypt."

Phillips grunted. "There's a fair amount of Christian history in these parts," he said. "I think Lady's Well used to be associated with some old saint—whatshisname."

When Ryan opened his eyes again, they were full of humour. "Ah, yes, that well known apostle of the border, Saint Whatshisname."

"It'll come to me," Phillips said, and began massaging his temples, as if that would help to jog his memory.

While he did that, Ryan took out his smartphone and ran a quick Google search, to save time.

"N—" he began.

"Norman?" Phillips interrupted him. "No, that's not it."

"Ni—"

"Nincompoop? No, that's definitely not it. I reckon it was Saint Ninny-Ann."

"*Ninian*," Ryan told him. "Saint Ninian, fifth-century apostle of the borders."

"Ayc, that's what I said."

With a short laugh, Ryan slid his phone back inside his pocket and turned on the engine.

"Well, this Ninian used to baptise loads of people in the well, back in the Olden Times," Phillips continued, affecting an air of sage wisdom.

"Olden Times," Ryan repeated. "Which would be when, exactly, oh Wise One?"

"*A long time ago*," Phillips snapped. "Don't interrupt your elders when they're laying down some knowledge on you, boy. As I was saying, later on, folk started calling the place 'Lady's Well' after the Virgin Mary."

"Very informative," Ryan said, with a grin. "We've got a meeting with the team from Northumbrian Water and Environmental Health tomorrow morning, so we can see this famous well for ourselves—although, you know, I have a funny feeling that, for all the heads that might have been dunked over the years, it was probably just used as a watering hole for passing travellers."

"Oh aye? I wonder what gave you that idea?" Phillips asked, pointing towards the wooden sign flapping from the side of the pub of the same name. "But, you're probably right. This'll turn out to have nowt to do with religious voodoo, Hallowe'en or anythin' like that, and everythin' to do with some unscrupulous factory owner dumpin' illegal chemicals in the water supply. We've been gettin' the heebie-jeebies about it but, I'm tellin' you, Fred Humble would've been dead as a doornail, even without the problem with the water, mark my words."

"I'm not so sure, Frank."

"Eh? What d'you mean?"

"The television—it was on, and then it was off."

"Have you lost your last marble?"

Ryan laughed. "Not yet, but there's time," he replied. "Think about it, Frank. Nick Humble says the television was on when he discovered his father's body, and is adamant that he didn't turn it off. For all their faults, the first responders didn't interfere with it either, because they were too hapless to do more than poke their noses in and run straight back out again—I checked, just to be sure. Where does that leave us?"

Phillips thought back to the crime scene, and the penny dropped.

"Somebody entered the house and turned the television off, sometime after Nick Humble discovered his father's body and before the police went in. How long would that have been?"

"They could have had a window of up to half an hour," Ryan said. "But, as we know, the back door was closed and locked from the inside. They must have gone through the front door, bold as brass."

"Why would they turn the telly off?"

"Who knows, Frank? Maybe they just didn't fancy it. The point is, somebody went back inside the house for a reason; to retrieve something, to finish the job, to plant something…we don't know yet. All I know is that, if there was nothing amiss, they'd have seen the body and run straight out of the house to report it, like any honest person would. There haven't been any reports made by *any* material witness, aside from the victim's son."

"Who had a key, and could let himself in at any time, without looking suspicious," Phillips pointed out. "Didn't seem all that cut up about his da's passin', either."

"Exactly what I thought, too."

Phillips looked across at his friend, who was smiling in the semi-darkness of the car. "What on Earth are you grinnin' about?" he exclaimed. "We've got a load of poisoned villagers, a bloke as dead as a dodo and a journo sniffin' around like a basset hound. That's usually enough to give us both a pain in the arse."

Ryan's grin widened a fraction. "I was just thinking the other day, 'I could do with a good mystery' and here we have it."

"Takes all sorts," Phillips muttered, and reached for the last eyeball.

CHAPTER 8

"*Boo.*"

Ryan froze in the act of reaching for a glass, while a pair of slim arms wrapped themselves around his torso.

"I thought I'd have to send out a search party," his wife said.

"There were a couple of hairy moments," he admitted, and leaned down to bestow a thorough kiss. "I missed you."

"Same goes, Chief Inspector."

"You didn't have to wait up for me," he said, frowning at the time. "No need for both of us to be exhausted, tomorrow."

"I wasn't tired," she said, although it was unlikely she'd have been able to sleep while she knew he was out there in a remote corner of Northumberland at night.

"How's the little one?"

Their daughter, Emma, was growing bigger by the day and, at two years old, was rampaging around the house with all the grace and elegance of a miniature bull in a china shop.

"She had a lot of fun at the nursery's 'spooky party,'" Anna said, leaning back against one of the countertops.

"She must have worn herself out with all the dancing, because she's out for the count."

Ryan smiled, thinking of his little girl.

"What about you?" she asked him. "I caught a story on the evening news—something about rivers running red up in Holystone and people turning up dead?"

Anna delivered her summary with the kind of detachment he might have heard from one of his detectives in an incident room back at CID, and wondered whether that was a good thing or a bad thing.

"The two factors might be completely unrelated," he said. "I think somebody's killed a man in the village—or, at least, his death is suspicious—but whether contaminated water played any part in it remains unclear."

"Why would anybody kill him?"

"That's always the million-dollar question," he said, downing the rest of his water after having inspected its colour thoroughly. "And it's what I plan to find out."

Anna smiled to herself. "I almost feel sorry for them," she said.

"Who?"

"Whichever poor sod has you on their tail," she laughed. "They probably thought they'd covered all the bases, and then you come along to throw a spanner in the works."

"They all think they're committing the perfect crime," he said, with a tigerish smile. "But, as somebody famous once said, *every contact leaves a trace.*"

They made their way upstairs, turning off lights as they went, and then sank onto their bed with a collective sigh of relief. After a moment, Ryan turned to his wife with a troubled expression that marred his handsome face.

"Do you think we're getting old?" he asked.

Whatever she'd expected him to say, it certainly wasn't that.

"Eh? Speak for yourself!" she told him, with a playful jab to the ribs. "As far as I'm concerned, it's about how you feel *inside*, and I think we'll always feel like a couple of kids when we're together."

He reached across to take her hand.

"Whatever made you think of that?" she asked. "You're not usually one to worry about the passage of time."

"I just don't want to miss a moment," he said. "I don't want to be so busy working that I forget to live, then open my eyes one day to find that I don't have as much time left as I thought."

Anna gave his hand a quick squeeze. "We won't let you forget," she promised, with a soft kiss. "Which reminds me, Denise rang earlier to say that she's signed you up to be a guinea pig for the self-defence class she's running, next weekend. I said you'd be delighted."

"You're so thoughtful."

"Don't mention it, Greybeard."

With a decidedly youthful burst of energy, Ryan tugged his wife across the bed towards him.

"It seems there's life in the old dog, yet," she teased.

"Woof," he said softly, before lowering his head to hers.

"Not a chance, Frank Phillips."

These stark words came from the mouth of Detective Inspector Denise MacKenzie, who lay on her side with her eyes firmly shut.

Phillips, who'd tiptoed into the house and made his way upstairs to snuggle into his wife's warm body, froze in the act of reaching for another kind of…pillow.

"I was just…"

"Aye, I know what you were 'just'," MacKenzie snapped. "You can just think again, boyo, because I'm in no mood for any funny business—not after you abandoned me with all of those kids, right before the sugar started to kick in."

Phillips flexed his fingers, and began to rub slow, soothing circles on her back.

"I know, love," he said. "If it hadn't been an emergency, I'd have been right there with you."

Earlier that evening, their adopted daughter, Samantha, had played host to several of her school friends for a Hallowe'en party, complete with toffee apples and a donkey-shaped piñata, while *Casper* and *The Addams Family Values* had played on the telly in the background. He and Denise had agreed to it as a reward for consistently good behaviour at school and outstanding grades which, given Sam's tough start in life and limited access to early mainstream education, was no small achievement. Besides, they were glad to throw as many parties as they could, in the hope that it would make up for all the ones she'd missed. Still, it didn't mean they had to enjoy the practicalities, nor the clean-up operation that followed.

"Water spilled all over the lounge floor, from the apple-bobbing bucket," MacKenzie wailed softly. "Then, the bowl of popcorn went flying…"

"You've been a trooper, love, a real trooper," he said quickly, and began kneading her shoulders.

Against her better judgment, MacKenzie began to soften.

"Don't think I don't know what you're doing," she mumbled, when he brought out the big guns and started to massage her scalp. "I'm immune to…to…"

"To what, love?"

MacKenzie turned over and smiled up at him.

"To you, Frank," she said, and grasped his ears so that she could pull him in for a kiss.

Just before his lips could claim the forbidden fruit, she sprang up again.

"What's that smell?" she demanded.

Phillips was instantly contrite. "Sorry, I *did* spray a bit of air freshener in the en-suite—"

"Not that," she said, and leaned forward to sniff his breath, her fine nose stripping back a liberal use of mouthwash to detect the mysterious scent that lingered beneath it.

Phillips held his breath.

"*Chocolate*," she hissed, and he could only be grateful the light was too dim for him to see the look in her eyes.

"Be gentle with me," he pleaded. "I can't help being a chocoholic, I was born this way—"

"Tell it to the judge," she said, and then smiled. "Luckily for you, she's very lenient."

Phillips gave a laugh that would have made Sid James proud.

"In that case, bang me up, yer honour, 'cos I'm guilty as sin!"

CHAPTER 9

The next morning

"Thank you for agreeing to see me, ma'am, at such short notice."

Chief Constable Sandra Morrison waved away the formality and indicated that Melanie Yates should take a seat in one of the chairs arranged in front of the desk in her office, which occupied one of the plush corner spots of the executive suite at Northumbria Police Headquarters. Not that anyone would have known the difference, given an indiscriminate use of beige paint and brown carpet tile throughout the building.

"Coffee?"

Melanie nodded gratefully. "Thank you, ma'am."

"I'm not her late Majesty," Morrison said. "Call me Sandra, unless the situation calls for something fruitier, in which case I'd rather be called 'Chief' and, even then, only if absolutely necessary."

It brought a smile to the young woman's lips, which was a welcome change from the general air of fragility she wore like a second skin.

"So, how can I help?" Rather than heading for her usual spot at the desk, Morrison changed course and decided to take a chair beside Melanie. There was a shared history between the two women and, she hoped, a degree of trust. Melanie Yates had been a girl of sixteen when Sandra had first come across her in the family room of their former offices, standing beside her parents while they waited to receive the devastating news that their daughter and her twin sister, Gemma, would not be coming home. She'd seen the core of strength in the girl she'd met; the same strength that was displayed time and again in the able detective Melanie had become. Yet, for all her resilience, the question of whether she was strong enough to withstand her most recent experience remained unanswered.

"I planned to discuss this with Ryan before coming to you with what is, essentially, an HR matter," Melanie began, in what she hoped was a professional tone. "Unfortunately, he's tied up with a case, and this can't really wait. The fact is, I'd like to come back to work—just for a trial period, to begin with."

Morrison heard the hesitation beneath the bravado and took a thoughtful sip of coffee.

"Do you think you're ready?"

"I—" Melanie set her cup down, not trusting herself to keep the liquid steady. "The honest answer is that I don't know. All I *do* know is that I'm going out of my mind staying cooped up at home. I'm developing claustrophobia and agoraphobia—at the same time, if you can believe it—not to mention a host of other syndromes that would give the occupational therapist a field day. It's quite possible that, the first time I clock eyes on a fresh DB, I'll hurl up my breakfast and turn into a gibbering wreck."

Morrison raised an eyebrow. "You're not filling me with confidence, Mel."

"I thought honesty was the best policy," she said, stoically. "I think I should try coming back, Sandra. I think I *have* to, before things get past a point of no return."

Morrison rose to her feet and walked to the window, where a couple of pigeons had settled their squat bodies on the extreme edge of the sill, feathers fluttering in the morning sunshine. Free to fly, if they wished, or free to stay there for as long as their bodies would hold them, before they fell.

Much better to fly.

"All right," she said, turning back. "You're back on the team, effective immediately. But, Melanie, I always want complete honesty from you. If you feel it's becoming too much, or you need more time to recover, I want to know about it. Is that a deal?"

Melanie rose to her feet, and held out a hand.

"You have my word."

While Melanie Yates prepared to face her peers in the Major Crimes Unit of the Criminal Investigation Department,

Ryan and Phillips found themselves confronted with something far more terrifying, in the form of the Holystone Parish Council.

Consisting of a collective of individuals voted in by their fellow residents to manage the shared interests of the village, the Council was regularly employed in the task of writing letters—*copious* letters—to their Member of Parliament and Local Authority; fundraising for the repairs of the church roof; entering the flower-beds into the bi-annual 'Britain's Most Beautiful Borders' competition alongside a multitude of other small but necessary civic endeavours designed to preserve the contented life the residents of their parish enjoyed.

On that day, the Council had convened an emergency meeting of its members, led by Councillor Karen Russell who, when not engaged in the laudable task of "fighting for everyday rights, for everyday people", was otherwise kept busy as the owner of the village store and tearoom—"Russell's Teatime Treats"—which put her at odds with fellow Council member, Lynn Gibbins—who, as landlady of The Watering Hole, should really have known better than to start serving scones and clotted cream on her afternoon menu which had, for many years, kept to an uncontentious selection of pub classics.

Blissfully unaware of these troubling undercurrents, Ryan and Phillips entered the pub's private dining area, set up to resemble a Council Chamber, and surveyed the row of surly faces awaiting their arrival.

"Are you Detective Chief Inspector Ryan?"

Councillor Russell addressed Phillips, who was the elder of the two men, if not the most senior in the police hierarchy.

"I'm just his lowly sergeant," he said, with good humour. "This here's the feller you're lookin' for."

He jerked a thumb towards Ryan, who then found himself the recipient of a very thorough inspection.

"We'd like some straight answers," she said, once she'd finished looking him up and down for longer than was strictly necessary. "As you can imagine, we've been inundated with queries from villagers who'd like to know what the *heck* is going on, and how quickly their water supply will be restored. Some of them have young children—"

"May I?" Ryan tapped a finger to one of the chairs that had been laid out, and made himself comfortable without waiting for her response.

"Thanks," he said, while Phillips availed himself of the chair to his right. "Now, before we go any further, I'd like to have the pleasure of knowing who I'm speaking to."

Phillips retrieved a notebook from his pocket.

"Let's start with you," Ryan said to Karen, though he was already broadly aware of her credentials. "Your name, please?"

"Councillor Karen Russell, Chair of the Village Council," she said, with a degree of smugness she made no effort to disguise. "I run the tearoom on the high street, as well."

"Nice lookin' cakes," Phillips put in, with his usual nose for sugar and flattery, when the occasion demanded it. "We'll have to stop in."

"Our scones are to *die* for," Karen couldn't help saying. "You'll not find anything to match them around here. Of course, I've been forced to close the tearoom until we can get the water back up and running safely—"

A woman they recognised as the pub landlady huffed audibly, and crossed her arms over her chest.

"They understand perfectly well the problems we're facing, Karen," she said, through gritted teeth. "None of us can run a decent trade until the water is fixed, which is a crying shame when you think of all those passing journalists who keep popping their heads around the door, but there you have it. We should think of poor Fred."

Karen snorted. "*Poor Fred*, indeed," she sneered. "You weren't saying that when he was alive and kicking, that's for sure—"

"And your name, please?"

Their voices came to a shuddering stop and both women turned back to Ryan, who awaited their full attention with the patient air of a man who'd faced worse things than council quarrels in his time.

"Lynn Gibbins," came the dutiful reply. "I own the pub, here."

"Very nice, too," Ryan said, before turning to the remaining three members of the council, who'd done little more than murmur, 'Good morning'. They consisted of two men and another woman of around sixty, who wore a serene smile on her attractive face, which was framed by a riot of grey-blonde corkscrew curls and a pair of enormous, hooped earrings. Silver rings adorned her fingers, aside from a pretty sapphire which graced the third finger of her left hand. If he hadn't known better, he'd have guessed she was either a pirate or a hippy.

"I'm Sabrina Graham," she told him. "I run the holistic shop, beside the village store."

"And tearoom," Karen put in, sharply.

Sabrina raised an eyebrow, then looked Ryan dead in the eye and said, very seriously, "And *tearoom*."

His lips twitched. "Yes, I've seen it," he said. "Love and Light."

From the outside, it looked like one of those catch-all, jingle-jangle shops that sold everything from healing crystals and dreamcatchers to homemade soaps, and was the kind of place a person might easily have lost an hour of their life perusing the bookshelves and sniffing the homewares before having their palm read or their fortune told.

"That's the one," she said, beaming at him.

Ryan nodded, and turned to the man seated beside her, whose body language indicated a certain familiarity. Of a similar age, if not a few years older, he was tall and broad-shouldered, with a military bearing and a weather-beaten face that spoke of time spent outdoors in all conditions—features which reminded him very much of his own father, Charles Ryan.

"David Hetherington," he said, plainly. "Most people call me, 'Davie.'"

Ryan thought of Nick Humble, who had first been alerted to the water contamination by this man, whom he'd described as owning a farm on the outskirts of the village.

"I've got Coquet Farm," he said, confirming the matter. "It isn't far from the well."

"Davie was the first to notice any trouble," Karen butted in, again. "It's a *miracle* he wasn't struck down—"

The man himself gave a discreet roll of his eyes. "Aye, it's nowt short of a miracle," he said. "Either that, or plain good sense in decidin' not to chug down a litre or two of bright red water."

"Shush," Sabrina chided him with a nudge of her elbow.

"Well, I don't think my suffering from gastric poisoning is a matter of being without *sense*," the fifth voice chimed in. "Not all of us spotted the danger before it was too late. Even after we ran our taps for a while, the water only looked pinkish to me."

Phillips surmised that there'd been a significant case of the runs in that man's household, and tutted sympathetically.

"Ian Bell," he supplied. "I'm the archaeologist in charge of Project Holystone, but I happen to live in the village."

"Ian is one of our *newer* residents," Karen intoned, and gave Ryan a look that suggested he was not to be trusted for that very reason.

"Project Holystone," Ryan repeated, while his brain flipped through a back catalogue of discussions held with his wife, who was herself a well-known local historian. Academic history and archaeology were different disciplines, but Anna had friends far and wide and, whenever there was a new dig underway in the region, she liked to know about it.

"It's been underway for a year," Bell explained. "We started over on the site where we know for certain there was an old Augustinian priory, and then pushed out from there. There's a long history of Christian settlement in these parts, especially in the fertile areas immediately beside the river—"

"And even longer before that," Sabrina said, with quiet authority. "Pre-Christian faith dominated for centuries before Christianity, Ian."

"This is all very *interesting*," Karen rode across them, obviously irritated. "I'm far more concerned with the here and now, if it's all the same to you. We've got a village full of people clamouring to know when they'll be getting their drinking water back. Over and above the logistical nightmare we're facing, I can't be the only one who wants to know who poisoned the water in the first place. I'm sure you feel the same, Chief Inspector? *Obviously*, whoever poisoned the well must also be responsible for killing Fred."

The assumption was delivered with such confidence, Ryan might almost have believed it.

"We can't say there's any connection at all until further investigations are complete," he said mildly. "On that topic, we'd be grateful if any theories surrounding Mr Humble's cause of death were kept to yourselves."

Karen narrowed her eyes at his tone, and the implication that she or anyone else would gossip about Fred's death…I mean, who *hadn't* spoken to a few people, here and there?

"What about the water?" she demanded.

"Team's already up there tryin' to work out what happened," Davie reminded her. "We've got some big tanks on the way that should be with us by lunchtime, so that'll keep people going till the system can be flushed out—"

Ryan leaned forward. "Who authorised the system to be flushed out?"

Davie frowned. "Well, nobody, I s'pose, but that's what the water folk have suggested, so we'll be takin' their advice—"

By 'The Water Folk', Ryan imagined he was referring to representatives of Northumbrian Water, who managed the supply from Lady's Well, and perhaps also an officer of the Environment Agency.

"I'm sorry, I can't allow the pipework to be cleaned out," he said simply. "Not until our forensic examination is complete."

Five faces stared at him in surprise.

"Isn't it obvious that somebody dumped a load of red dye into the water?" Lynn remarked. "Surely, there's no need to delay flushing out the pipes?"

"Our team will be working as swiftly as they can," he assured her, in a tone that brooked no argument. "In case I haven't made myself clear, we are treating Mr Humble's death as suspicious. That includes the potential of *murder* and, as such, we will cover all possible lines of enquiry."

"Murder?" Ian said, and laughed in disbelief. "Who'd want to kill Fred? He might have been a difficult sod, at times, but he was a permanent fixture in these parts."

Ryan looked at each of them, in turn.

Small towns had their secrets, he thought.

"That's just what I mean to find out," he said.

CHAPTER 10

"I don't know what I can possibly tell you."

In a sharp reversal of fortunes, it was now Councillor Karen Russell who found herself on the receiving end of some forthright questioning, having been sequestered to a smaller room supplied by Lynn Gibbins to allow Ryan and Phillips to conduct their interviews in private.

"Why not start by telling us where you were yesterday, from around three o'clock?" Ryan said.

Karen ran an agitated hand over her hair, feeling suddenly hot in the confined space.

"I was in the tearoom," she said. "It closes at five, so I must have been there until half past, cleaning up and so on."

"Do you work with anyone else?" Phillips asked her.

"Yes, I have a girl who helps me with the waitressing," she said, and gave her name. "Look, I object to this line of questioning. I don't have any reason whatsoever to have disliked Fred, let alone—well, whatever it is you imagine has happened to him!"

Ryan gave her a quiet look, and then changed direction. "Tell us about the fracking dispute that's been going on."

Caught off guard, Councillor Russell recovered swiftly. "Plans have been put forward to allow fracking on a designated site to the west of the village," she said, in what Phillips might have described as a 'telephone' voice.

"What stage have the plans reached?" Ryan asked.

"Well," she said, and shifted in her seat. "It's a matter of…ongoing debate."

"Very diplomatic," Ryan said. "Could you be more specific?"

Karen pursed her lips. "Look, if you *must* know, the majority of residents are in favour of the plans," she said, with a hint of defiance. "We're talking about a rocky scrubland area with very little agricultural value. The potential for fracking has attracted interest from a number of energy suppliers who'd be willing to purchase the land for a very good price, and many people could benefit."

She thought of the eye-watering offer that had been made for her own small portion of that land, which formed part of her back garden. She'd have accepted in a heartbeat if it weren't for the small minority of difficult people blocking her way.

"I presume there were also some objections to the plans?"

She swallowed the bitter taste of disappointment, and gave a short nod.

"Yes."

"From whom?"

"Well, there's Ian," she said, straight off the bat. "He's *never* been in favour of the plans, because he believes the scrubland area has historic value and fracking would alter the character of the village and its surrounds."

"You disagree?"

"I think it's all a storm in a teacup," she said, dodging the question. "There's absolutely no reason to assume the heart of the village should change, at all. If anything, an injection of funds for local people might *reinvigorate* the place."

"I see," Ryan said. *And he did see.* Tearooms were hardly multinational corporations, and Holystone was not on the main tourist trail, despite its beauty and all the history to recommend it. Its relative seclusion made the village a popular destination for die-hard walkers and fans of Northumberland landscapes, but their trade might not have been enough to keep things afloat in a changing economy.

"Who else raised objections to the fracking proposals?" he asked.

Karen rubbed a hand across the back of her neck.

"Well, since you ask…Fred was one of the objectors," she admitted.

Ryan raised an eyebrow. "Did he say why he was against it?"

"He said he liked things just the way they were," she replied. "Fred was very much stuck in his ways, you have to understand, and he didn't like large businesses—he thought all the energy companies were crooks and charlatans. His final word on the matter was just over a week ago, actually. He came along to our last meeting, where the proposals were discussed once again, and said that we should all stop trying to interfere with things that should be left alone."

"What do you think he meant by that?" Phillips asked.

"Fred was a difficult man—God rest him," Karen tagged on, swiftly. "The fact is, if he wasn't complaining about this or that, he was moaning about the other." She leaned forward, her voice persuasive. "I sat with him, more than once, to try to explain the benefits," she said. "I told him he needed to move with the times, but it just wasn't in his nature. He was stubborn as an old mule."

"Did anybody else raise an objection?"

Karen listed a few names from the village, then sighed heavily.

"Not forgetting the *protesters*," she said, as if it was a dirty word. "When the plans were raised, two young men and a woman turned up a few days later and set up a camp on the outskirts of the village. We're having a devil of a job trying to get rid of them."

"Do you have their names?" Phillips asked, and twiddled his biro.

Karen shook her head. "I only know one of them—a young lad by the name of Zachary. He's the leader of their group, if you can call that bunch of ill-mannered, entitled young miscreants an organised group."

She sniffed.

"If you ask me, one of them *must* have been responsible for dyeing the water red," she said. "Not a doubt in my mind, it's a publicity stunt that went too far and ended up making people ill. When I *think* that any one of us could have wound up like Fred…"

She trailed off, clearly horrified by the prospect.

"Once again, we have no evidence presently to suggest any causal link between the contaminated water and Fred Humble's death," Ryan said.

Karen was unconvinced.

"Well, I'll tell you something *else*," she said, pointing a finger at them both. "If those young layabouts haven't anything to hide, I want to know where they've been for the past twenty-four hours. Up until now, they've made a thorough nuisance of themselves, canvassing everyone in the village and harassing every visitor. Only yesterday, I saw Zachary had planted himself on the main street again, with another placard pinned to his chest. In fact, I'm surprised Fred didn't chase him off, since he was shouting the ends just outside his front window."

Karen folded her arms.

"But, lo and behold, as soon as people start to become ill, suddenly the protesters are nowhere to be seen. That's fishy, if you ask me."

Though it might have irked him to admit it, Ryan agreed with her. "What time did you see Zachary on the street?"

"Oh, it must've been around four o'clock," she said.

Something flickered in Ryan's eyes. "You've already told us Ian Bell is against the fracking plans," he said. "Does that mean he supports the protesters, since they're of the same mind?"

"You'd have to ask him," she said, and her mouth screwing into an expression Phillips had seen many times on the rear end of a cat. "I suppose, in his defence, Ian hasn't ever *said* as much, but neither of them wants the fracking to go ahead, for different reasons."

"Thank you, Councillor Russell."

There was a brief silence in the wake of her departure, then Phillips blew out a long breath, stretched his arms above his head, and turned to his friend.

"Bet you're thinkin' the same thing I am," he said, with a knowing twinkle.

Ryan smiled. "If you're thinking something along the lines that Karen Russell couldn't possibly have been at her tearoom at the other end of the village until five-thirty, if she was able to witness Zachary sitting near Fred Humble's window at four o'clock, then, yes, we're thinking the same thing."

Phillips looked crestfallen. "Actually, mate, I was thinkin' it's almost time for a bit o' lunch," he said. "I'm clammin' for one of those scones everyone keeps bangin' on about."

Ryan cocked his head to one side, and considered his friend as if for the first time.

"Frank, somewhere far, far back in the 'Olden Times' you were telling me about, was one of your relatives a Labrador, by any chance?"

Phillips gave a bark of laughter. "Don't talk about Granny Phillips, that way," he said.

CHAPTER 11

An hour's drive south of where Ryan and Phillips argued over the merits and demerits of cheese versus fruit scones, Doctor Anna Taylor-Ryan stood on the threshold of a different world entirely, one she knew very little about.

Creative writing.

Armed with her laptop and a stomach full of nerves, she stepped inside the hallowed walls of the Literary and Philosophical Society of Newcastle upon Tyne, where a creative writing group met weekly to console and cajole one another through the process of writing and publishing works of fiction. It was a grey day in the city, and a film of drizzle coated the surrounding buildings, lending a sheen to the stonework whenever a rare shaft of light happened to break through the clouds. Its roots might have dated back to pre-Roman times, but Newcastle had been fashioned and moulded by Victorian hands, and their architecture was reflected in the neo-Classical columns of its train station and in the curved grandeur of the streets around the oldest part of the city, known as Grainger Town. There was a proud beauty to the place, which Anna had always thought was a fitting reflection of the people who had toiled to build it.

"Are you looking for something?"

Behind the reception desk, a lady smiled at her, and Anna nodded. It was silly to be nervous, especially for a woman so accustomed to academic environments, but storytelling was an entirely new venture and, as yet, she had no idea whether she was any good at it. Family and friends had been very positive, of course, but, with the exception of Ryan, who knew how much value she placed upon the truth, Anna felt they would be unlikely to tell her if her fledgling effort was a load of old codswallop.

"Yes, I'm looking for the creative writing group, please?"

The woman pointed towards a stairwell. "Head upstairs to the Committee Room—you can't miss it."

Anna thanked her and made her way up to the first floor, which gave way to a pretty galleried area overlooking the main library, where rows of books were illuminated by a set of impressive domed skylights through which a weak morning light filtered. She followed the gallery until she spotted a door with a placard that read 'Committee Room', alongside a paper sign which had been tacked to its exterior and read, 'CREATIVE WRITERS IN HERE'.

Feeling very much like a child reliving their first day of school, Anna stepped inside and found that, much to her chagrin, the meeting was already underway.

She was sure the flyer said eleven o'clock on Monday mornings...

A quick check of the time told her it was just before eleven, which should have made her dead on time. Anna had gone to a bit of trouble swapping her own workdays at the History Faculty in Durham in order to attend the group, so to say she was disappointed was an understatement. However, there was no time for self-recrimination before another person proved themselves more than happy to do the job for her.

"Oh *dear*!" A woman's voice carried across the room, and the fifteen people seated at its long oval committee table paused in the act of packing away their papers and turned to face the source of her disquiet. "It seems we have a latecomer."

Anna clutched her bag and stepped into the room, pinning a friendly smile on her face. "Sorry," she said to the group at large. "I thought the group met at eleven—"

"Normally, we do, but the time was changed for this week," the woman said, as if it was something a new member should have known by telepathy, if not by ordinary lines of communication. "Well, you might as well come in and introduce yourself, but there won't be time for much else, today."

Anna fought against the strong urge to turn and run in the opposite direction, but instead lifted her chin and walked past a number of interested faces to take the only remaining chair, which happened to be placed beside the group's leader. *Definitely like being back at school,* Anna thought, but her mama hadn't raised a quitter, so she bore down against the urge to escape and smiled at the rest of the table of interested faces.

"I'm Anna," she said, leaving off the various letters and academic accolades she might have added. "I was born in the North East and it's still my home…the place I love."

There were smiles around the table from those who understood the depth of feeling towards the sea, the beaches and hills, castles and rivers that made up the place where many of them had been born.

"That can't be your author name."

Anna's smile slipped, and she turned to face the predictable source of this interruption, wondering what it was about the scathing tone some people employed that just rubbed the wrong way.

"I don't think you mentioned *your* name," she said.

The group's leader glanced at the others around the table, her expression seeming to convey just the right mix of self-deprecating indulgence and outright surprise at not having been recognised on sight.

"Lin Oldman," she replied. "You've probably seen my books."

Anna hadn't.

"Mm," she said, politely.

"When I'm not writing, signing books or chairing an event, I like to give back in this way," Lin said, spreading her arms like some sort of Mediaeval queen doling out scraps to her serfs. "I find it *so* rewarding to be able to give people a nudge in the right direction…"

Several dutiful heads bobbed up and down in effusive agreement.

"So, tell us what it is you want to write."

Anna set her misgivings aside and tried to remember why she was there. "I've written a supernatural murder mystery," she said.

"*Lovely*," Lin said, as though speaking to a very slow child. "Why don't you give us the synopsis—that's a summary, by the way."

Anna had written more synopses than Lin Oldman had probably eaten hot dinners, but she brushed off the condescension and rattled off a summary of the storyline. By the end, she was encouraged to see more smiles burgeoning on the faces of those around her.

All except one.

"It's certainly a start," Lin said, doubtfully. "Have you thought about how to plot your novel? What about character development? Try not to be intimidated; *many* new writers feel overwhelmed, at first. It's only when you've been going for as long as I have, that you can truly feel confident to sit and write, straight off the bat…"

"Actually, I've already written the story," Anna said, tentatively. "I was hoping the group could tell me if it's any good."

"*Well*," Lin said, with an edge to her voice. "I should manage your expectations, dear. *Many* would-be writers think they've written their story, only to find several more edited drafts are required before they have something *approaching* the standard good enough to query agents—"

"Actually, you know, I was thinking of publishing independently, rather than trying to find a traditional publishing deal. I've been looking into it, and I think it makes the most sense."

In the wake of this statement, Anna could have heard a pin drop.

"You mean, *self-publish*?" Lin whispered; the scathing tone having returned in full force.

"Why not?" Anna asked.

"Well, you know, it's not…" Lin's lips puckered, as though she'd sucked the juice from a ripe lemon. "It's not the *usual* route. Surely, you'd like to know whether your work is good enough to be published—?"

"I was rather hoping my peers and the reading public could tell me that," Anna replied, with irrefutable logic. "I can't really think of anybody better qualified."

Lin guffawed. "I realise you're very *new* to this," she said. "But ask yourself this: do you ever want to be considered for an award? Do you want to be taken seriously by the rest of the publishing world? Do you want to be *accepted*? If so, the best way to achieve that is to toe the line and find yourself a publisher, if you can."

Anna heard the words, looked into the other woman's eyes, and realised something very important in that moment.

Lin Oldman was afraid.

Afraid of failure, and of ridicule.

But was she? Anna asked herself. Was she frightened of what another person she'd never met might say about the story she'd so lovingly written?

She came to her feet. "Thank you," she said quietly. "I'm grateful for your time; this has been very informative."

Lin's shoulders sagged with relief, though she couldn't have explained why. "Not at all," she said. "Now, come along next week with your first chapter and we'll have a look at it. I'm sure it isn't half as bad as you might think."

Anna knew that she would not be returning the following week, nor any week after. It was small wonder people lived in fear of shadows, she thought, when those they trusted to guide them were so quick to issue judgment and disdain. However, she need not be one of them, for she knew the meaning of *real* fear. She'd lived it, body and soul, and survived. She did not fear shadows any more, nor the unkind word of a stranger and, as she left the building with its beautiful décor and musty scent of books, she told herself that, one day, she'd see one of her own novels sitting on the shelves. Every day, she encouraged her students at the university to be brave, enquiring, and to live life to the fullest, so she would have to start taking her own advice.

When Anna stepped back onto the busy pavement outside, she looked up to see the sun breaking through a blanket of clouds, and a shard of brilliant light fell over the city of Newcastle. She stood there for a moment or two with her eyes closed, feeling the unexpected warmth against her skin, and when she reopened them, they were full of purpose.

Lin Oldman watched Anna leaving from the gallery above, feeling something stir in her belly, something bitter and acrid.

It might have been jealousy.

Her mouth opened to call down to the woman, to tell her that she'd left a copy of her manuscript on the table upstairs, but no sound came out. Instead, her fingers curled around the wad of paper, and she tucked it into her leather satchel, casting a swift glance this way and that, pleased to see the action had gone unnoticed. She felt it burning a hole through her bag on the journey home.

Thief, her mind whispered.

"Shut up," Lin muttered, and threw her satchel down before sinking onto the edge of the sofa in her living room.

It had been three long years since her last book had been published and, even then, its reception had been lukewarm at best. Her publisher had gone quiet and, worryingly, so had her agent. The invitations to appear at the best literary festivals were beginning to dry up, and it was becoming harder to fool herself that she was the roaring success all those glossy magazines had proclaimed her, back in the early days. She wished she could think as Anna Taylor-Ryan did, and brush aside the terrible need for her work to be validated by somebody who was a member of all the right circles.

If only she could be so free.

But the more pressing concern was that she'd run out of ideas. She needed to come up with some new concepts, fast, or the prospect of a new publishing deal would become even less of a reality than it was now. Yet nothing came to mind at all.

Her eye fell on the satchel.

It wouldn't hurt to look, would it?

CHAPTER 12

Sabrina Graham entered the little interview room at The Watering Hole in a cloud of perfume, something earthy and spicy that made Ryan and Phillips think of the Far East. It went well with the floating, multicoloured kaftan she wore and the bold red lipstick, which gave one the overall impression of a woman unafraid to follow her own style.

"Please take a seat, Ms Graham."

"Sabrina," she corrected. "It's only Davie who's allowed to call me 'Rina.'"

Ryan lifted an enquiring eyebrow.

"Of course—you wouldn't know. Davie and I are engaged," she said, waggling the sapphire stone on her finger and turning a sweet shade of pink that belied her advancing years. "It's only taken us decades of living in the same village to realise we're in love!"

She laughed and Phillips, for one, smiled with her. He understood how cupid's bow could strike at the most unlikely moment, and it wasn't always while you were in your twenties or thirties, either.

"Congratulations to you both," he said, warmly. "I hope all this disruption won't interrupt your plans?"

She shook her head. "No, we'd planned to have the ceremony in a few weeks' time," she said. "We both like the idea of a winter wedding, even though it'll be cold underfoot—you may have guessed that I follow the Old Ways, and Davie is happy to oblige me, providing we make a quick trip to the Registry Office, too."

"I'm sure our investigation will be over and done with, by then," Ryan assured her.

The joy leaked from her eyes, as the reason they were all there came to the forefront of their minds once more.

"I was sorry to hear about Fred," she said, and seemed entirely genuine. "Oh, I know what people say about him, and it was all true. He wasn't a nice man, and never had been. I know that better than most, considering he was married to my sister for twenty years and led her a terrible life. That being said, I would hate to think he was poisoned, as Karen seems to imagine."

They thought of the woman in the old photograph at Fred's house, and, if they had looked closely enough, they could have seen a family resemblance around the eyes.

"And your sister's name?"

"Diane," she said.

"You seemed to imply Fred wasn't the best of husbands to your sister," he said. "What do you mean?"

Sabrina sighed. "Fred was old-fashioned," she said. "Believe it or not, as a younger man he was very handsome and could be charming when he wanted to be—before life and bad living took its toll. Diane met him on a rare night out in Newcastle and was smitten. He courted her, and they ended up getting married very quickly and moving here, because our parents had recently died, and I've always preferred to stay here. I was the only family she had left, and I think Diane had an idyllic notion of us all being one big, happy family. That's before the bruises started turning up on her wrists and arms," she added.

A couple of seconds passed by, in which they could imagine everything she'd left unsaid.

"Where's your sister now?" Phillips asked. "It would be good to have a word with her."

Sabrina's eyes glazed with tears, and she blinked several times.

"I wish I knew," she replied. "Diane left, very suddenly, twenty years ago. She just couldn't take it anymore, and something snapped. She ran away, leaving a note for me and Davie, begging to be left alone."

"She left without taking her son?" Ryan said softly.

Sabrina nodded, and dashed away an errant tear. "I don't think Nick ever forgave her for that," she whispered. "He loved her, so much." She dragged in a shaking breath, surprised by her own depth of feeling after the passage of time. "I stepped in, where I could," she told them. "I'm his aunt, not his mother, but I've done my best to bridge the gap Diane left in his life. Lord knows, Fred wasn't able to offer the lad any real affection. But, really, it's Davie who brought Nick up, and taught him how to be a man. It's part of the reason I find him so lovable."

And it certainly explained why Nick Humble hadn't rushed to his father's side, Ryan thought.

"Do you agree with Karen, about Fred having been poisoned?" he asked.

"I really don't know what to think," she said. "I was up at Lady's Well last night, with a few members of our usual circle—"

"*Circle?*" Phillips asked, sharply.

"Yes, you know, our Wiccan circle," she explained, not understanding his sudden suspicion. "Quite a few people in these parts follow the Old Ways, and our ceremonies are in line with Wheel of the Year. Last night was Samhain."

Not the same as the Circle they'd known, Phillips reminded himself, thinking back to a time a few years earlier when a group of corrupt men and women with a taste for violence had infiltrated the highest orders of industry and power, wielding it to their own ends. Their group had called themselves, 'The Circle', and their practices had been a bastardised mix of Pagan ritual and devil worship. Theirs had been a false worship, based not on true beliefs but a need to lend sordid acts of murder a veneer of respectability, which was not the same thing as those harmless men and women who prayed for a decent harvest.

Ryan had been thinking along much the same lines, and made a conscious effort to set aside any residual bias that might have lingered.

"Could you tell us about your movements from around three o'clock yesterday afternoon?"

She took a deep breath, and cast her mind back to the previous day. "Of course. I was at the shop until around four, when I decided to close a bit earlier than usual and pop around to see Davie…" She paused, looking mildly embarrassed. "After that…um, I went home at around five-thirty to collect some things for the ceremony—candles and things like that—and then wandered up to Lady's Well to meet the others. I got there just before six."

They asked for the names of those who'd attended the ceremony and Sabrina gave them all, including Lynn Gibbins, before going on to describe what happened, right up until she'd plunged her hands into the water.

"I got quite a fright," she admitted. "That water is a protected source, so it's usually crystal clear. It seemed prophetic, somehow, to find it blood red and, later on, to learn that Fred was dead. It's shaken me up, to be honest."

"Who do you think is responsible for contaminating the water?" Ryan asked.

She was quiet for a long moment. "The Wicca in me would say this was a sweeping out of the old, to make way for the new," she said. "But I don't expect others to believe that, so I'll also say, if you're asking me who was guilty of contaminating the water, it was probably one of those protesters who're camped not far from the well."

"One final question, Ms Graham," Ryan said, choosing to keep things strictly formal. "You've admitted your former brother-in-law was not the nicest of men. Do you know of anyone who might have wanted to kill him?"

She grew serious. "Fred made enemies wherever he went," she said. "If it wasn't my sister, it was his son, who he barely acknowledged for most of Nick's childhood. He refused to sell Ian a bit of useless land he owned, because he didn't like the cut of the man's jib. He blocked Karen's fracking proposals, which could help a number of the small businesses in this village to prosper a bit, and a number of families to have a little injection of cash…"

She looked between the two men, and shook her head. "Fred just didn't know when to stop," she said. "Although I wouldn't like to think that *any* of us was capable of something so deliberate, there's no denying that Fred's death will have benefited some people and made life easier for others."

"How did Davie feel towards Fred?" Phillips asked.

She gave a mirthless laugh. "He's always hated Fred, and he'd tell you that himself. But there's one thing my Davie isn't, and that's a killer. I know it, in *here*." She tapped her chest, somewhere in the region of her heart.

"Thank you, Ms Graham."

The door clicked shut behind her, and Phillips gave a long whistle.

"Well, there's a turn up," he said. "Fred was married to her sister."

Ryan nodded.

"Talk about motives poppin' up all over the place," Phillips continued.

"And yet, we still don't know if we're dealing with a murder, to warrant any motive at all," Ryan reminded him, before pushing up out of his chair to pace around the room like a caged tiger. "I need those toxicology results, and Pinter's verdict on the post-mortem."

"Can't rush him," Phillips cautioned. "You know he doesn't respond well to pressure, that one."

"No, but he responds to overtime pay," Ryan shot back.

He came to a sudden standstill and turned back to his friend.

"I think it's a good idea to find Diane Humble," he decided. "In the meantime, why don't we take a walk up to see this Zachary, and get a lay of the land?"

"Would it take us past the tearoom?"

Ryan swore softly. "Yes, I suppose it would."

"In which case, lead on, Macduff."

CHAPTER 13

The walk from the centre of the village towards Lady's Well took only a few minutes, and was a scenic meander off the beaten track. The sun was already making its descent, and long, mellow rays of light shone down over the valley, lending the small cluster of houses and surrounding countryside an ethereal glow.

"I've been thinkin'," Phillips said, after they'd walked in companionable silence for a minute or two.

"A dangerous pastime."

"I know."

Ryan smiled. "Well? What is it you've been thinking?"

"Well, the fact is, Denise and me've been wonderin' about makin' a move to the country," he said. "We've lived in the city a long while and we're ready for a bit of quiet. Besides, Kingston Park isn't the same anymore."

He referred to the estate where he and Denise MacKenzie lived with their daughter, on the western edge of the city of Newcastle.

"It's still a canny place for young people and families to grow up, but people move in an' out all the time and you never really get to know anybody."

Ryan nodded, although he was of a misanthropic nature that would have preferred it to an alternative reality of street barbeques and coronation parties.

"What about Samantha's school?"

"Well, aye, that's another thing," Phillips said. "I wouldn't like to move her, now she's made some nice friends. On the other hand, she's still horse mad. We're keepin' her pony, Pegasus, at the livery near where you live at Elsdon, but I know she'd love to be there more often. If we were nearer, or had somewhere with a scrap of land ourselves, it would tick all the boxes."

"Do you think Samantha would mind moving to the country?"

"Are you jokin'? That lass is never happier than when we take a ride out to your gaff," he said. All I hear is, 'It's so quiet out here, Dad' and 'I wish Ryan had a younger brother.'"

Ryan rolled his eyes at the last part. "She doesn't still—"

"Have an enormous crush on you, since you're the spitting double of Superman? Whey aye, she does."

Ryan's face was pained. "Is there anything I can do about it? For God's sake, Frank, I'm old enough to be her dad."

"Well, there's nowt you can do to prevent a hormone-addled teenage girl from lookin' up at you with stars in her eyes, but if you wanted to do the rest of us a favour, you could start by losin' your hair and pilin' on a bit more beef."

Ryan laughed. "I'll see what I can do, if only to stave off the hormonal teenagers."

"Good lad."

"Speaking of hormonal teenagers, is that the camp up ahead, d'you think?"

They'd reached the edge of the village, where well-tended gardens gave way to open farmland. A single-track lane led towards a grove of trees which sheltered the by-now *infamous* well that provided water to the village. Just beyond it, they spotted a campervan.

"Must be," Phillips intoned. "Howay, let's have a word with the youngsters."

"They could be as old as the hills," Ryan said. "Not every protester happens to be under twenty-five."

"No, but the ones over thirty've got the good sense to book into a bed and breakfast at the end of a long day's protestin'," Phillips pointed out, tapping the side of his temple. "When your arse has been on a cold, hard pavement for twelve hours, you appreciate the benefits of a hot bath when you're of a certain age. These young'uns don't know what it is to feel a draught in the mornings."

Ryan turned to him. "Ever wish you'd been more of a rebel, Frank?"

Phillips looked back at him and smiled slowly, affecting an air of Jimmy Dean. "Son, I never stopped bein' a rebel, with or without a cause. I just wised up about how not to get *caught*."

Ryan clucked his tongue. "Denise found out about the chocolate, didn't she?"

"Course she bloody did."

They trudged up the single-track road towards Lady's Well but, instead of ducking inside the trees, they circumvented the grove and made their way towards a rusty campervan that had seen better days.

"It's no Mystery Machine," Phillips remarked, thinking of his own little slice of heaven which had ferried him and his family around various beauty spots in the North East.

Ryan was less interested in the vehicle's bodywork, and more interested in the fact that nobody seemed to be home.

"Councillor Russell told us nobody had seen the protesters since yesterday afternoon," he recalled. "Maybe they've abandoned their camp."

"They wouldn't leave their wheels," Phillips said. "These aren't Sloane Rangers, lad. They're idealists, most likely without two pennies to rub together. There's no way they'd abandon their transportation. They're probably still asleep inside, or off behind a bush somewhere sufferin' a bit, if they've been using water from the well."

Ryan made a non-committal sound, and stepped towards the sliding door to knock against its metal wall.

No response.

He stepped back, and then began to walk around the van, more out of habit than anything else. He'd barely reached the rear of the campervan when his eye fell upon something curious.

"Frank!"

Phillips hurried to join him, and one look at Ryan's face was enough to tell him something was badly amiss.

"Wha—?"

He followed the direction of Ryan's finger, which pointed towards the vehicle's exhaust. A long, green hosepipe had been secured to its tailpipe and, with dawning horror, they followed the line of it along the grass and up again, where it fed through a narrow gap in the driver's window.

Ryan was galvanised. "Frank! Quick!"

Both men moved like lightning, each taking a doorway on either side of the van, yanking them open so that fresh air rushed inside while the stench of petrol fumes poured out. Coughing, they covered their noses and mouths with the only thing to hand, which happened to be their clothing, and tried to peer beyond the cockpit of the vehicle to the living space beyond.

Eyes watering, Ryan waved Phillips back and went ahead, needing to see with his own eyes that which his mind already knew to be the truth.

Zachary White's body lay crumpled on the floor, curled into a foetal position as though he were asleep. His head did not rest against any pillow, but rather against the hard edge of a metal toolbox, which had cracked his skull with such force Ryan could see brain matter, even from his position several feet away.

Stomach heaving, Ryan stepped outside and dragged in several deep breaths, coughing up the fumes and the sight of death, before turning to his sergeant who waited patiently beside him.

"He's gone," Ryan said, in a voice carefully devoid of emotion. "Call it in, Frank, and find out his next of kin. Somewhere, a mother will be missing her son."

CHAPTER 14

Bad news spread quickly.

"Keep them back," Ryan instructed the local bobbies, after spotting the return of a number of familiar faces from the press, many of whom he'd seen less than twenty-four hours before.

Faulkner's team had also returned, this time to pore over the compact space that had been Zachary White's final residence. A police line had been set up at the base of the hill to prevent access, and to allow his team to conduct a search of the road leading up to the camp site, while a number of powerful mobile spotlights had been positioned in the immediate vicinity of the van to compensate for a lack of natural light, which was fading quickly, and a large forensics tent erected for reasons of privacy and to protect any residual evidence. Once the interior of the van had been aired and was considered safe to re-enter, Ryan steeled himself to look once again at the body of Zachary White, this time with a critical eye for detail.

"I wonder if the cause of death was carbon monoxide poisoning or that head wound?" It was a question he posed to himself, as much as to anyone else within earshot.

"Hard to say," Faulkner replied, and snapped another shot of the gaping wound on the dead man's skull. "I can't give you any clinical finalities, but I can give you a working theory from the placement of the body and surrounding furniture, plus blood spatter patterns."

Ryan gestured for him to continue.

"The chair, here?" Faulkner began, indicating a fallen stool which lay tipped over on the floor. "The legs have fallen forward, which would be consistent with somebody having been seated there before tumbling in the same direction, which would tie in with the placement of the body, *here*."

He indicated the position of Zachary's body, using his hands to demonstrate the likely direction of the fall.

"So, you're thinking he set up the hose to asphyxiate himself, and then sat down to wait," Ryan said quietly, imagining the process, piece by piece. "As the carbon monoxide took hold, he fell unconscious and his body tipped forward, taking the chair with it. His head connected with the edge of that metal tool box and the injury was enough to kill him, if the carbon monoxide hadn't already."

"That's certainly what it looks like, at least at first glance."

Ryan crouched down to consider the dead man's skin. He was looking specifically for any blanching, which was when the skin took on a whitish appearance when pressure was applied, owing to the diversion of blood flow from the pressurised region. In cases where carbon monoxide poisoning was suspected, the question of whether skin was 'blanchable' was an important one, for it was an indicator of the degree of livor mortis in a body, which could help to determine an estimated time of death. Blanching could still happen up to twelve hours post-mortem, but, after twelve hours, the skin tended to be fixed or 'unblanchable', such that no whitish discolouration would occur because the blood in the body had succumbed to gravity.

Ryan reached forward and pinched the dead man's cheek with two gloved fingers.

"The skin's unblanchable," he said. "We're looking at more than twelve hours, post-mortem."

He wound back the clock in his mind.

"That would put time of death sometime before four a.m. this morning," he said.

Just then, Phillips stuck his head around the door.

"Got a minute?"

"Several," Ryan muttered. "What's up?"

"Somethin' you should look at," came the reply.

Peeling off his gloves to replace them with a fresh pair, Ryan followed Phillips back outside, where large sheets of tarpaulin had been laid out to protect any trace evidence that might lie beneath the grass. Their footsteps crunched against it as they made their way around the back of the campervan, which had been left open for inspection.

"I think we've found the person responsible for contaminating the water," Phillips declared.

Ryan saw three large containers, one of red sheep dye powder and another two of pesticide, every one of them empty. "Any sign of his fellow protesters?"

Phillips shook his head. "Their gear isn't here," he said.

"Sir?"

Both men turned to look at one of the younger members of the forensic team.

"It's just that—you might want to know there was an anti-war rally today in Newcastle. They might have gone to that."

Ryan nodded. "Thanks," he said, and mustered a smile. "That's helpful to know."

The young man smiled happily, and went back to his task of inspecting the underside of the van, while Ryan and Phillips stepped away from the small melee of police and forensic personnel to take stock of what they knew, so far.

"First, the water was contaminated, then Fred Humble turned up dead," Phillips said. "Now, we find this lad a goner, with all those empty containers. Seems cut and dried, doesn't it?"

Ryan watched as the windows of the houses in the village half a mile away began to light up, like blinking eyes.

"I suppose it does," he replied. "It looks very much like Zachary White poured the sheep dye and pesticide into the water source at the well over there, which wouldn't have been hard for him to do, considering both of those things can be acquired from any farm supplies shop in the county and it's a short walk over the brow of that hill to do the deed. He probably thought it would give people a bit of tummy ache but cause enough of a stir to catch the headlines and spotlight his greater cause, which was to oppose the fracking."

"He must've heard about what happened to Fred," Phillips said.

"It was impossible to miss the furore last night, no matter what Karen said about the protesters not having been 'visible,'" Ryan agreed. "Word spreads, and Zachary must have heard about Fred's death and the suspected cause having been the water. That would make him guilty of manslaughter, if we assume a lack of requisite *mens rea* to elevate the action to murder."

"He couldn't live with himself," Phillips said, and there was a tremor to his voice he couldn't quite hide. "Daft young bugger. If only he'd waited, he could have spoken to us—"

Ryan said nothing, but looked out across the landscape, listening beyond the sounds of their immediate company to the more subtle melody of nesting birds and the thrum of insects making their home at the riverside.

"Sir?"

They turned to see the same young man as before, who stood before them clutching a laptop in his gloved hands.

"What is it?"

"We found this inside the campervan," he said, flipping it open so they could see. "It was already open on a web page—it looks like the deceased's own YouTube channel. There was a new video uploaded early yesterday morning that you might want to see."

Ryan wasn't sure he wanted to see it at all, but he had to.

"All right," he said, and moved to look over the man's shoulder. "How did you unlock the computer?"

"I tried out a couple of passwords, sir," the CSI replied. "Turned out to be 'CHEGUEVARA'. He had a poster of the man tacked to the wall of the van."

"Smart thinking," Ryan approved, and waited while he brought up Zachary White's YouTube page.

After a couple of clicks, a very earnest young man came back to life, if only briefly, to tell his online followers that he had important work to do in the fight against environmental pillage. He urged his comrades to find novel ways to impart their message and became emotional towards the end, real tears flowing as he described his belief that he had no future.

"Do you think he was suicidal?" Phillips asked, once the message ended. "Is that what he meant when he said he had no future?"

Ryan shook his head.

"I think he was trying to say there'll be no future for *any* of us, if we don't take his message about the environment seriously," he said. "However, this video was posted before he found out about Fred Humble, so, if he committed suicide, this video certainly wasn't a suicide note."

Phillips gave him a sharp look.

"If?"

"Hm?"

"You said, 'if' he committed suicide."

Ryan gave a brief nod. "It's too neat for suicide, Frank, and too convenient."

As always, Phillips played devil's advocate. "Sometimes, they are neat," he said. "We do occasionally get an easy case."

Ryan closed the laptop and handed it back to the forensics team. "Call a briefing for tomorrow morning," he said. "We've got two deaths on our hands in an area barely larger than a postage stamp. That's at least one too many, Frank."

"Consider it done."

CHAPTER 15

Davie Hetherington looked around the kitchen of his old farmhouse, which he'd lovingly restored over the past thirty years. Now, rather than the ramshackle place it had been in his father's day, it was warm and homely, the stonework mellow against marble countertops and fine oak cabinetry he'd crafted and built himself. His mother's old brass pots and pans had been polished to a high gleam, and hung from hooks on the wall to remind him of his childhood. In the centre of the room was a long table that could seat ten but was presently playing host to four other people who meant all the world to him, and for whom he'd do almost anything.

"Come and sit down, love, before your dinner gets cold."

Sabrina reached out a hand to guide him into the seat next to hers, and he leaned in to press a kiss against her soft cheek. She was a good woman, one he'd never truly appreciated for a long time, until he'd woken up one day and seen her with fresh eyes. It was funny the way the world turned, but he thanked his lucky stars they weren't too late to make the most of the years they had left.

As for Nick, who sat on the opposite side of the table beside his own wife and child, the boy made him proud every day.

Because, who else besides himself had really been a father to Nick?

Certainly not the man who made him. It took much more than that to bring up a child. For years, he'd suffered the pain of watching Nick grapple with the guilt of having a father in name only, one with whom he shared no common interests or values, but who expected blind allegiance, nonetheless.

Now, they sat down not to mourn but to celebrate his passing, whether they admitted it to themselves or not.

"Did you hear about Zack?" Nick asked them, once little Mia had skipped off to the lounge to watch cartoons. "According to Ian, who had it from one of the press pack, he committed suicide. Those two detectives found him in his campervan a couple of hours ago."

Sabrina made a strangled sound of horror, and put a hand to her throat. "Oh, no," she murmured. "That poor boy. He couldn't have been more than twenty."

"Nineteen," Davie said. "Always polite, too, which is why I let him use the land."

Nick was surprised. "I didn't know you were anti-fracking, Davie?"

"It's not so much that I'm anti-fracking, as pro-freedom-of-speech," he said. "There's nowt wrong with peaceful protest in my book, so long as no harm comes to others. Funny enough, I popped up to see Zack earlier today to have words about the water, and to ask if he was responsible—face-to-face, man-to-man. As I say, I don't condone any actions that harm other people, and I was ready to tell him that and ask him to move off."

Sabrina rubbed his arm in silent agreement. "You must have been one of the last to see him alive," she murmured. "What did he say?"

"I didn't see him at all," Davie said. "I went up there just after lunch, but the place looked deserted. The other two who're normally with him must've been somewhere else, because I couldn't see their tents pitched up anywhere nearby."

"Even if he *did* pollute the water," Nick said. "There was no need for him to—" He lifted his hand and let it fall away again with a sigh.

Davie put a hand on his shoulder, and then reached for a tea towel to begin drying the dishes they'd washed.

"Sometimes, people do things you can't understand," he said. "You have to accept it."

He looked up to find Sabrina watching him, and smiled at her.

"Life goes on."

A couple of hours later, Frank Phillips stepped through the front door of his home in Kingston Park, allowing the comforting smells and sounds to surround him as he toed off his comfortable Hush Puppies and hung his coat on a peg in the hallway.

"Only a burglar!" he called out.

Seconds later, the door to the living room opened and a small, freckled face appeared, belonging to his daughter, Samantha.

"Hi, Dad!" She bounded out like a puppy, all arms and legs, and barrelled into him.

"Hello flower," he said, catching her up into his arms for a big hug and a smacking kiss on the forehead. "How was school today?"

"Long," she said, dramatically. "We had *double* maths."

"At least it wasn't triple or quadruple," he said, forever tracking the positives. "Whatsamatter? Don't you like maths?"

She pulled a face. "It's okay."

"Are you findin' it a bit tricky? Me or your mam can help out, if you need it."

Her face took on the determined look he loved so much, and she shook her head. "I'll keep trying, and if I still can't do it, then I'll ask."

"Good lass," he said. "That's the spirit."

"Besides, since I always win at Monopoly, I don't know whether either of you will be up to the task," she added, with an impish smile.

"It's 'cause you cheat, that's what it is," Phillips shot back, with an accusatory finger. "Funny how you're always the banker, that's all I'm sayin'…"

"That's because it helps with my addition and subtraction," she said, innocently.

"Aye, and helps line your pockets so you can scoop up Mayfair 'n' Park Lane, n'all," he grumbled, but kissed the top of her head as she ran off again. Smiling to himself, Phillips wandered on towards the kitchen, where Denise had made a start on some dinner.

"Hello, love," he said, leaning in to give her a kiss.

MacKenzie smiled, but saw the sadness behind his eyes. "Everything all right?" she asked.

Phillips thought of the young lad who'd seen fit to end his life, and then of his own child. "Fine, pet. It's just been one of those days."

MacKenzie had seen her equal share of sad cases, and needed no further explanations. "You're home now," she said, putting a gentle hand on his cheek.

"Aye," he said, and caught her hand to kiss it. "Anythin' I can help with?"

"Sit yourself down," she said, with a nudge. "I'll cook, and you can do the washing up."

He pulled up a chair at the kitchen table.

"So, what happened?" she asked, and began to chop carrots for the casserole she was making. "At least you're not back too late."

"We caught another one, today," he said. "Nineteen-year-old lad with his whole life ahead of him. It looks like he topped himself the old-fashioned way, with a hosepipe connected to the exhaust on his campervan."

Without a word, she set down the knife and came to sit beside him. "I find suicides the hardest, too," she said. "Do you know what prompted it? Did he have a history of depression?"

"That's just it," Phillips said. "He was full of energy, and righteous indignation about the various things that are wrong with the world. He was protestin' some proposals for a fracking site up at Holystone. In fact, it's lookin' like he might've been the one to have polluted the water source—as a bit of a stunt, to get some media attention."

"Then he succeeded," she said.

"Aye, but with Fred Humble dyin', it went further than he might've planned," Phillips pointed out.

"Was he…what's the word…*extreme*?"

Phillips thought back to the video they'd found, and the others he'd watched from Zachary White's YouTube channel, where he'd encouraged his followers to take all action necessary to bring about meaningful change.

"We need to do a bit more legwork to find out about his character but, from what I've seen of his public persona, the lad was definitely a risk-taker," he said. "He was all for doing whatever was necessary, which could be considered extreme in its own way."

MacKenzie was thoughtful. "It just strikes me as funny," she said. "If his goal was to get some attention from the mainstream press, then surely Fred's death and a whole village full of people coming down with gastric problems is media gold. The village must be crawling with journalists, by now."

He nodded, thinking of the ones who'd plagued them for much of the day.

"Have you confirmed that Fred Humble died because of whatever contaminant was in the water?"

"Not yet," Phillips admitted. "Pinter's takin' his sweet-arsed time about finishin' that autopsy."

"In which case, you don't know for certain if there's any causal link between the water and Fred's death."

"Have you been speakin' to Ryan?"

She was surprised. "No, why do you ask?"

"No reason. Carry on," he said.

"Well, I was only going to say that, if the young man who died *didn't* kill anyone, or even if he *might* have made a few people unwell, it doesn't seem like reason enough to take his own life," she said. "He'd be punished, but that would only add to his credibility as a serious activist, wouldn't it? His friends would get a video of him being dragged off to the clanger by the men in uniform, and it would probably go viral."

Phillips sat back, considering all she had said. "That's an interestin' perspective," he said. "I'd been thinkin' the lad was eaten up with guilt, but that's me already assumin' he's guilty of anythin' at all. He might not be."

"Exactly."

"Mind you, there've been some crackpots who've martyred themselves for a cause," he offered, although it didn't ring true in the present case.

"Usually religious fanatics," she said. "It's a different mentality entirely."

Phillips smiled suddenly, and leaned forward. "I'm a lucky one, aren't I?"

"Oh?"

"The woman I love isn't just my boss at work—"

"She's also your boss at home?"

He laughed, and rubbed his nose against hers. "Aye, but I don't mind at all, lass. In fact, I wouldn't change a single thing. You know why?"

She shook her head, feeling warmth spread from her chest to all corners of her body as he spoke softly to her, right there at their kitchen table. "Why, Frank?" she whispered.

"Because there's nowhere else I'd rather be than here with you and our Samantha," he said. "There's nobody else I'd rather work and strive for, than you and that littlun."

She grinned, and stroked his cheek. "It's the same for us, Frank. We wouldn't want you any other way."

He opened his mouth.

"No, you can't," she said smoothly, pressing a finger to his lips. "Not until after dinner."

"You don't even know what I was goin' to ask!"

"Frank, if you think I didn't clock your eyes straying over to that box of chocolate macaroons on the counter from the *moment* you walked in here, you must think I've lost my touch."

His mouth fell open in admiration. "Teach me your ways," he said, reverently.

She laughed, and chucked him a carrot stick instead.

CHAPTER 16

After Ryan swung into his own driveway and unfolded his tired limbs from the car, he took a moment to stand in the quiet night air and look up at the stars. They were spectacular that night, abundant across the sky and shining like brilliant diamonds against a canvas of deep, midnight blue. As always, he felt his own insignificance; nothing but a tiny, minute speck of being in comparison with the vastness of space and time, and, despite having no belief in any deity looking down upon him, he took comfort from the knowledge there were things far greater than himself.

The wind was biting on the brow of the hill, and eventually Ryan made his way towards the front door of the home they'd built together. It was a beautiful place, one where he'd thought to remain for a very long time to come, but it had been tainted by the interference of others; he would never forget when men had broken inside to take his wife away and attack his mother. He'd hoped time would dim the memory but, as he stepped into the same hallway where Eve Ryan had been struck down, anger reared up again, as ripe and potent as it had ever been. It was a worrying phenomenon, and he'd been meaning to speak to Anna about it, but had never really found the right time nor the right words.

Unexpectedly, the conversation with Frank popped into his mind.

We've been thinkin' of makin' a move to the country…

Samantha's horse was already stabled at the livery at the end of their garden, and Ryan knew that Denise and Frank had come to know the village of Elsdon very well, not merely as guests of Ryan and Anna, but as lovers of the countryside themselves.

An idea began to brew…

No, Ryan thought. *They'd never agree.*

He was still mulling it over when Anna called out to him from the living room, where she was sitting with her feet up on the sofa, laptop open on her knees while Emma sat on the rug beside her, happily turning the pages of her books with careful, chubby fingers.

Anna looked up as he entered the room and felt her stomach trip, even after all the years they'd spent together. "Hello," she said, drinking in the sight of him.

"Hello," he returned, and walked across to take her face in his hands for a long kiss.

"*Daddy!*" Emma hurried up onto her feet and stampeded towards him, where she was caught up into her father's arms.

"Hello to you, too," he said, nuzzling her neck to make her giggle. "Have you had a lovely day at nursery?"

"I hurt my finger," she declared, raising her right pinkie for him to inspect.

To the naked eye, it looked absolutely fine.

"Ah, yes," he said, seriously. "I see what you mean."

"Ollie did it," she continued, and Ryan supposed she was too young to learn the questionable adage that 'snitches got stitches'.

"Accidents happen," he said, kissing it better.

"Is *your* finger sore, Daddy?"

Ryan was taken aback. "No, sweetheart. Why did you think it was?"

Emma raised one of her little hands and rubbed the side of his face, as she'd seen her parents do many times before, as a mark of affection. "Your eyes are sad," she said. "My eyes get sad when I hurt myself."

The reasoning was so simple, Ryan was lost for words. He held her close, feeling her dark hair brush his chin while a fierce wave of love overwhelmed him. In that moment, he wished he could shield his little girl from all the bad things in the world and promise her that life would be one long holiday. But, as he knew only too well, that simply wasn't the case. What he *could* promise her was that he'd spend every day striving to make it a better place, and trying to keep the sadness of what he'd seen during his working hours from sullying her happy world for as long as he possibly could.

"My eyes aren't sad anymore," he said definitively, once he could trust his own voice. "They're happy when they see you and mummy."

Emma inspected his beautiful grey-blue eyes for herself.

"Okay," she pronounced, and then wriggled out of his arms to toddle across the room, kiss her mother goodnight and select a book. "Bedtime story now, Daddy."

Ryan grinned over his shoulder as he was led from the room, and Anna blew them both a kiss before returning to her manuscript.

Half an hour later, Ryan returned to the living room looking bleary-eyed.

"She's a tyrant," he declared, lovingly. "A two-year-old tyrant with an insatiable love of reading."

"And rice pudding," Anna put in. "Don't forget the rice pudding."

He smiled and plonked down onto the sofa beside her, where he proceeded to read over her shoulder.

"This is my favourite part of the story," he said, and she tried not to be distracted by the smooth tenor of his voice so close to her ear. "It's where the heroine of the tale meets the hero and dislikes him on sight."

She turned, and found his face very close to hers.

"This isn't a love story, you know. It's a crime thriller, or something like it."

"Aren't detectives allowed to have love lives?" he asked. "Seems a bit unfair."

"Apparently, it's not the 'done' thing."

"Ah, I must remember that," he said, and kissed her again. "How did it go over at the Creative Writing Group?"

Anna gave a small, very eloquent sigh. "I don't think I'm going to fit in very well, there," she confessed. "The group's leader is an author—of some note, if she's to be believed—and I don't think she takes kindly to new members who aren't wallowing in the depths of despair, or drowning in their own low self-esteem, in need of her omniscient advice. I'm afraid I gave her a bit of a shock."

Ryan could see that, behind his wife's bravado, there was genuine disappointment.

"It's hard to travel your own road," he said quietly, and took her hand in his own. "Not everybody appreciates it, because it threatens their status quo."

Anna nodded. "I've seen a bit of that, working at the university all these years," she said. "Academics can be precious about their research work, to say the *least*. I don't know why, but I imagined creative circles to be different…less egoistic, maybe. I thought writers would be more concerned with telling their stories and having them read and enjoyed, than with accolades and applause."

Ryan wondered how such an intelligent person could still remain so idealistic, but knew that he wouldn't have her any other way.

"People are people, all the world over," he said. "If anything, I would imagine those who work in creative circles are more prone to flattery—their work is an extension of themselves, isn't it?"

"Look, just promise me this: if I ever start acting like a prima donna, you'll nip it straight in the bud."

Ryan laughed. "I can't imagine it, but, if the worst should happen, I'm pretty sure Emma will be the first to let you know about it."

Anna could only imagine what her daughter might have to say, considering she hadn't learned any of the finer subtleties of conversation, including the meaning of 'tact'.

"Never mind about my foray into the literary world," she said. "How was your day? Emma wasn't wrong, was she? Something did happen to upset you."

He leaned back against the cushions and closed his eyes. "No, she wasn't wrong," he said, at length. "We found another body today, which looks like a suicide."

Anna was instantly upset, despite knowing nothing of the person who'd died. "That's dreadful. Who?"

"A young man of nineteen, who was protesting some fracking proposals that had been put forward in Holystone," he said. "It seems he could have been the one to contaminate the water at Lady's Well and, after hearing about Fred Humble's death, he might have assumed responsibility for it."

"His protest went too far, you mean?"

Ryan nodded. "Apparently."

She studied his face, the contours and lines of which she knew so well. "You think he was murdered," she said, after a second or two.

His eyes flew open, and he turned to her with a lopsided smile. "I can see where our daughter gets her insightful nature," he said. "And to think that, for years, people used to say I had an inscrutable face."

"Are you sure they didn't just think you were a grumpy git?"

He threw back his head and laughed. "Come to think of it, you could be right."

They sat comfortably for a while in each other's arms, staring at the log burner whose dying embers crackled mesmerically, and then he spoke again.

"I meant to ask whether you'd heard of an archaeologist called Ian Bell," he said. "Runs an outfit up at Holystone."

Anna thought of her various contacts in the field of academic history, and of archaeology, and came up blank, at first.

Then, a memory surfaced.

"Just a minute," she said. "I seem to remember an Ian Something-or-Other who used to run a dig up beside the Coquet, but that was a few years ago. He didn't get anywhere with it, and was struggling to renew his funding…although, if he's still going, I suppose he managed it."

"Anything else you can tell me about him?"

She shook her head. "Not this time. It's a small world, up here, but, even so…" She shrugged. "Why? Is he under suspicion?"

Ryan smiled, while reflected flames from the fire danced in his eyes. "They all are," he said, and drew her against him. "In my experience, the smallest places harbour the biggest lies."

CHAPTER 17

The next morning

Two men stood in the shadows, their voices hushed.

"I thought we had an agreement," the shorter one said, with just a touch of desperation.

"We did, mate, but—"

"But what? Haven't I been a good customer, all these years?"

"Aye, o' course, but—"

"Well, then."

The taller man sighed, folded his arms, and glanced across the car park, which was beginning to swell with people clocking into work for the day.

"Look, she'll get suspicious."

"You've got to hold your nerve, man, that's all. She might *suspect*, but she doesn't know for sure."

"Easy for you to say, Frank, but it'll be me who gets it in the neck from Denise MacKenzie when she finds out I've sold you a bacon buttie outside of the agreed times."

Phillips eyed the owner of the Pie Van with resignation.

"She got to you, n'all."

"Aye, Frank, she did, and to be honest I don't blame her," came the reply. "You've been doin' canny these past few months, and I won't be the one to push you off the wagon. You're lookin' better than I've seen you in years."

Phillips could hardly blame the man for having scruples, especially in a world where they were a rarity, but the scent of frying bacon was a powerful corrupting force.

"You can have your regular bacon stottie on a Friday morning, as agreed, and any of the salads or smoothies from the fridge section until then."

Phillips' lip wobbled.

"I s'pose those banana smoothies aren't so bad," he said, to convince himself. "I could force one down."

"You know it makes sense."

"Can you at least put a dollop of Nutella in it, to sweeten the blow?"

"Not worth my life, mate. I've got cacao or chia seeds?"

Phillips felt his stomach turn over.

"I'll stick to milk and banana," he said.

"What kind of milk d'you want?"

"Eh?"

"Cow's, oat or soya?"

"Aye, that one."

The man blinked, shook his head, and then made his way back around to the front of the van where a queue of customers was already beginning to form in the layby nearest to the car park at Northumbria CID.

And there, standing right at the front, was Denise MacKenzie.

"Good morning," she said, sweetly. "I'll have a banana smoothie—extra chia. Oh, and tell Frank I'll meet him at the briefing in five minutes, will you?"

"I—er—"

"Thanks," she said, and toasted the cup he handed to her.

"*Mm, mm, mm*…y'nah, the great thing about these smoothies is that they're not only healthy, they're *tasty*, n'all."

Phillips made this pronouncement from his seat at the long table in Conference Room B, where he and the rest of Ryan's immediate team had assembled for a briefing.

"*Mm*," he said again, and licked his lips.

"All right, Frank, that'll do," MacKenzie told him, with a roll of her eyes. "For pity's sake, anyone would think you'd been forced to eat gruel."

He eyed the residue at the bottom of his takeaway cup, and set it aside with a shudder.

"Never realised how much I hate bananas," he said.

"Considering how hairy you are, that's surprising," Ryan chimed in, as he finished the task of scribbling a timeline along the whiteboard at the front of the room.

Just then, the door opened to admit Lowerson and Yates, the latter coming as a surprise—but not an unpleasant one.

"Morning," Melanie said, shyly. "I hope you don't mind an extra pair of hands."

Ryan walked around to greet her properly.

"Welcome back," he said. "I'm sorry, I had no idea you were due to return this week—"

"I wasn't," she said quickly. "I had a word with the chief—I hope you don't mind."

Everything was bound up in that simple statement, and Ryan shook his head. "Pull up a chair," he said. "I can always use another set of eyes on a problem."

She nodded her thanks and moved off to see the others while Jack remained, his expression troubled.

"We'll be careful," Ryan promised quietly, in answer to the unspoken plea.

"Thanks," Jack said. "She isn't out of the woods, yet."

"No, but maybe we can help her to find a path."

"Right, let's get down to it."

Ryan took up his usual position at the head of the room, leaned his long body against the wall and rapped a knuckle against the whiteboard.

"Everything you need to know is in the file," he said, having spent hours the previous evening typing it up. "Let's recap what we know so far."

He pointed to the first marker on the timeline he'd drawn.

"The first report of red water running through household taps in Holystone was made at seven-thirty-three. It was called in to the Northumbrian Water 24-hour helpline by David—or "Davie"— Hetherington of Coquet

Farm, which is the nearest of all the dwellings in that area to Lady's Well."

He gave them a moment to locate its position on the maps he'd printed out, before continuing.

"The well, which is more of a pool of water, is fed by an ancient spring which, in turn, provides water to the whole village and is treated and managed by Northumbrian Water. We could deduce from the timing and geography that Hetherington was in a position to make the first report because his household water was probably one of the first to be affected by the contaminant. We know that, following his discovery, he contacted Nicholas Humble, and the two men went about the business of checking on their neighbours in the village, eventually coming to Frederick Humble, Nicholas' father, at exactly eight o'clock."

Ryan paused to tap the next marker on his timeline, which read, 'DISCOVERY OF FRED'S BODY' and featured a printed image of the man himself tacked directly above, taken while he'd been scowling at the camera inside a passport booth, by the looks of it.

"After receiving no answer to his knock at the door, Nicholas Humble proceeded to access Fred's property with his own key, whereupon he found his father dead in his chair in the living room with the television still playing. As you can see from our preliminary observations, and Faulkner's, the body did not appear to have suffered any form of attack and displayed no defensive wounds."

"Have you had that confirmed?" Lowerson asked.

Ryan shook his head.

"Still waiting for Pinter to complete his post-mortem report," he replied. "Obviously, there's been a lot of speculation around the water having been the cause of death, but we won't know for certain until the toxicology and autopsy reports come through."

Lowerson nodded.

"Extensive house-to-house enquiries have been made, which was difficult considering most members of the village were suffering gastric poisoning to some degree in the immediate aftermath, on the evening of 31st October," Ryan continued. "Yesterday, Frank and I continued our enquiries and spoke to key members of the community who sit on the Parish Council; they're concerned to reinstate the water supply, of course, and to allay any fears surrounding Fred's death."

"How long until the supply is up and running again?" MacKenzie asked.

"It should have been reinstated last night," Ryan replied. "Faulkner's team completed an examination of the pipes feeding into the village, and, with the cooperation of members of Environmental Health and Northumbrian Water, was able to pinpoint the likely entry point for the contaminant, which appears to have been straight into the well itself. Once that work was complete, I was able to give the go-ahead for the pipes to be flushed out and the water supply reinstated."

"How do they know it wasn't contaminated further down the line?" Phillips asked him.

"The pipes between Lady's Well and the village were stained, but there was no staining in the spring feeding into the well further up," Ryan replied. "Which brings us onto the question of who might have been responsible."

He pushed away from the wall and pointed to the next marker, above which had been tacked an image of Zachary White. Looking into the young man's eyes, which stared back at him from the snapshot provided by his grieving parents, Ryan thought of the painful conversation he'd held with his mother the previous day and hoped he'd never need to be on the receiving end of such a phone call.

"This is Zachary White, aged nineteen," he said, in a voice that was carefully stripped of emotion. "He was a student of Philosophy and International Development at Durham University, and a keen protester. As one of the leaders of a small army of similarly charged activists known as 'Northern Resistance', he and his comrades made their feelings known about everything from climate change to parking tickets."

"Can't disagree with the last one," Phillips said, as a man who'd been caught out many a time for unpaid toll charges while passing through the Tyne Tunnel.

"Sadly, he won't be standing up for the victims of debateable ticketing offences anymore," Ryan said. "We found him shortly after noon yesterday, dead on the floor of his campervan. It was parked on land to the south of Lady's Well, which I found out earlier this morning forms part of a broader stretch of land incorporated into existing proposals for fracking in the area, and is owned by the same Davie Hetherington."

Ryan turned away from the board and walked over to the table, where he took a seat opposite his colleagues and friends.

"A hosepipe had been rigged from the exhaust in through one of the windows," he said quietly. "It bore the hallmarks of suicide."

"Frank told me a bit about the circumstances," MacKenzie said. "Apparently, empty barrels of red sheep dye and pesticide were also found nearby?"

Ryan nodded, and clasped his hands together.

"It looks very damning for Zachary White," he agreed. "But we're awaiting further information from the forensic team as well as Pinter's autopsy report. Let's not jump to any conclusions."

"Aye, but you've got to admit, it all looks very neat," Phillips remarked. "Zach got carried away with an idea to get a bit of media attention for his cause and decided to stain the water red—which is symbolic, as we all know. He might've banked on a few people gettin' stomach cramps, but nothing more than that. Instead, when Fred turned up dead, he felt terrible about it and couldn't live with the guilt—or, if he was indoctrinated to his cause more than any of us imagine, he could've decided it was a good idea to capitalise on Fred's death and make a martyr of himself."

"That's all well and good," Ryan said, taking a sip of his coffee, which had, by now, developed a milky crust. "However, it doesn't explain the engine having been turned off."

"Eh?" Phillips was confounded, and looked it.

"What're you on about?"

Ryan leaned forward. "Think about it, Frank," he said. "If you were acting alone, you'd leave the engine running for as long as it took to get the job done because, if all went to plan, you wouldn't be around to turn it off, would you?"

Phillips gave a reluctant nod. "Aye, I s'pose. What's your point?"

"The engine *wasn't* running when we arrived. Everything was silent."

"Fuel could've run down," Lowerson offered.

"Aye, what Jack said," Phillips agreed. "Or maybe the battery died?"

Ryan had already checked out both possibilities.

"I looked at the fuel gauge, and there was still a quarter of a tank left," he said. "When I tried the key, the engine started again without any battery failure."

"You turned the key?" Phillips said, finally catching on. "How—?"

"Exactly," Ryan breathed. "The key was already in the 'off' position when I came to try it. I know that neither of us tampered with it when we arrived on the scene, which leaves only one conclusion: somebody turned the engine off again once their task was complete." He finished off his coffee and set the cup down again. "We know the engine was turned off by a third party because Zachary couldn't very well have done it himself."

"Not terribly bright, whoever they are," MacKenzie observed.

"Either that, or they're inexperienced," Ryan said. "Executing the perfect murder is an extreme rarity and not something we've ever really come across, when you think about it. There's always some little slip, some 'tell' that gives the game away, but they're harder to spot when you've got an experienced hand who's used to covering their tracks and traces."

The faces of some of the men and women he'd brought to justice swam briefly in his mind's eye, rising to the surface like spectres at a wake, but he thrust them aside.

"In this case, whoever we're dealing with has done a competent job; they've capitalised on the general feeling that the water killed Fred Humble and used it as motive for Zachary White to have killed himself. However, now that I know the engine was turned off by a third party, I have to ask myself: why would anybody want Zachary dead, and are their motivations linked to the death of Fred Humble?"

"It's the same question for Humble, if you assume he wasn't killed by accident," Yates ventured, her voice rusty from disuse. "Why would anybody want an old man dead, either?"

"Fred seems to have been a difficult customer," Phillips told her. "Everyone we spoke to tended to agree; even his new neighbours, the Harveys, who told us he was rude and obstructive when they were trying to arrange for their septic tank to be emptied."

"*Obstructive* seems to have been a watch-word for him," Ryan agreed. "If Fred Humble wasn't blocking the drainage of a septic tank, he was frustrating the fracking proposals or refusing to sell a bit of old scrubland to Ian Bell so he could carry on with his digging."

"What about his personal life?" Yates wondered. "I know Nicholas Humble was his son, but what about a wife or any other family?"

"As always in small villages and towns, more and more connections come out of the woodwork every day," Ryan said. "Humble was married but his wife left him years ago and never looked back, leaving their son behind—and, by all accounts, it's Davie Hetherington who was more of a father to the boy, which explains why he went to Nick Humble straight away after finding the water red. One of the members of the council, Sabrina Graham, is the younger sister of Humble's former wife, Diane. She told us he treated her sister very badly, so she wasn't surprised that Diane left him."

"Can't imagine she was very happy to lose her sister, either," Yates whispered, and several heads turned towards her in sympathy.

"In other words, quite a few people had a motive to have wanted Fred Humble out of the picture," MacKenzie surmised. "I wonder if young Zachary saw something he wasn't meant to?"

"It's possible," Ryan agreed. "But, at the moment, the engine being turned off is all we have to support any notion of third party interference. We're still waiting on the forensics and autopsy data to come back, which could tell us more."

"What time did Zachary die—roughly?" Lowerson asked.

"More than twelve hours before we found him," Ryan said. "And he was last seen on the main street of the village around four o'clock, which puts his death somewhere between four o'clock and midnight on 31st October."

"If we're talking about death having occurred between four p.m. and, let's say, ten p.m., it would have been harder for anybody with a family to slip away to see Zachary without somebody wondering where they were off to," Phillips pointed out. "On the other hand, if the lad died sometime after then, say, between ten and midnight... *whey*, a person could sneak out while everyone was asleep in their beds or laid up with gastroenteritis."

"Which anyone bar the most elderly and infirm in the community could have done," Ryan said, with a flash of anger at the very thought of it.

"If you're right, and we find this boy *was* murdered," MacKenzie began, "Zachary must have been comfortable allowing his killer inside the campervan, mustn't he? There were no signs of forced entry, nor any defensive wounds from what you could see?"

Ryan and Phillips shook their heads.

"Nothing obvious," Ryan agreed. "I'm willing to bet we'll find Zachary White died from blunt force head trauma, which doesn't match the trajectory or velocity of his fall against the edge of the metal tool box that was placed conveniently beside him. Far more likely, he let person or persons unknown into the van and was taken by surprise with some other weapon. Afterwards, they staged it all to look like suicide."

Phillips rubbed the side of his nose.

"That's an awful lot of hypothesizing', if y'ask me," he said, folding his hands. "You willin' to put your money where your mouth is, lad?"

It would be highly unprofessional, Ryan thought, to place bets during the course of an investigation. Highly unprofessional.

All the same...

"What're you thinking?"

Phillips leaned forward. "Here's the deal, son. You can keep your money but, if I'm right and everythin' is just as it appears, here's what you've gotta do...strip off that shirt o' yours and pose up a storm for the charity Christmas calendar," he said, and, held up a finger to stave off Ryan's objections. "Now, now, lad. Modesty is nothin' in comparison with the needy who rely on the Police Benevolent Fund, is it? And, y'nah the lasses round here would pay top dollar to get a peek o' you in your birthday suit wearin' nowt but a hat, so it'd bring in a pretty penny for the cause. You wouldn't want them wonderin' if you've got a third nipple you've been tryin' to hide all these years, would you?"

Ryan sighed, then leaned forward so they were eye to eye.

"All right," he said, shocking the others with his apparent capitulation. "But, if *I'm* right, and this whole thing was a stitch-up, then it won't be *me* getting my kit off for the camera, it'll be *you*."

He pointed a finger towards Phillips' chest.

"Think of it, Frank. You'll be hanging on the kitchen wall of every member of CID as of January...in nothing but a pair of boxers and one of your favourite ties."

"Maybe the Benevolent Fund will pay both of you *not* to get naked," MacKenzie murmured, which elicited laughter all round.

"You've grown too accustomed to seein' the real thing, every night," Phillips told her, with a wriggle of his eyebrows, then turned back to his friend. "Well, I'm game if you are! Do we have a deal?"

He held out his hand to Ryan, who, feeling very much like he was making a Faustian pact with the devil, shook it.

"*Deal.*"

"Right, well, if you've both quite finished, shall we get back to the business of policing?" MacKenzie drawled. "What *I* can't understand is, how could people have drunk any of the water, if it was bright red?"

"The working theory is that the barrels of sheep dye and pesticide were emptied into the well one at a time, rather than all at once," Ryan said. "The first waves of contamination would have been very diluted by the time the water reached households in the village, and might have appeared very pale pink to the naked eye. It was only by the time all the barrels had been emptied into the water source that the dye's concentration would have built up in the pipework and become obvious."

"Which means that the process of contaminating the water must have begun much earlier than seven-thirty, when the first reports were made," Phillips said, and Ryan nodded. "And it's more likely someone was acting alone, otherwise the dye would've been emptied in much faster with more hands making light work."

"Exactly. As it was, the dye would have been hardly noticeable to begin with, which is why so many people came down with mild gastric poisoning rather than a more severe version."

"There's—"

Just then, the outer door swung open, and, to their surprise, Chief Constable Morrison entered the room with a face like thunder. All five hurried to their feet, chairs scraping against the carpet tile.

"Ma'am, this is an unexpected—" Ryan began.

"Would one of you like to tell me what the hell is going on up at Holystone?" she demanded, without preamble.

They looked at one another, then at her, unconsciously mimicking the actions of PCs Waddell and Elliott from the Berwick Office.

"Ma'am, the scenes were all under local control when we left—" Ryan said.

"I'm not talking about the scenes of crime," she said, and barged past to seek out a television remote for the flatscreen that was fitted to one of the walls. "Have you been living under a rock, for God's sake?"

Morrison jabbed an angry finger onto one of the buttons and the television burst to life, whereupon she proceeded to find the news channel. In silent dismay, they watched a local reporter tell them what they should have known already, which was that, overnight, members of Northern Resistance had mobilised to form two human road blockades: one preventing ordinary access in or out of Holystone, which was inconvenient for residents, and another spanning the A1 dual carriageway in both directions, effectively halting the flow of traffic through the main arterial roadway connecting England and Scotland, used by thousands of travellers each day.

"Balls," Phillips said, into the residual silence.

"Shit," Lowerson muttered.

"Bugger," MacKenzie added.

"Arse," Yates breathed.

"Quite," Morrison snapped.

Ryan turned away from the screen. "Meeting's adjourned," he said. "Frank? You're with me. Mac? I want you to take the reins of the main investigation; dig into Fred Humble's early life, his marriage, and then move onto his wider family. I want to know about his financial affairs, who inherits…everything you can find out. Light a fire under Pinter's arse and tell him I want those post-mortem results within forty-eight hours, or he'll have to start thinking about who'll be conducting his own."

"Consider it done."

"Yates, Lowerson? Find out everything you can about Zachary White and Northern Resistance, then get on the road as fast as you can. We're going to need all hands on deck."

He caught Morrison's eye, who gave a satisfied nod. "Good," she said, and pointed towards the television that was still running. "I want this mess under control within the hour, and those people in custody and booked for public nuisance by close of business."

Only after she'd left the room did Jack say what had crossed all their minds.

"There's never any 'close of business' in the work we do. Crime doesn't clock off at five-thirty."

Ryan shrugged back into his jacket and scooped up his files, preparing to move out. "Yeah," he muttered. "I'd noticed."

CHAPTER 18

Never in a million years would Frank Phillips admit that the journey back to Holystone had been *fun*.

He'd grown accustomed to Ryan's unique driving skills over the years, which were the product of several advanced police training courses and early driving lessons from his father, Charles Ryan, who'd allowed his son to take the wheel on their private estate in Devon at the tender age of fourteen and proceeded to impart his wisdom without the long arm of the law having anything to say about broken hedgerows or ruined lawns—though his wife had made up much of the shortfall in that area. Consequently, Ryan had grown to be a confident driver of almost any motorised vehicle and, much to Phillips' initial surprise, was equally capable of making engine repairs and getting his hands dirty whenever the situation called for it.

By contrast, it had been a number of years before the young Frank Phillips had taken a driving test and, even then, it had been spurred on by necessity and social convention. As with most things, the task presented no challenge to him, but it was certainly not in his nature to drive *fast*, as MacKenzie and most of the standing population of the North East of England could readily attest. He preferred to take in the world at his own pace and, as he'd often remarked, 'if God had intended any of them to hurtle along a road at breakneck speed, he'd have given them wheels instead of hands and stuck an exhaust pipe up their backsides.'

That being said, Phillips was not immune to the occasional thrill of a journey with his friend at the wheel, and this was the case as they powered along the dual-carriageway northbound with their blue light spinning like a disco ball and cars full of angry motorists watching as they whipped along the empty right-hand carriageway, which could not be used by southbound vehicles held up by the blockade further ahead.

Keeping one hand firmly clamped to the edge of his seat and a boot braced against the bodywork, Phillips risked a glance at Ryan, whose profile was focused entirely on the road, eyes sharp for any hazard that could present itself. He thought of all the elements that had gone into the making of such a man: the privileged birth, the boarding school education and academic excellence, the early career in London which—curiously—Ryan seldom spoke about, not to mention all the experiences and losses that life had thrown in his pathway during the past fifteen or more years since he'd known him.

"Stop staring at me," he said. "It's creepy."

Phillips blustered, red-faced at having been caught out. "I wasn't...I mean to say—"

Ryan's lips curved into a smile. "Look, Frank, I've told you before. Despite your raw, animal sex appeal, I just don't see you that way and I don't think Anna or Denise would be terribly happy about it, even if I did."

Phillips couldn't help the laugh that bubbled up. "Divn't flatter yoursel'," he said, all bravado again. "You'd be punchin' well above your weight, n'all."

Ryan chuckled. "What's on your mind, anyway? Do I have something on my face?"

Phillips sighed, looking out of the passenger window as they passed by the line of stationary cars whose drivers stood outside, stretching and chatting to one another while they waited with rising impatience to be told whether they could continue their journey north. "I was just thinkin' about all the things that make us who we are, I s'pose."

Ryan turned away from the road briefly to look at his friend. "What's prompted this introspection?"

Phillips scratched an imaginary itch on his left ear. "I s'pose, just for a minute there, I was wonderin' what it might've been like to have swapped places with you—just for a day. I don't mean *now*," he added swiftly. "I mean when we were both kids, y'nah? Just to have a taster of what life was like on the other side. I wonder if it would've made a difference to me, in the early days."

Ryan listened to his friend's faltering explanation, heard the awkwardness behind it, and understood why. "Would you really want to swap?" he asked. "What difference do you think it would have made to the man you are today?"

"I dunno," Phillips muttered, waving away his own silly thoughts. "Must be too long since I had a bacon butty…the lack of meat has addled me brain."

Ryan was quiet for long seconds, thinking of how best to say what he wanted to say. "In case you ever catch yourself wondering whether you'd have been *more* of this or *less* of that if you'd had my upbringing, I feel I should tell you something important," he said.

"Oh, aye? What's that, then?"

"For all the material advantages, all the love my parents showed me, their capacity to demonstrate compassion and empathy for certain things was limited by their own life experience," he admitted. "When I first arrived here, I was cold and detached—"

"No, you—" Phillips started to object, but Ryan shook his head.

"My heart was in the right place," he continued. "I had the makings of a good man, but it wasn't until you made me your friend that I began to learn how to connect with people on a meaningful level. All the qualities that come so naturally to you are ones that can't be bought, Frank, and, honestly, if I hadn't learned from your example, I don't know that I'd have recognised the life and happiness Anna offered me when she came along. I'm a better father because I see how you love Samantha; a better husband because I saw how you cared for Laura before she died, and how you care for Denise now; a better friend and a better man. So, I want to thank you for sharing that with me."

Phillips looked away sharply to stare out of the window, while his throat worked. "You're welcome," he said, when he trusted his own voice. "But I didn't have to teach you a thing you didn't already know."

Ryan lowered the sunshield to block the sun's glare, which was obviously causing his eyes to water. "Right, well, that's enough of that," he said. "I feel the *need*."

Phillips raised an eyebrow. "The need…for *speed*?"

Ryan grinned broadly, and reached across to press a button on the central console. A moment later, the theme tune to the movie *Top Gun* blasted around all four walls of the car and the two men riding inside it continued north, feeling as rich as kings.

"I'll meet you in the car park in two minutes."

Melanie Yates called back to Jack Lowerson and then made a sharp detour towards the ladies' room. Once inside, she threw herself into an empty cubicle and fell to her knees, where she emptied the contents of her stomach into the industrial white porcelain. She stayed there for long minutes, hands shaking as she gripped the rim of the toilet for support and continued to retch until there was nothing but the acid flavour of bile on her tongue and an uncomfortable ache in her belly. Eventually, she dragged herself up again and began the clean-up operation, stumbling towards the bank of sinks to scrub her hands and face clean.

Bracing herself on the edge of the unit, Melanie stared at the pale face of a woman in torment and wondered what she should tell her to do.

Go home, a voice whispered. *Go home, and never leave again.*

You're safe there.

"No, I'm not."

"You're not what, love?"

MacKenzie stepped out of the neighbouring cubicle, where she'd been debating whether to remain for a while longer and allow her young friend some privacy, or emerge and offer the hand of friendship instead.

Friendship had won out, as it always did.

Melanie hadn't stopped to wonder if the other cubicles were occupied during her desperate flight to rid herself of the churning anxiety in her system, and could have kicked herself at the lack of foresight. Denise MacKenzie had always been a good friend to her, but, even so, she felt her own weakness keenly and wished there'd been nobody there to witness it.

"Here," MacKenzie said softly, holding out a bottle of water she kept in her bag. "Drink some of this."

Melanie chugged down a few mouthfuls. "I suppose you heard me," she said, staring at the bottle she held in her hand. "I'd appreciate it if you wouldn't mention this to Jack, or anyone else."

"Mention what?" MacKenzie said. "I'm not here to tell tales on you, Mel. But, as your friend, I do care about your wellbeing. Are you sure you can manage? Sometimes, rushing the recovery process can put you back—I know all about that."

Her hand strayed to her leg, which bore the old scar of a slashing knife wound and still ached in cold weather. For a while, her mobility had been affected, as had her physical strength, but it had been the mental impact that had proven the most difficult to recover from.

"I'll be fine," Melanie said brightly, but the smile didn't quite reach her eyes. "Absolutely fine."

MacKenzie stepped forward and put a hand on her arm. "You don't have to bear this alone," she said. "All of us have been traumatised at one time or another. It's very normal to feel what you're feeling."

"Is it?" Melanie put a hand to her head, and shook it. "I feel like I'm going crazy, Mac. I'm talking to myself… replaying the same scenarios over and over in my head, re-enacting what's already been and gone. It isn't getting any better."

MacKenzie recognised all of the symptoms, for she'd suffered them herself. "Believe me, it can get better," she said. "I had the night terrors, the sweats, agoraphobia…and a list of other syndromes as long as your arm, after what happened with Keir Edwards. You need to remember something."

Melanie's eyes were bleak. "What?" she asked, listlessly.

MacKenzie took her in both hands, and looked her in the eye. "We're the lucky ones," she said deeply. "We're alive, and our captors are dead and buried. They aren't coming back, whereas we've got the rest of our lives to lead. Some people weren't so lucky."

Melanie thought of her sister and all the others, and knew she spoke the truth. "But, how do I carry on living, enjoying everyday life, when…when…"

The words caught in her throat.

"Have you been back to Blyth?" MacKenzie asked. "Have you been back to where he died?"

Melanie shuddered, the motion racking her whole body. "I couldn't."

"I disagree," MacKenzie said. "You can, and I think you *should*. You need to exorcise this, Mel, expel his memory from your system because a small part of you is still thinking he's alive, still worrying he'll come back and try to finish what he started. But that isn't the case. He's dead as a doornail and, maybe, seeing the place will replace old memories with new ones."

Just the thought of going back to where she'd been bound and drugged was enough to bring her out in a cold sweat, but Melanie could see the sense in it. "Did you?"

"Did I go back?" MacKenzie nodded. "Yes, I did. When I was well enough to walk again, I went back to High Force with Frank, who held my hand while we walked through the trees and retraced the steps I'd taken that night. We went back to the farmhouse where I'd been held, and I stood there and looked at it. You know what? A young couple bought it for peanuts and they're slowly renovating it into something lovely, so their fresh stamp had removed the stain of everything it had been before. They invited us in for a cup of tea in the kitchen, and it felt like a totally different place. By the time we left, I felt liberated."

Melanie listened, and felt embers of hope. "Would you come with me, Denise?"

MacKenzie agreed, and pulled her in for a hug. It was only later, when Melanie had left to catch up with Jack that she found herself wondering why she hadn't asked her boyfriend to hold her hand, instead.

It could mean nothing.

On the other hand, it could mean everything.

CHAPTER 19

Pandemonium.

It was the only word Ryan could think of to describe the scene that awaited them on the A1 dual carriageway, where a blockade had been set up by a small tribe of people who'd glued themselves to the tarmac and would not be moved. They wore high-vis jackets over combat trousers, sat cross-legged in one long row spanning both lanes and, to top it off, they held placards which read, 'FRACK OFF'.

"Not exactly poetry, is it?" Ryan remarked, as they pulled over on the hard shoulder.

"Aye, but it's catchy," Phillips said. "So, how d'you wanna play this?"

"Let's have a word with their ringleader. That's if we can get past the bloodthirsty mob."

Phillips peered through the windscreen at the crowd of angry motorists mingled with journalists and television cameras capturing the mood of the protest. A line of officers formed a protective barrier but, even from a distance, they could sense rising tension.

To make matters worse, at that precise moment, the heavens opened.

"Typical," Phillips tutted. "Didn't bring a rain jacket, either."

"I think your hairdo will survive."

Before Phillips could tell him what a cheeky git he was, Ryan stepped out of the car, where he was greeted immediately by a hawk-eyed journo who hurried across to get the inside scoop.

"*DCI Ryan*! How do you feel about the fact this protest comes so soon after Zachary White's suicide? Do you think the protesting has gone too far? Why did Zachary kill himself?"

It hadn't been confirmed as suicide, and Ryan cursed whichever blabber-mouthed constable had spilled their guts.

"No comment," Ryan said, and began shouldering his way towards the picket line with Phillips at his side.

"*Chief Inspector*! Is there any connection between the deaths of Zachary White and Fred Humble?"

"No comment."

"What about the water contamination?" another one cried out. "Was Zachary White responsible? Did he murder Fred Humble? Is that why he killed himself?"

Ryan swung around, eyes blazing.

"*Look*," he ground out. "You can see we've got a situation here. Why don't you stand aside and let us do our jobs? You should know by now that we can't comment on an active investigation."

They stared at him like lemmings, then began to squawk again.

"*DCI Ryan—*"

"*Chief Constable—*"

"Do you think this is the work of the Circle?"

The last voice belonged to Marcus Atherton, whose measured, no-nonsense tone sliced through the rest and caught Ryan's attention.

He turned, more puzzled now than angry.

"The criminal association known as 'the Circle' was disbanded and brought to justice years ago," he said, although Atherton should have known that already. "There isn't any evidence to suggest the death of either Fred Humble or Zachary White was the handiwork of a copycat."

Atherton opened his mouth to say something, then shut it again.

Ryan didn't wait, but turned on his heel and stormed towards the picket line with a gaggle of reporters nipping at his ankles. Atherton watched him go, then drew the hood up on his all-weather coat and began to walk back to his car, which was parked over a mile away down a country road, which had been the only way to gain access to the site without being able to use the A1.

Some sixth sense prompted Ryan to turn back, to seek Atherton out and ask why he'd thought of the Circle, but the man had already gone.

He shoved it aside, and focused on the task in hand.

"We want justice for Zach!"

Ryan kept his eyes fixed on the young woman seated in the middle, her face slick with rainwater while her body shivered uncontrollably.

"Very laudable," he said. "But don't you think this is a dramatic way to go about it? Staging a protest at a key moment in our investigation won't help us to find the justice you're looking for, it will distract us and add to an already heavy workload."

"If the tools of the State won't listen to our message, then we have to use all means necessary!"

"What is your message?" Ryan asked. "Are you here because of Zach or because you don't want any fracking in Northumberland?"

She was granted a short reprieve from having to answer that probing question, when one of the bystanders succumbed to temper.

"You're wasting everybody's time, for God's sake!" they cried out. "I need to visit my mother at her care home—we visit every day! She has dementia and, if she doesn't see us, she gets upset! You're nothing but a bunch of selfish—"

Before he could finish, the man was led away by one of the police constables, and, when he turned back, Ryan caught a flicker of discomfort in the woman's eyes.

"Listen to me, Moss."

Apparently it was her real name, and the irony wasn't lost on any of them.

"These motorists have places to be. Some need to go to care homes, others to hospital or to help others. Do you think it's fair that you're preventing them from exercising the same freedoms you enjoy?"

She looked away. "If people won't help themselves, we have to be the ones to do it," she said, with what Ryan considered to be breath-taking arrogance. "The government won't listen to us about the fracking, so we have to *make* them listen."

"I thought you were here to expedite 'justice for Zach', whatever you imagine that to be," Ryan murmured, and she became flustered.

"I—of course we are. *We are*. But we're also continuing to fight for the cause," she added quickly. "Zach would have wanted it this way."

A sigh escaped Ryan's lips—he couldn't help it—and her face hardened.

"You're all alike," she spat. "You're an agent of the government and can't see past the end of your own nose. Well, we won't be moved. *Will we?*"

Another cheer rose up although, in his idle estimation, Phillips thought it sounded less passionate than before.

"Howay, pet," he said, stepping forward and bending down a bit so he could be heard above the patter of the rain and the murmur of the crowd beyond. "Don't you think you've made your point? Why not call it a day?"

"Not until the government changes its policy on fracking," she parroted. "It's a travesty they would allow rural areas of outstanding natural beauty to be butchered, and oil and gas conglomerates to cash in. Well, if others won't stand up and be counted, we will."

Another cheer, this time for the benefit of the mobile phone footage being taken by a skinny young man in a black beanie, and the television cameras who filmed the action from the sidelines.

Phillips looked to Ryan, who made a gesture that he should try again. He had an easy likeability that had been known to soften even the hardest of criminals, let alone a young idealist with dreams of changing the world, and it was worth a try.

"I think it's grand that you've got a vision and that you're willin' to stand up for what you believe in," Phillips said, and that happened to be true. "But, listen, there's more than one way of going about things y'nah. Pullin' this sort of stunt won't get you much sympathy amongst ordinary workin' folk, or persuade people to agree with your line of thinkin.'"

And that, he thought, was also true.

"I'm not looking to win any popularity contests," she shot back. "We're doing what's *right*, whether people realise it or not."

Phillips was astonished. "What about the people who don't agree with you, love? Don't their opinions count?"

Moss Green—her real name, incidentally—had tried to rationalise her own ideology of freedom with the competing freedoms of others but, ultimately, had abandoned the endeavour because the two were utterly incompatible. It was only when she thought of herself as a freedom fighter, protecting people from threats within and without and thus safeguarding the future, that she could continue along the road she'd chosen.

No pun intended.

"The masses are uninformed, fed misinformation by a useless media," she threw back at him. "Take the people in those cars over there. They're so stupid, they probably believe anything they're told. That's if any of the people in that queue of cars ever *read* the news, let alone fact-check it or do their own research. I bet they don't even know what 'fracking' is!"

Phillips frowned now, as a father would to a wayward child. "Now, look here," he said. "Even if other people *don't* happen to know what fracking is, that doesn't make anybody stupid, or give you the right to be makin' decisions for them, *or* to go around thinkin' you're holier than thou. Don't you think it's a bit much to assume everyone aside from yourself and your merry band are tone deaf and misinformed?" He tutted and shook his head, which brought a flush of shame to her frozen cheeks. "It's one world, hinny, and we've all got to share it," he said softly. "Besides which, there's a lot of good out there, if you look hard enough to see it. I'm all for progress and improvement, but you can't force things, you have to allow people to come around of their own volition. You can't remove people's right to choose or make their lives a misery if they don't agree with you, or else all you've got is an empty win."

Moss looked into the button-brown eyes of a man who reminded her so much of her father. Recognising the danger of allowing his particular brand of mesmerising kindness to undermine her resolve, she looked away and into the distinctly chillier gaze of his friend, who towered above her from a height well over six feet.

"It wouldn't matter too much to me if you stayed out here and caught frostbite," Ryan said, without a scrap of remorse. "I've got far more important things to be dealing with than having to babysit the lot of you—as have all these officers. For one thing, I could be investigating your friend's death, so we can give his family the answers they deserve."

Moss thought of Zach's mother, who'd called her the previous day to impart the news.

"The bottom line is that you and your friends will be *forcibly removed* from this spot and arrested for public nuisance if you aren't out of here within the next ten minutes. In addition, you will make yourselves available for questioning—you, and anyone else who's been camped on the land beside Zach's campervan for the past three weeks."

"Wh—why do you want to question me about that?" she gasped, and almost jumped to her feet before remembering she was supposed to be glued to the floor. "I don't know anything about it. A few of us left the campsite on Hallowe'en morning to get back to Newcastle in time for the anti-war rally, so I wasn't around when… when he died."

Her voice wobbled, and Ryan softened his tone.

A bit.

"Is there anyone who can corroborate your whereabouts?" he asked.

"Any one of these guys," she gestured to the row of students beside her. "And hundreds of people who saw me at Grey's Monument with a megaphone."

Fair enough, Ryan thought.

"Look," he said wearily. "It's been a long couple of days. Why don't you do us all a favour and go home?"

"We'll go home when the government decides to change their policy."

"Right," he muttered, and was about to signal for one of the officers to begin the process of removal when Phillips stayed his hand.

"Hang on a second," he said, keeping his voice low. "I might have just the thing that'll get these boys 'n' girls movin'."

"A flame-thrower?" Ryan said, deadpan. "Scratch that. The power of your farts alone would be enough to move mountains."

Phillips couldn't deny it. "Even better," he said. "There's one way to a student's heart, and that's through their stomach. One sniff of something delicious and they'll be out of here faster than a rat up a drainpipe."

Ryan was doubtful.

"Trust me," Phillips said. "Students love nowt better than a good freebie."

He waggled a thumb towards the motley crew seated behind them, huddled into puffer jackets which couldn't prevent the uncontrollable shivers brought on by a cold sheet of rain that was blowing in sideways.

"I could save us the trouble, and ask the uniforms to sling their arses in the back of the van," Ryan said, conversationally.

"Next time," Phillips promised. "Let's try my way first, and resort to the nuclear option if it doesn't work, eh?"

Ryan let the air hiss out between his teeth. "Fine."

"Right, then. First thing's first, I need provisions," Phillips said, rubbing his hands together. "Let's find a way back to Holystone, so I can pop into the tearoom. We could call Jack and Mel and ask them to keep an eye on things here—"

"Speak of the devil," Ryan said, and reached for his mobile which signalled an incoming call from Lowerson. "Ryan here."

"What's up?" Phillips asked, once the call ended.

Ryan began walking towards the car, and his friend kept pace.

"Davie Hetherington just went up in my estimation, that's what. Jack and Mel turned up at the road block in Holystone to find him being detained by local constables—apparently, he threatened to dump a load of slurry on the protesters over there."

Phillips scratched his lip, to hide a smile. "Well, I mean, obviously that's the wrong way of handlin' things," he said.

"Naturally."

"We couldn't condone it," Phillips continued, as they reached the car and huddled inside.

"Of course not."

"All the same—"

"I know," Ryan said, and gave him a wicked smile. "It's a pity the constables didn't arrive five minutes later than they did."

Phillips laughed, then grew serious.

"What d'you reckon to all this?" he asked, thinking of the fracking protesters who were now a speck in the rear-view mirror. "Do you think they're doin' the right thing?"

Ryan performed a slow U-turn, wary of the people who milled around both lanes.

"We all think we're doing the right thing in the moment," he said. "It's only with the benefit of hindsight that we know whether it actually *was*."

He rolled his shoulders, trying to see beyond his official role and a conservative upbringing, both of which had instilled in him a general respect for the Rule of Law and a sense of order and balance in society. That wasn't to say he was averse to a spot of rule-breaking, when the occasion called for it, but it went against the grain.

"I think their hearts are in the right place and plenty of people don't agree with fracking, so they'd be in support of their cause. It's the way they're going about things that might bother people in general, and me in particular. I could do without the drama, the press interference or the added pressure of Morrison breathing down my neck; not when there's a stack of unsolved cases sitting on my desk back at CID."

Phillips understood his concerns and found himself thinking back to his younger days, and the causes people had fought for and against.

"When I was comin' up, it was all about the miners' strikes," he recalled. "That was the talkin' point back then, and it affected so many people in this part of the world.

There was a big outcry, a big support network whichever side of the fence you were on, because people had a stake in the outcome and they knew the government's decision would affect them *immediately*, not just ten or twenty years later."

Ryan slowed to turn off the dual carriageway onto a smaller B-road, which would take them in a roundabout way back to Holystone.

"It's all well and good to speak of climate *this* and fossil-fuels *that*; to talk about protecting the long-term future for our kids," Phillips carried on. "I don't know anyone who doesn't agree with the idea of a cleaner planet, in principle; you'd have to be bonkers not to want clean water and unpolluted air, wouldn't you?"

The question was a rhetorical one, so Ryan continued to listen.

"On the other hand, folk have to feed their families and for a lot of 'em it's hand-to-mouth. If y'ask me, it's hard for some to find the energy to worry about the future when they're strugglin' to survive in the present, and even harder to be lectured by youngsters who haven't had to graft or go without, but seem to have no qualms askin' those who *have* to mend their ways. It's a tough pill to swallow."

"Having principles can be an expensive business," Ryan said. "That's what some of those kids are forgetting. It isn't necessarily that people would disagree with their cause...but, they've come from comfortable homes and are enjoying a university education, which puts them in something of a rarefied, academic bubble—and I should know, because it's the same bubble I was in at their age, and I was probably full of my own self-righteousness—"

"Never," Phillips quipped.

"As I was *saying*, they're so wrapped up in their own ideology, they start to think anybody who disagrees with it must be heartless, cowardly or stupid. Perhaps it's none of those things. Maybe it's a simple case of having lived a bit more of life to be able to take a step back and see both sides. It's conceited to think other people are all incompetent or unable to think for themselves, and to imagine you should do the thinking for them. That's irrespective of what I might happen to think about fracking, war, or any other contentious issue you'd care to mention."

Ryan paused, thought of some of the scrapes he'd seen people get themselves into over the years, and conceded there was probably a contingent of the general public who *could* use a nudge in the right direction.

"I mean, obviously, some people are…" He cast around for a nice way of putting it.

"Nincompoops?" Phillips offered, with a smile.

"You said it. There's a reason they put safety warnings on things," Ryan added.

"Careful, lad. That kind of talk'll have you cancelled on *Twatter*."

Ryan didn't correct his pronunciation, because he preferred Phillips' version.

"I'm quaking in my boots at the very thought. Now, which way to Holystone from here, or are you thinking of doing some more sightseeing?"

Phillips gave him a friendly punch on the arm which, considering he was an experienced amateur boxer, packed quite a bit of force. "Anyone'd think you enjoyed this lark," he said.

Ryan smiled as they wound their way through the Coquet Valley which, even on a rainy winter's day, was a sight to behold.

"Anyone would be right."

CHAPTER 20

"What's all this, then?"

While Ryan took himself off to speak to Yates and the other protesters, Phillips and Lowerson peered into a squad car parked near to another picket line, this time blocking the main access road into Holystone village. In the back, Davie Hetherington was seated with his arms folded across his broad chest, staring through the windscreen, bearing the look of one who could happily have put his fist through it.

"Reports were made by several protesters about harassment and intimidation," Lowerson explained. "Apparently, Mr Hetherington threatened to, and I quote, 'cover them in a mountain of shit if they didn't move their sorry backsides.' It appears Mr Hetherington planned to make good his threat, considering the vehicle he brought with him."

He indicated a large slurry spreading truck parked down the street.

"Is this true?" Phillips asked the farmer.

"The drum's *empty*," Hetherington barked, only just keeping a rein on his temper. "The threat was supposed to get them to move out of the way, that's all. I've got some livestock I need to see to in one of the far fields, but I can't get a trailer past this bunch of louts, can I? They refuse to budge, and none of those bloody flatfoots have done a thing about it."

He referred to the small contingent of local constables, one of which Phillips recognised as PC Waddell.

He wondered if there were any more chocolate eyeballs to be had…

"So," he said briskly. "If the slurry drum is empty, we can be fairly certain you *didn't* intend to follow through on your threat?"

Hetherington neither confirmed nor denied, which Phillips could only admire.

"Well," he said, turning to Lowerson. "Since nobody was harmed and there's been no damage…I think we can let this one go, don't you, Detective Constable?"

Lowerson adopted a straight face. "Just this once," he said gravely.

"Howay then," Phillips said, and held the door open for the farmer to step out.

Hetherington joined them on the pavement, stretching out his long body.

"What're you doing to do about it?" he wanted to know. "I don't mind a peaceful protest, but this is disruptin' people's lives. It isn't just that I've got livestock to think about; there are people in the village with elderly relatives still in hospital, and this whole thing is making it difficult for them to visit or bring them home."

"I understand your frustration," Phillips said, and he really did. "Leave this to us, Mr Hetherington, and we'll see if we can't get things moving sooner rather than later."

Hetherington recognised a kindred spirit when he met one, and didn't ask any further questions. "Right then," he said. "I'll be off, if it's all right with you?"

At their affirmative, he headed back towards his slurry truck, ambling through the rain like a disgruntled bear with a sore head.

Speaking of sore heads, Ryan could feel the beginnings of a low-grade migraine forming in the base of his skull, and it had nothing to do with unexplained deaths, disruptive protests or the prospect of facing the Chief Constable's wrath.

Councillor Karen Russell stood before him in full makeup, dressed for the weather in a stylish outdoor ensemble featuring all-Northern brands, which was a conscious decision of hers, intended to look good for the cameras and maximise her chances of re-election when the time came. She'd also found the time to give lengthy interviews to almost every available reporter, whether they'd asked for one or not. Now, after what she considered to be a productive morning, she found she had the energy to deliver one last rant before lunch.

"—and *another* thing, Chief Inspector. I know I speak for everyone on the Parish Council and certainly in the village when I say we've been thoroughly disappointed by the slow response from your department and the wider police force," she was saying, in a voice that carried and grated on his last nerve. "For one thing, we're acting entirely within our rights in putting forward proposals to the Council for fracking sites on the outskirts of our village. It's all above board and legal. It's thanks to these protesters and the extreme lengths they've gone to for media attention that two people are now dead—including one of their own. It's a disgrace that each and every one of them isn't already behind bars!"

Russell had brought along with her a couple of cronies, who Ryan recognised as her employees from the tearoom, and they took their cue to mutter agreement.

Ryan ignored them. "In the first place, Councillor, your rhetoric is dangerous and misinformed," he said, in a voice that carried even further. "There is no evidence that any one of the protesters was responsible for either death and, certainly, if there was, my department would have taken the appropriate steps to bring those individuals into custody."

Russell opened her mouth as if to argue, but he silenced her with a look—which, to the minds of those who looked on, was no small feat.

"Furthermore, I would be very careful, if I was you, to consider the ramifications for a person in your position," he said.

"What on Earth do you mean by that?" she snapped. "I'm only speaking the truth, or at least what everyone is thinking—"

"No, you're publicly defaming these individuals," he said, and watched her eyes widen. "You're smearing their names to anyone who will listen, without anything currently to substantiate your accusations despite my clear warning to you yesterday morning about not doing that very thing. If I were you, Councillor, I would think carefully before giving any more interviews, and I'd make it a priority to apologise to every person you have named. Then, I'd pray that these people are more forgiving than you."

After that final, blistering remark, he turned away.

"Yates?"

Melanie tried not to jump, but couldn't quite prevent the nervous jolt that ran through her system. Ryan saw it, as well as her attempt to hide it, and added the information to a mental pile of 'Things to Talk About Later'.

It was becoming a hefty pile.

"How's the mood amongst the locals?" he asked her.

A small crowd of residents had gathered around the protesters that morning to complain or cajole, depending on their mood. However, as the rain continued to fall, many had returned to their homes and businesses, while the reporters stowed their mics and sought shelter at The Watering Hole where they sampled Lynn Gibbins' afternoon tea special—much to the consternation of her competitor, who began the task of issuing grovelling apologies to a line of student protesters she'd branded as murderers to the world's press.

"They've calmed down a lot," Yates replied. "The local bobbies tell me the protesters turned up at the crack of dawn and nobody's been able to get past them since then, so most people gave up trying—aside from Davie Hetherington, of course."

"The protesters arrived at the crack of dawn, you said?"

"According to the local officers, yes."

Ryan pinched the bridge of his nose. "And yet they didn't think it would be a good idea to pass on that kind of pertinent information. Who was the first responding officer?" he asked, but had a funny feeling he could guess.

Yates checked her notes. "Couple of guys from Berwick," she said. "PCs W—"

"Waddell and Elliott?"

"How did you know?"

"Call me psychic."

Yates smiled. "They tell me they thought they could get things in hand without needing to call in the big guns. I had the impression they were trying to impress you with their crowd management skills."

Now, Ryan managed a smile. "The way for Laurel and Hardy to impress me would be to stay *away* from anything involving brainwork", he said. "What about the protesters? I take it they're still married to their cause?"

She nodded.

"They're sticking to the party line," she said. "They refuse to move until the government agrees to listen and change their policy on fracking—they've glued themselves down."

"Phillips has a plan," he said. "It involves food."

"When doesn't he have a plan that involves food?"

"Good point," he said. "But, in this case, it's food he intends to use as a bribe—"

"I'm sure you mean 'an incentive', sir."

Ryan's lips twitched. "Quite so."

"You know, that isn't as crazy as it sounds," she said. "I remember, when I was a student, I ate like a horse... mostly, to soak up the bottomless 2-4-1 shots I'd downed at the student bar, but that's another story."

At that moment, they spotted Phillips emerging from the tea room with Lowerson. Both men carried large cardboard trays in their arms, filled to brimming with rows of pastries and takeaway cups of hot tea and coffee.

"May the Force be with you," Yates said, raising a hand towards them both.

Ryan turned to her in surprise. "I didn't know you were a Star Wars fan."

"Learn something new every day, you will."

CHAPTER 21

Within half an hour of leaving the village, Phillips and Lowerson re-appeared on the horizon like a desert mirage. They led a convoy of squad cars carrying bedraggled and rain-soaked protesters, all of whom had abandoned their picket line and made a run for the jam doughnuts faster than any of them could say 'apostate'. Furthermore, when the secondary blockade at Holystone saw that their comrades had packed up for the day, they disbanded too, which elicited an almighty cheer from the residents and a grunt from Davie Hetherington, who had been Googling the maximum punishment he'd get if he decided to revisit the slurry-dumping idea.

"Processed sugar," Phillips would later say to the younger, more impressionable members of CID. "It works greater miracles than God Almighty."

Ryan and Yates met their colleagues at the doorway of the pub, where its landlady had agreed to provide a space they could use to question the protesters in private. Rural Northumberland might be an area of natural beauty, but the nearest major police station was miles away and there was no time to waste driving back and forth.

"Howay then," Phillips said to Ryan, cupping his ear. "C'mon, you know you want to say it…"

Ryan rolled his eyes. "Fine. You pulled it off. I don't know how you managed it, but you did."

"It's like I told you, son. Young'uns like food; it's as simple as that."

"That's their excuse, but what's yours?" Lowerson joked.

"I'm a young'un at heart," Phillips said. "Not that I got a look-in with those doughnuts, or much else. They wolfed it all down like a bunch of half-starved gannets."

"Well, now they're suitably fortified, they can talk to us," Ryan said. "Let's start with their leader, Moss Green, and the other one who was camping next to Zachary until a couple of days ago. What was his name, again?"

Yates checked her list. "Rain," she said. "Rain…M—oh, no. You're not going to believe his surname."

Ryan shook his head slowly. "Don't tell me it's—"

"Maker," she said bluntly. "His name is Rain Maker."

The four detectives waged an internal battle to contain their laughter.

"Okay, all right, that's enough," Ryan said, studiously avoiding Phillips' eyes. "It's supremely unprofessional to laugh at other people's names. Frank, I can still see your shoulders shaking."

"Can't—can't help—it—" Phillips wheezed. "Moss Green and Rain Maker…it's too much, man. I can't—stop—"

"Yes, you can. We're going to conduct a serious interview with Rain Maker, while Lowerson and Yates re-interview Moss Green, and we'll reconvene afterwards to compare notes."

"All we need now is a Willow Tree, or a Sandy Verge—"

"Don't start, Frank. I'm barely keeping it together, as it is."

"Hey man, thanks for the pastries. That was solid."

To counteract a fit of the giggles, Phillips was now seated with a serious, no-nonsense look on his face, the folds of which had sunk into a frown to prevent the smallest ounce of laugher from escaping his lips.

"Don't mention it," he said, gruffly.

"I'm sure we're all glad you could join us here, Mr Maker," Ryan said.

"Call me Rain, man."

Ryan and Phillips stared at him, the muscles in their jawlines twitching with the effort of keeping their composure. First Rain Maker, now Rain Man. They couldn't have made it up.

"What can you tell us about the late Zachary White?" Ryan asked.

"What d'you wanna know?"

Rain Maker turned out to be the young man they'd spotted earlier on the A1, whose task it had been to capture Northern Resistance's protest on film. Once the beanie hat was removed, they found he was the spitting double of Ed Sheeran, ginger hair and all.

"Anyone ever tell you that you look like that singer—" Phillips remarked.

"Ed Sheeran? Yeah, I get that a lot."

"Must make you popular with the girls," Phillips said, affecting a cosy, man-to-man demeanour he'd found effective when questioning the younger generation. "But do you play the guitar?"

"Nah, but I have a recorder," he said. "Some girls like that."

Ryan and Phillips were silent for another long moment, each man checking his notes with sudden, curious intent.

"Getting back to Zachary White," Ryan said firmly. "How did you know him?"

"We both go to Durham Uni," Rain said. "I ran into Zach at the Fresher's Fair last year, and we hit it off. There was this hot tutor handing out leaflets, and we bonded over it. She was older but *so* fine, man. She was from the History Faculty, though, and neither of us are reading History, so…"

He shrugged it off, like a man who would otherwise have had a look-in.

When Ryan didn't ask the obvious question, Phillips dived in.

"Oh, aye," he said, trying not to sound too interested. "What was her name?"

"I dunno. Doctor something double-barrelled. Doctor Taylor-Bryan, maybe? Taylor—"

"Ryan?" Ryan suggested.

The man still didn't connect the dots.

"Yeah, yeah that was it. Doctor Taylor-Ryan," he repeated, and patted his chest to imitate his heart racing. "It was almost worth changing courses, just to see her—"

"Let's get back to the point, shall we?" Ryan interjected, in a tone that reminded Phillips greatly of a bloodthirsty serial killer they'd once questioned at Broadmoor. "You were telling us about Zach, and how you became acquainted—aside from lusting over unsuspecting older, married women that were well out of your league."

Rain frowned at the last part, but acknowledged it was probably true.

"Right, yeah. We get angry about the same things, so, after a couple of months, we set up Northern Resistance as a club meeting every Friday night with Moss, and it kind of grew into this...*beast*. Zach was good with tech stuff, y'know? He set up the YouTube channel, the JustGiving page, the website and all that, so people know where we'll be if they want to turn out and support us."

"You'd say he was your friend?"

"Yeah, he was my friend. He didn't have to go and do what he did."

It seemed that the reality of having lost him only just hit home, for Rain's young face began to crumple and Phillips handed him a small packet of tissues he always kept on hand, for emergencies.

"Thanks," he muttered. "The thing is, when we left him on Sunday, he was in a good mood. He said he planned to sit on the main street in Holystone because the weather didn't look too bad, that day."

"That's all he said?"

Rain nodded. "More or less," he replied. "We would've been back in a couple of days anyway, because we know there's another meeting planned between the Parish Council and the CEO of Bernicia Energy. We didn't want to miss it, for obvious reasons."

So much information, Ryan thought.

"When is this meeting scheduled to take place?"

"There's an open discussion for residents to ask questions and all that on Friday morning. Councillor Russell arranged it, probably because she's still trying to win everyone over."

"Not everyone is pro-fracking, then?" Phillips said, playing dumb.

"Not by a long shot," Rain replied, with a broad smile. "Davie might not like the roads being blocked, but he's no fan of fracking, not on land that's been in his family for generations. As for Ian, he's desperate to extend his archaeological site, so the last thing he wants is some big energy company turning up and damaging anything precious that might lie beneath the surface. There are others, too—and old Fred wasn't keen, come to think of it."

Ryan made a note, then fixed the young man with a stare. "I'm going to ask you a question, and I'd prefer the truth. It will make everything easier in the long-run, okay?"

Rain grew nervous, no doubt thinking of minor drug offence charges.

"Did you, or any of your friends, contaminate the water at Lady's Well?"

Immediately, the cloud lifted. "That was nothing to do with any of us," he said, with some relief.

Ryan and Phillips looked at one another, then back at him.

"How can you be so sure?"

"Well, I guess I can't say for definite, but we all work together, we plan things. There's a kind of hierarchy and we don't go off on tangents, we stay focused on a plan, whatever the plan might be. If anyone had an idea about doing this or that, we'd have heard about it *way* in advance. Nobody talked about dyeing any water red."

"Not Zachary?"

"He never said a single word about contaminating the water."

"You sound very sure," Ryan said, and decided to give away a small piece of information in order to progress their discussion. "I know we discussed this in the standard caution at the beginning of our chat, but, if you'd like to change your mind and have a lawyer present, that's your right."

"I don't have anything to hide."

"Fair enough," Ryan said, and considered his duty discharged. "In that case, let me ask you another question. Were you aware that several large, empty barrels of red sheep dye and pesticides were found hidden in bushes near to Zach's campervan?"

Rain was taken aback. "Woah, man. I don't know anything about any sheep dye or pesticides," he said, holding both hands up. "You're saying you think Zach had them?"

Ryan said nothing. He'd found that silence could be a valuable tool in questioning a witness, because they tended to fill it.

"I mean, sure, Zach was a bit of a hothead, if I'm being honest," Rain said, almost talking to himself. "There were times I had to tell him to chill. But...nah, man. I can't see him pulling something like that. It goes against his ethos... or, you know, *went* against it."

Sadness crept into his voice again, and he looked away, through one of the windows of the pub's function room to the village beyond.

"What ethos was that?" Phillips asked.

Rain dragged himself back. "Chemicals and stuff. He hated anything like that. We protested about the water pollution in parts of the River Tyne a few months ago," he said, and both detectives sat up a bit straighter. "He'd only wear organic clothing...he was vegan, too."

Ryan leaned forward. "When did you stage an anti-water pollution rally?"

"I dunno, maybe back in February? Look, there's no way Zach would've poisoned people," Rain said again. "He was outspoken, yeah, and not everybody agreed with him. But he wouldn't have poisoned anyone."

"Not even by accident?" Phillips wondered.

Rain let the idea roll around his head, then shook it. "I'm telling you, it wasn't his style," he repeated. "I dunno why he would kill himself, either. Maybe all this stuff just got out of hand, you know, in his own mind..."

His voice trailed off, and he rubbed a tired hand over his face, obviously reaching his limit. Ryan recognised it, and knew he only had so much time left before the witness began to shut down. "Can you tell me if Zach had any enemies that you know of?"

They saw the precise moment the penny dropped in Rain's mind, and the moment directly after that, when surprise was replaced with fear.

"Wh—why do you want to know? Do you think he was…you know, *killed*, or something?"

"Perhaps."

Rain goggled at them. "Okay. Okay. This is…I dunno what to tell you. Yeah, of course some people didn't like him. He rubbed people the wrong way, like Marmite. You either believed in the same things, or you didn't, and Zach wasn't one to back down. But you could say the same for any one of us."

"How so?" Ryan prodded. "Who really stands out for you as having an issue with Zach, or your group?"

Rain ran shaking fingers through his hair, thinking of all the altercations, the crossed swords with so many people, and felt tired just thinking about it.

"Anyone with an interest in fossil fuels, for starters," he said. "The bloke who runs Bernicia Energy already hates us because we keep popping up whenever he's trying to run a positive PR campaign for some new site he's opening."

"And this 'bloke' would be?" Phillips waited, with a biro.

Rain grinned. "He's got a ridiculous name," he said, and Ryan considered it a small miracle that neither he nor Phillips so much as batted an eyelid in response to the overwhelming irony of that remark. "The CEO is called Hector Farquhar. It's a family business, and he runs it alongside his son and daughter, who are both obscenely spoilt, obscenely overweight and generally not worth the time of day. But Hector, he's a character."

There was a grudging respect in what Rain had just told them, but it did not undermine the general message of overriding contempt he held for the man he considered to be the antithesis of everything he stood for.

"All right, thank you for sharing that with us," Ryan said. "Anyone else?"

Rain was suddenly defensive, in no small part because the act of being made to think of Zach's enemies had brought home just how many he might have made for *himself*.

"There are probably hundreds, okay? Too many to count. Could be the mother or father of some kid who didn't make it to hospital because we blocked a road one day. Could be some other suit who didn't make it to the airport on time for a fancy meeting in Zurich. Could be the Art Director at the museum where we paintballed one of their statues the other week."

Listing all the possibilities was overwhelming, so Rain fell silent.

"Does it worry you, thinking of them all?" Phillips asked quietly.

If it did, Rain would never admit as much. Although, if there was a chance Zach had been killed, maybe it was worth playing things safe for a while.

"Do you have any idea who might've killed him, if Zach was killed?"

Ryan shook his head. "It's why we're talking to you, now. We're trying to put the pieces together to find the answer to the puzzle."

Rain nodded, and the men seated opposite thought he appeared very young. "All I know is, Zach's a hero," he said. "He's a martyr, whether he killed himself or somebody else wanted to snuff out everything he stood for, and we still stand for. You might be able to silence one voice, but you can't silence them all. Nobody will forget Zach's name or the reason he died—to prevent Big Oil from taking over the land. In fact, I wouldn't be surprised if they just hired somebody to assassinate him, so they can push through the fracking deal."

Ryan wanted to think it was a ridiculous notion, but stranger things had happened.

They asked a couple more questions to ascertain Rain's whereabouts during the critical periods when either Fred Humble or Zachary White might have died, and concluded that neither he nor Moss Green could have been anywhere near the village.

"At least we can start ruling people out," Phillips said, once they were left to themselves again.

"Yeah, that still leaves a big pool of suspects who might've had reason to want either Fred Humble or Zachary White out of the picture...maybe both. That's assuming the same person killed both of them—"

"If they were killed," Philips reminded him, thinking of their private wager. "*If.*"

"We might be able to find out which one is true, if Pinter would only call and give us an update," Ryan complained. "I wonder if MacKenzie has managed to hurry him along."

"She's got ways and means, that one," Phillips said. "Ways and means."

CHAPTER 22

MacKenzie certainly did have ways and means.

For instance, she happened to know that their esteemed Senior Pathologist, Jeffrey Pinter, was presently walking out with a lady by the name of Lisa, who, in turn, was the sister of her long-time hairdresser, Una. Now, Una happened to be very protective of her younger sibling, and there had been several occasions when MacKenzie's opinion alone had been enough to extinguish a budding romance, when word had reached her ears of a gentleman's dubious history. Up to that point, MacKenzie had spoken only very highly of Pinter's good character while Una took care of her roots—but, as she told Pinter in no uncertain terms, that could very easily change and wasn't it *amazing* how women listened to other women about the things that really mattered.

Upon hearing this, Pinter overcame his initial outrage at so blatant a threat, and found he was left with two residual thoughts: firstly, that life had been far brighter since he'd met Lisa, and he didn't want to run the risk of losing her.

It had been difficult enough to overcome her natural aversion to dating someone whose hands were mostly occupied in handling dead people and, sadly, they hadn't yet reached the next level of their relationship so that he might convince her that being a surgeon of any description came with additional benefits—chiefly, being *very* dextrous. Secondly, and more concerning, was his certain belief that any attempt to call MacKenzie's bluff would be a fool's game; when she meant business, she meant business, which was one of many reasons he'd always admired her.

Consequently, when she arrived at the electric double doors which gave access to the basement mortuary of the Royal Victoria Infirmary, he welcomed her like a visiting monarch.

"*Denise!*"

He hurried across the wide, open-plan space with a smile so blistering it could have cracked his face.

"Jeff," she said. "*So* kind of you to fit me in, today."

A hoot of laughter escaped his lips. "I don't think I had too much choice," he said, pushing his glasses back onto the arch of a long, thin nose. "All the same, it's good to see you. Shall we take a look at Mr Humble?"

By then, she'd scribbled her name into the logbook by the door and slipped into one of the visitors' lab coats.

"Lead on," she said.

Whilst MacKenzie couldn't claim to enjoy the mortuary environment, she, like Ryan, was capable of detaching her senses to a greater extent than some of their colleagues. She thanked Providence for this as they walked across the main floor, passing a couple of technicians on the way who raised a gloved hand in greeting before continuing with their respective Y-incisions, or whichever unenviable task they happened to be performing on one of the two fresh cadavers delivered to them that morning.

"You seem busy at the moment."

Pinter held open the door to a private wing of the mortuary, which held a number of individual examination rooms, and waited for her to precede him.

"We are, as a matter of fact," he said. "It's part of the reason I wasn't able to get around to Fred Humble as soon as I would've liked. We're also down a mortuary technician at the moment, which doesn't help."

He led her to a room signposted 'EXAMINATION ROOM 1' and entered a code on the side of the wall before buzzing it open.

"Here we are," he said, with a singsong cheerfulness that was at odds with the environment.

In the centre of the room was a shrouded figure, who was laid out in preparation for their discussion. MacKenzie's stomach gave a little pre-emptive jitter but, after a couple of seconds, she had it in check.

"I'm ready whenever you are."

Pinter pulled back the covering to reveal the waxy remains of Frederick Humble who, at the age of sixty-eight, had been heavily overweight, which was somewhat predictable given his penchant for home-brewed beer and starchy foods. There were sagging lines around his face and deep grooves across his forehead that told of a lifetime's worth of frowning but, otherwise, if it hadn't been for the setting and the slow putrefaction that was underway despite a liberal use of chemicals, she might've thought he was sleeping.

"What was the cause of death?"

It was the most important question, and one that could swing the focus of their investigation.

"Cardiac toxicity leading to massive heart failure," Pinter said, without any of his usual propensity for drawing things out, which made a pleasant change.

"So, he *was* poisoned?"

Pinter nodded. "Whether by foul play or by accident, I can't tell you," he said, just to be clear. "What I *can* tell you is that Fred Humble's heart muscle was damaged by a toxin called *thiacloprid*. The impact brought on a massive arrhythmia, which ultimately caused his heart to fail."

The information would be in his report, no doubt, but MacKenzie made a note for easy reference when she relayed everything to Ryan and the rest of the team.

"What sort of symptoms would he have experienced?"

Pinter removed his glasses and began to polish them, while he spoke.

"Dizziness, fatigue, chest pain, shortness of breath... some fluid retention in the legs, which is one of the few things we can measure post-mortem, as you can see in the calves here."

He replaced his glasses and then took out a retractable pointer to indicate the dead man's swollen calves.

"Having said that, Humble was approaching an age where sustained inactivity can also lead to problems with lymphatic drainage," Pinter said. "So, in this case, it's hard to determine whether the retention was a side effect of the toxin or not; you'd have to cross-check with his medical record, to see if he was on any medication. In the meantime, I can also tell you the post-mortem interval would suggest Mr Humble ingested the toxin at least three hours prior to his death, so there may not have been time for this level of fluid to build up in that period, but that really depends on the body's own responsiveness."

MacKenzie frowned, and looked up from where she'd been studying the dead man's hands, which were encased in two clear plastic bags.

"Wait a minute," she said sharply. "Did you say you thought he'd ingested the toxin two or three hours before he died?"

Pinter nodded, and raised a pair of eyebrows tamed recently by the Turkish barber.

"Yes. The toxin didn't take immediate effect but was reasonably slow-acting, which would suggest it was ingested in diluted form. I take it that's significant?"

MacKenzie nodded. "Very possibly," she said. "Contaminated water didn't reach household taps in the main village of Holystone until around seven-thirty on the thirty-first, which is when the first report came in. For some households, it would have been later, because the pesticide was drawn down only when people came to use a tap. Humble was found dead in his chair at eight o'clock, by his son, Nicholas. From what you're telling me, it's more likely he ingested the toxin around five or six o'clock, long before the first report of contaminated water?"

Pinter understood her difficulty. "I thought it was possible this gentleman might have been unlucky," he said. "Perhaps he'd used his taps at just the wrong moment, drawing down an undiluted quantity of contaminated water, which would have had a more potent effect on him than on other people in the village, but…"

He shook his head.

"There's something else to bear in mind, which rather blows that theory out of the water," he said, laughing at his own joke. When MacKenzie didn't join him, he cleared his throat and pointed towards the desktop computer on the workstation to his left. "Come and look at this."

Pinter brought up a report on the screen which turned out to be the analysis of the pipework leading into Humble's house, and then a second report which was an analysis of the cocktail of toxins found within Humble's body.

"Here, you can see the list of individual chemical concentrates found to have been in the water supply, in diluted form," he said, tapping the screen. "And, *here*, you can see the list of chemical concentrates found within Humble's bloodstream. Do you notice anything unusual?"

MacKenzie was past hoping he would just come out and tell her, and, knowing that Pinter lived for drama, she indulged him by making a show of studying both tables.

"There's no mention of thiacloprid having been present in the pipework," she said, after a swift comparison of both.

"Nor in any of the water samples taken from Lady's Well. I thought thiacloprid was the fatal toxin?"

"It was," Pinter said, eyes twinkling with an excitement few people beyond those four walls would understand, but MacKenzie happened to be one of them.

The body behind her forgotten for the present, they put their proverbial heads together.

"So, if thiacloprid was the fatal toxin but it wasn't present in the household pipes, it must have been administered by another means," she said. "What about the bottle of beer found on the floor beside him?"

Pinter clicked another data sheet, and pointed to the analysis.

"Here's the analysis from the samples taken from the bottle, as well as the carpet. Neither contained any trace of any of the chemicals, let alone thiacloprid."

"What about—"

"The other bottles found at his home, alongside other drinking vessels and foodstuffs?" Pinter interrupted, and gave a small smile. "I took the liberty of ordering full analysis of all the bottles, and, of course, the samples taken from any other glasses or vessels were also considered. No trace of thiacloprid found on any of them, nor any of the other chemicals found in agricultural pesticides." He paused. "However, finding myself *intrigued* by all this, I decided to do some cross-checking."

"Go on," she said.

"Well, first of all, I looked at the samples Faulkner took from the scene at Zachary White's camp," he said. "Specifically, the two empty containers of pesticide."

She nodded. "They strongly suggest Zachary White was responsible for contaminating the water."

"Well, the samples were very interesting," he said, and scratched the side of his cheek. "There was no trace of thiacloprid found in one of them, but there *were* traces found in the other."

MacKenzie opened her mouth to speak, but he was already moving on to his next sleuthing discovery.

"I found this even *more* intriguing, because both containers look identical—except that the one containing thiacloprid looked older than the other container. Both containers bore identical labels and, on the list of ingredients printed on the underside, neither mention the presence of thiacloprid."

"Even though one *did* have it?"

"Exactly."

MacKenzie pulled up the only other chair in the room and sank onto it, feeling the old injury in her leg beginning to ache after standing around for too long. It was a weakness she detested in herself, one she tried to stave off through regular exercise and physio, but there was only so much she could do. "Let's consider the possibilities," she said. "Is it possible that someone added the thiacloprid to one of the containers?"

She wasn't really seeking an answer from him, Pinter knew, but he was enjoying the conversation so he was happy to be a sounding board; it was better than being wrist-deep in bodily matter, for one thing.

"Is it easy to source neat thiacloprid?" he wondered aloud.

"You can get anything on the Dark Web, really," MacKenzie muttered. "So, yes, I'd have to say it's possible. The better question would be to ask *why* anyone would want to add thiacloprid to only one container and not the other."

Pinter shook his head. "I should mention the other interesting facet of that chemical," he said. "Thiacloprid is never ordinarily found in pesticides in the UK or in the European Union, because it has carcinogenic properties and was banned a few years ago. However, it's still found in pesticides in the United States."

"And, you said the labelling was identical?" she queried. "One container wasn't shipped in from the US?"

"I couldn't comment on the shipping, but the labelling was certainly identical as you'll see from the images in the file," he said, and clicked a few times to bring up the photos.

After a brief inspection, she nodded.

"Both seem to originate from the UK," she confirmed. "Is thiacloprid more toxic than any of the other chemicals ordinarily found in pesticides? What I mean is, would the other chemicals have been enough on their own to have killed Mr Humble?"

Pinter flipped back through the list of chemicals found in the ordinary agricultural pesticide, and then nodded.

"I'd say several of those could have proven fatal, if administered in a high enough dosage," he said. "Which is what happened, really. As you can see from the percentile spread of chemical compounds found within Mr Humble's body, thiacloprid didn't make up any significantly greater percentile than the others."

"In which case...I can't understand why anyone would deliberately add it to the formula, if the existing compound would have done the job, so to speak."

Pinter shrugged his bony shoulders. "That's a mystery for you to solve, I'm afraid," he said, and yawned. "You know, this might be well off the mark, but—" He stopped himself.

"But, what?" she prompted him. "Spit it out, Jeff."

"I was only going to suggest that it's possible whoever used the containers of pesticide didn't *know* that one contained thiacloprid. They might not have added it in at all."

"You know, I'm inclined to agree with you," she said. "We need to find out where the containers were sourced in the first place. Were they bought or stolen? That should help us to answer that particular question."

She swung back around in her chair to look at the dead man, whose sagging jowls were on a level with her eyeline.

"Because of what you've told me today, I think we can say for certain that Frederick Humble was not only murdered, but murdered in a premeditated fashion. We know that the contaminated mains water had nothing to do with it, but a separate, slow-acting dosage administered to him was likely the means, approximately two or three hours prior to death, although we're yet to establish the way the toxin was imbibed. We also know that the two compounds—the pesticide in the mains supply and the pesticide Humble ate or drank—were almost the same, but not quite." MacKenzie turned to him, one professional to another. "You've been very helpful, Jeff, and I'm grateful to you."

Pinter found himself tongue-tied. "Not at all," he mumbled. "All in a day's work."

"You know, I would never have said anything to Una," MacKenzie admitted. "You're one of us, Jeff, and I'd never do such a mean-spirited thing, even if I *was* desperate for a post-mortem report."

Pinter smiled at her. "I know that, Denise, but sometimes we all need a boot up the arse, as your Frank would say."

She had to laugh. "That we do—and, in the spirit of things, that reminds me to ask you about Zachary White."

Pinter blew out a long breath. "I walked straight into that one, didn't I? Speak to me again tomorrow, and I'll be able to tell you more—I'm waiting for some lab results which are due in the morning."

MacKenzie nodded. "Appreciate it, Jeff."

CHAPTER 23

Bernicia Energy LLP held offices around the United Kingdom, with strongholds in London, Aberdeen and Newcastle. The latter was its original base and, over a hundred years after it was first built, the Farquhar family still retained their impressive four-storey headquarters on Newcastle's Quayside, which bore the family's crest above its columned entrance alongside a Latin inscription loosely translated as 'He Who Dares, Wins'.

A motto shared by one Derek Trotter, if Phillips' memory of classic British comedy served him correctly.

Hector Farquhar Sr. wasn't wholly unlike Del Boy in attitude or temperament but, as the family's patriarch and Chairman of the Board of Directors at Bernicia, Farquhar bore more of a physical resemblance to Donald Trump, though his tan was slightly less pronounced. When Ryan and Phillips were shown into his sprawling office by an attractive young woman, hot on the spiked stiletto heels of two other attractive young women seated at the front desk, Ryan and Phillips could only assume that Hector liked the ladies in his office to fit a certain mould, which told them a lot about the old man's mindset long before he opened his mouth.

"Tea and coffee, Kelly," he ordered his personal assistant, without any additional niceties.

Phillips held open the door for the young woman, who looked at him as though he was some sort of unicorn, before vanishing down the corridor towards the kitchen.

"Thank you for finding the time to see us," Ryan said, having judged it best to approach the man with a certain deference he might not otherwise have shown, but for the generational gap and their need to elicit information from him. "We'll try not to take up too much of it."

Farquhar nodded, and shooed them both towards a couple of visitors' chairs arranged beside a long leather sofa set against one wall of the office.

"Might as well sit down," he said, and heaved himself out of his desk chair to join them. "I've only got twenty minutes. What's he done, this time?"

"Who?" Ryan wondered.

"Don't play games with me," Farquhar said, pointing an imperious finger at them both. "I'm in no mood for it. Just tell me what the blighter's been up to, and we can agree an appropriate slap on the wrist…"

Ryan held up a hand. "Mr Farquhar, I think there's been some misunderstanding," he said, crossing one leg over the other. "Sergeant Phillips and I are here in connection with two murders committed in Holystone, and to discuss the proposal put forward by your company to the Holystone

Parish Council and individual members of the community for the acquisition of land for the purpose of fracking in that area."

Ryan held out his warrant card and, after a quick inspection, Farquhar relaxed back into the buttery leather armchair he occupied.

"CID, eh?" he said. "I s'pose you're looking into the water contamination deaths everyone's been rabbiting on about. Last I heard, it was that young lad, Zachary White, who was responsible for all that, and he's no longer with us—*sadly*," he tagged on.

"Where might you have heard such a thing?" Ryan asked, in a tone that was deceptively mild. "Certainly not from the police team."

"I keep my ear to the ground, Chief Inspector."

Ryan was sure of it. "I see. Well, perhaps you could start by telling us why your company decided to target Holystone as a potential fracking site?"

Farquhar made an expansive hand gesture. "Gentlemen, I can tell you that Holystone is just one of dozens of sites where my company is in the process of acquiring land and completing preliminary geological surveys to assess the viability of a fracking exercise," he said, clearly well versed in answering questions of that kind. "The geology of most of Northumberland is unsuitable, but Holystone is a rare exception, which makes it of interest to us and, I'm sure, other companies too."

He paused when there came a knock at the door to signal his personal assistant had returned with a large tray of teas and coffees. Without a second thought, both Ryan and Phillips stood up and made as if to help open the door, with Ryan doing the honours since he was closest.

Once they were furnished with caffeine that neither Ryan nor his sergeant intended to drink, Farquhar gulped his tea in three large swallows, inhaled a couple of shortbread biscuits and, brushing the crumbs from the front of his suit, picked up where he'd left off.

"In all these cases, we work with the community to obtain unanimous support wherever possible," he carried on, smoothly.

"What does that mean—in practice?" Ryan asked. "We're aware there were a number of objections raised by local members of the community, aside from any protesters from Northern Resistance."

Hector's face darkened at the mention of the group which had been a thorn in his side since its inception, but his voice was even when he replied.

"It means effective communication," he said. "Educating people as to what fracking really entails, and reassuring them as to the risks, which are very limited—"

"Maybe you wouldn't mind, ah, educatin' me a bit," Phillips said, giving his best impression of someone without a clue. "Seems there's quite a bit of opposition, for somethin' with limited risks."

Farquhar remained genial. "Of course, sergeant. 'Fracking', as I'm sure you know, is the process of hydraulic fracturing of oil and gas fields," he said. "Licences have been granted by successive governments over the years for the purposes of onshore shale gas exploration, a process already widely used in the US, which has created countless new jobs. As with so many things in life, there will always be *debate*—"

"I understand it was banned here in the UK," Ryan put in. "Chiefly owing to concerns around seismic activity brought on by the fracturing process."

Farquhar forced a smile.

"Full marks, Chief Inspector," he said. "We do, of course, have to respect the word of the Oil and Gas Authority, whose report into the safety of fracking operations precipitated an indefinite suspension back in 2019. However, the moratorium was lifted under Prime Minister Truss's leadership, which is a clear vote of confidence in the industry and what it can do for ordinary people, a view which is shared by the local councillor in Holystone, I might add."

They thought of Karen Russell and her tearoom, both of whom could use the financial boost the sale of land would bring, and wondered how unbiased a view she could ever provide as to the safety or viability of the fracking process. The protesters had branded her and her fellow supporters 'fracking mad', and, the more he learned, the more Ryan found he was inclined to agree with them.

But his first duty was to the families of Fred Humble and Zachary White, and that was never far from his mind.

"Did you have any personal dealings with either Frederick Humble or Zachary White?" he asked.

"I knew neither man personally," he said. "Of course, I'm terribly sorry for their families, and I know my team have already been in contact to offer our condolences."

And to reiterate an increased offer to buy the land from Humble's estate, he thought.

"In their own ways, both men had been flies in your ointment, hadn't they?" Ryan pressed him. "First, Fred Humble's very vocal opposition to your proposal, which swayed quite a few other members of the local community against it, we understand. As for Zachary White, his organisation, Northern Resistance, must have been on your radar for quite some time."

Farquhar had learned early on in life that, if you gave a little, it went a very long way. "Yes," he said. "It's true that we didn't see eye-to-eye on certain things, but that can be said of many people, Chief Inspector. I fail to see what I can possibly have to do with the death of either man, and, I'm afraid, if you have any further questions, I'll need to put a call through to my solicitor and make a separate appointment for another time."

"Understood," Ryan said, and thought it was unlikely the most senior person at Bernicia would have had any hands-on involvement in either death, although he didn't rule out the possibility of a hands-off approach, which he would be investigating. "Coming back to working with a local community, then. You spoke of education and reassurance but, let's put our cards on the table, shall we, Mr Farquhar? Surely, the most persuasive factor in securing support for any fracking venture is payment, or funding for other local community ventures?"

Farquhar stood up, partly to work off the stiffness in his legs, and partly to put some distance between himself and the two men who awaited his reply. "What if it is?" he answered, with surprising honesty. "The world needs cheap energy, and solar panels aren't going to cut it, especially in this part of the world. We can't keep relying on Russia, either, for obvious reasons."

He turned back to face them, and they saw a powerful man used to wielding it without question.

"I haven't been to Holystone, personally," he said. "As you can imagine, we have teams of liaison personnel who take care of business development nationwide. However, it's perfectly true to say that any locals in possession of land within the catchment area of our proposals would stand to benefit handsomely from its sale, and local businesses would also be likely to flourish alongside the creation of new jobs on-site. None of that is new information, and would be true of any similar site you'd care to mention."

"That's true, I'm sure," Ryan said. "However, to my knowledge, you aren't actively pursing any other fracking sites in the North East at the present time—am I right? That being the case, more is riding on the Holystone site as a commercial venture than might otherwise be the case and, as you said yourself, it's a geological rarity in terms of its suitability. It's a limited resource, therefore more valuable to you in terms of its potential, which has been expanded now that the opposition posed by Humble and White has been eradicated. Wouldn't you agree?"

"As I've said, the deaths of both men are a source of sadness to the community," he said. "Have you any suspects, yet?"

"I'm sure you understand, that information is confidential." Hector gave a little shrug and pressed a button on his desk phone to call for his personal assistant. "I'm afraid our time is up, gentlemen," he told them. "I'm sorry I couldn't be more help to you but, as I'm sure you'll appreciate, I'm a very busy man." After a brief internal battle, he decided to take a Parthian shot. "In any event, this is all likely to become academic," he said.

Ryan frowned. "How so?"

Farquhar smiled again. "You aren't the only one with access to confidential information, Chief Inspector, but it will become public soon enough. Best of luck with your continuing investigation."

Right on cue, his personal assistant opened the door for them, and they were ushered out.

Outside, Ryan and Phillips found that darkness had fallen over the city of Newcastle, and the bridges spanning the River Tyne were illuminated in a rainbow of multicoloured light. They began to walk east along the quayside, bundled up against the lash of cold air rolling in from the North Sea while they contemplated the man they'd just met, and all the others of his type they'd met before.

"Always brings back memories when we walk along this stretch of the river," Ryan said, as their footsteps fell into rhythm against the pavement.

To their left was the imposing courthouse, shadowed and shuttered for the day, but Phillips knew that his friend wasn't thinking of all the times they'd been called upon to give evidence there. He was thinking, as they both were, of times when the bridges had been under siege, and of when Ryan had lived in an apartment further along the riverbank in which some of his greatest heartache had been played out.

"You sold it, eventually, didn't you?" he said.

Ryan nodded, without needing to ask what he meant. "There's a young professional couple living there, now," he said. "I hope they've breathed new life into the place."

"D'you ever—" Phillips hesitated, not wishing to prod old wounds.

"Do I ever go back?" Ryan finished for him, and then shook his head. "Not if I can help it but, if we're ever called out somewhere nearby, I can stand to see it because I know it's just bricks and mortar."

Phillips was glad to hear it. "Time's a great healer," he said.

They crossed one of the smaller, modern bridges known as the Millennium Bridge, an elegant structure which had been rebuilt since its destruction a few years before. Looking at it now, neither man would have known it had been the target of a terrorist attack, had they not been the men called upon to put a stop to it.

Reaching the middle, they paused to look along the river at the coloured arches of six other bridges connecting Newcastle and Gateshead.

"That's a pretty sight," Phillips said, and smiled with civic pride. "Makes me proud to see it."

Ryan nodded, steadfastly ignoring the cold that seeped through the material of his coat.

"Reminds us what we're fighting for, doesn't it?" he said. "Seeing the city like this, thinking of all the people within it who're trying their best to lead decent lives…it outweighs all the other people we see, and outshines the underbelly."

Phillips smiled, watching the lights reflect on the water below. "Aye well," he said, pushing away from the handrail. "We can't stand out here all night, catchin' our deaths."

"You were the one waxing lyrical about pride in your city," Ryan pointed out.

"Aye well, now that's done, and I'm freezin' me nuts off," Phillips declared. "Howay, let's get back to the car and crank up the heat on our way to HQ. I'm doin' the school pick-up tonight, and I'm gonna need a cuppa and a KitKat before I can face all the golf dads and yoga mams in the playground."

"If you can't beat 'em, join 'em," Ryan teased.

"Lad, the day you see me rockin' up to CID in one of those little carts, dressed to the nines in all the gear with no idea, you can just send me off to the glue factory."

"Duly noted," Ryan said, and the white of his smile flashed beneath the passing streetlamps. "Does that count if you turn up in Lycra? It wouldn't be the first time—"

"You promised me you'd forget all about that."

"I lied, Frank. Some things are too funny to forget and, after all, the tale of your arse hanging out to all and sundry will have reached all four corners of the country, by now. You're a legend in your own lifetime, so you might as well embrace it."

"Aye, and I'll bet I know how every bobbie from here to Land's End heard about it," Phillips said, giving his friend the beady eye.

"News travels fast," Ryan said, innocently.

"So'll your obituary, if your lips don't stop flappin.'"

CHAPTER 24

The Holystone Parish Council convened for another impromptu meeting, this time in the back office of Sabrina Graham's holistic shop, Love and Light. It had not been Karen Russell's first choice, and Lynn Gibbins had been mildly put out, but it represented neutral ground and they couldn't deny that the setting was supremely comfortable. In addition to selling all manner of spiritual healing books and tools, gemstones and incense, Sabrina had converted the back part of her shop into a therapy space with two treatment rooms and its own waiting area where the five standing members of the Council were now seated upon its comfortable sofas, sipping herbal teas while breathing in the comforting scent of ylang-ylang and some other exotic spice. Music played quietly from a speaker she'd hidden in the corner, although she had a feeling it would take more than pan pipes and wind chimes to ease the overstretched nerves of all those present.

"The police are saying it was murder," Lynn blurted out. "I can hardly believe it…here, in our village."

"It doesn't help anyone to become hysterical," Karen said, although she'd had a few jitters herself. "As for *murder*..." She *harrumphed*, and took a sip of her tea. "What utter nonsense. If you ask me, the reputation of that chief inspector has been wildly exaggerated. It's perfectly obvious what's happened, but he's making a meal out of things, no doubt to attract some attention to his department."

"And why would he want to do that, Karen?" Davie asked. "He doesn't strike me as a man who courts the press."

"Oh, that's probably what he *wants* you to think, but they're all the same, aren't they? And didn't you see his sergeant handing out cakes and coffees to the protesters? I wouldn't be surprised if the police had encouraged them to block the road today—"

"That seems a bit far-fetched," Sabrina said. "If anything, the police were under pressure to move the protesters off, so they were probably trying all means necessary."

"Well, whatever way the wind blows, it has one outcome that I can see, and that's to scupper any hopes any of us might have had about the fracking venture," Karen said. "All of this negative attention and publicity is *exactly* what Bernicia wouldn't want, which must be why they've cancelled the meeting on Friday. It's a bad sign."

"You won't find me crying over that," Ian couldn't help but say. "You know my feelings about it, Karen, so I won't go over it all again. But, remember, there's a human and environmental cost to those things, and the protesters today had every right to bring it to the attention of the world."

Karen thought of mounting debts, and dreams of exotic holidays going up in a puff of smoke. "That's your problem all over, Ian," she snapped. "You live in the *past*, whereas some of us want to look to the future."

"There's no shame in wanting to protect our shared history," the archaeologist said. "Which reminds me to ask you, Davie. I realise it hasn't been long, so I don't want to pressure him in any way, but I was wondering if Nick's had time to consider my offer for that bit of scrubland, yet?"

Formerly owned by Fred Humble, it was a nondescript bit of land at the extreme edge of the village, useless for agricultural purposes but bordering on an area of historic importance that he'd be interested to explore.

"I couldn't say," Davie replied. "Nick's been tied up dealing with the police, and trying to get his father's affairs in order before they release the body back to him."

Ian nodded. "Of course—forget I mentioned it," he said.

"I heard from Fred's neighbour, Christine," Davie did say. "She was hoping I could help to clear her septic tank, now that Fred isn't there to object. I don't see any issue with it, if Nick agrees, but I wanted to double check that the police have finished with the house and garden?"

Karen nodded. "The forensic team have cleared out," she said. "That sergeant—Phillips, I think—said it was released back to the family, now."

"In that case, I'll get to it in the morning," Davie said. "It's past time."

Sabrina rose to refill their cups, and he noticed her hands weren't as steady as they usually were. "Are you all right, love?"

She sighed, and allowed him to draw her down beside him, where she could feel the comforting rise and fall of his chest.

"It's all the drama of the past few days," she said. "I can't believe anyone could murder Fred or Zach. I hope Karen is right, and this is all some dreadful mistake."

"People can surprise you," Lynn said. "I never thought his wife would leave him but she did, in the end."

Lynn looked across at Sabrina, and pulled an apologetic face.

"Sorry to rake over the past, I know it must be hard thinking of Diane, but it's testament to just how difficult Fred Humble could be," she said. "Thinking of all that poor woman put up with, and of how awkward he could be, it's a wonder somebody hadn't murdered him before now."

"Lynn, *really*—" Karen said, but she revelled in the gossip.

"Nick was wondering whether to try to find her again," Davie said, his quiet voice breaking through the idle chatter. "He was wondering if Diane would want to know what's happened."

Sabrina clutched his arm. "Oh, Davie, I really don't think…it wouldn't be a good idea, would it? Diane left a long time ago and hasn't kept in touch because she didn't want to. After a while, I came to accept it, and I thought he had, too. I don't want to see him hurt all over again."

Davie stood up suddenly and paced around the room, ostensibly to pour himself a glass of water from the dispenser.

"I told him the same thing," he said shortly, and consciously loosened the grip he had on the unoffending plastic cup he held in his hand. "Diane left us—left *him*—a long time ago. Besides, Fred's passing is all over the news. Wherever she is, she'll find out sooner or later."

Sabrina nodded.

"It isn't really about that, anyway," Davie continued softly. "Nick misses his mum. He's always missed her, whether she abandoned him or not. Diane is still—" He took a long gulp of water, remembering where he was, and with whom. "She's still his mother."

Sabrina would not say it aloud, but thought that her sister had lost that accolade a long time ago. She thought of the festival of Samhain they'd celebrated only days ago, of the veil separating their world from the Otherworld, and of sweeping out the old to make way for the new. Though it pained her to think of it, she wondered whether her sister's spirit had lingered amongst the little stone cottages and streets of Holystone long after she'd left, and whether the echo of her voice and the tread of her footsteps would remain etched upon the memories of those who lived there, forever preventing the emergence of new beginnings.

"Do the police have any idea who might have done it?" Ian asked, breaking into her reverie.

"Done what?"

"Killed Fred and Zach," he said, as though speaking to a slow child.

"Oh. They haven't mentioned anything to us, have they, Davie?"

He shook his head. "The police have been good at keeping Nick informed of any developments, but they haven't brought anyone into custody," he said. "The last I heard, someone called DC Yates was in touch to ask about Fred's regular habits."

"What does that have to do with anything?" Karen asked, in an impatient tone. "That's just another example, if you ask me. Why didn't someone ask that before now?"

"I think the local constable who took a preliminary statement wasn't exactly the brightest bulb in the box," Sabrina said. "This team are specialists from CID, so they're taking charge of matters."

"I should think so," Karen muttered. "I don't know how Fred's daily habits will help them to find out who killed him, since it was obviously Zach—although, perhaps by accident."

Davie shrugged. "We all know what Fred was like," he said. "Got up at the same time every day and was the first in the queue at your shop every morning to pick up his paper."

Karen nodded. "That's certainly true," she said. "He was always there, rain or shine, on the dot of nine, or ten o'clock on Saturdays and Sundays."

"Anyone could have known that," Sabrina murmured. "Maybe they're thinking his killer used his routine against him."

They looked amongst one another, a new kind of awareness dawning amongst them of the possibility that one of them might be such a person.

"*Poppycock*," Karen decided, and nobody dared to argue.

CHAPTER 25

"Talk me through Fred Humble's daily routine, one more time?"

Ryan made this request from one end of the conference table at Police Headquarters where he and his team had reconvened, with the exception of Phillips who was, at that very moment, turning down another invitation to play golf as he huddled with the other parents in the playground outside Samantha's school.

Thoughts and prayers.

"Fred was very much a creature of habit, according to his son," Yates said, reaching for the notes she'd made following her conversation with Nick Humble. "He got up at six-thirty every day, had a shower and breakfast, which was always buttered toast with marmalade and two cups of builder's tea, and then left the house to walk along to the general store to pick up a newspaper and a carton of milk or a loaf of bread, if he was running low. He was always there just before the shop opened, which is at nine o'clock on weekdays and ten o'clock on weekends, although it's closed on Wednesdays. He played the lottery on Fridays and, on Sundays, he treated himself to a Full English in the tearoom."

"Hallowe'en was Sunday, which means he would have been at the shop for ten o'clock that morning," Ryan said. "Does that tally with the witness statements?"

Yates flipped through the file and then nodded.

"Yes, Karen Russell and her staff confirmed it," she said. "He was there as usual on Sunday morning and seemed perfectly fine. Nothing unusual, apparently. Fred went into the shop and bought his paper, then took a table in the tearoom and had a Full English breakfast. He left just before eleven o'clock and went home, which was corroborated by several other locals who saw him."

"Which left a full hour during which time somebody could've gained access to his house," Ryan said. "I presume you've familiarised yourself with MacKenzie's update, following her meeting with Pinter earlier this afternoon?"

Lowerson and Yates both nodded.

"Then you'll know we're looking for the window of opportunity during which time person or persons unknown could have entered Humble's property and planted contaminated food or drink, probably while he was out having his breakfast. I think we can be fairly certain they re-entered the property after Humble was found dead by his son at eight o'clock, but *before* the police entered the scene half an hour later, to remove anything incriminating."

"How do we know they did that?" Lowerson asked.

"Well, for one thing, we didn't find any contaminated vessel or foodstuff," Ryan said. "Therefore, it must have been removed or washed. Not forgetting that the television was turned off when police entered, but it was still on when Nick Humble found his father."

"Who'd do that?" Yates wondered aloud. "Why fiddle with the telly?"

"Why turn off the campervan's engine?" Ryan countered. "It goes to the personality of our killer, Mel. We're dealing with an inexperienced but organised risk-taker, who is also slightly obsessive compulsive, if I'm not mistaken. My guess would be that this person couldn't help themselves; they were compelled to turn off the television and the van engine."

"Without knowing everybody in the village it's difficult to know who fits the bill," MacKenzie said.

"Even then, you can't mount a murder case against someone just because they fiddle with switches or have a thing about saving power," Ryan said. "All the same, let's keep our eyes open. Coming back to Fred Humble, I'd say we have two new urgent lines of enquiry: the *mode* of administering the fatal toxin, and the *means*. Tell me about Fred's drinking habits," he said to Yates. "Was he known to have one of his home-brews at any time of day?"

"Not according to his son, who says it was Fred's habit to drink three bottles at night, the first one at around five o'clock," he said. "That's been corroborated by Sabrina Graham, who knew him throughout the years he was married to her sister, and she agreed he would always drink a bottle at five o'clock and then continue after that, although she says he didn't always stop at three bottles."

Ryan nodded. "Again, very helpfully sticking to a routine which enabled his killer to concoct a plan. Did they find any trace of pesticide in the beer containers in Humble's shed?"

This last question was directed to MacKenzie, who shook her head.

"None whatsoever," she said. "The brew in his shed was clean."

"And since we already know the mains water supply wasn't responsible for killing him, by a process of elimination we also know the toxin was brought into Humble's house by some other means," Ryan said. "The question is, what? It seems to me, Fred's killer could be very sure that he would drink a bottle of his own home-brew at around five o'clock, so it would make sense to contaminate the bottles he kept in the cupboard in his kitchen."

"They were all tested," MacKenzie said. "They were clean, too."

"Did they have any fingerprints on them?" he asked.

MacKenzie skim-read over Faulkner's report, and then smiled slowly, following Ryan's train of thought.

"Nope," she said. "Not a single fingerprint; not even one belonging to Fred Humble."

"Which strikes me as extremely odd, since he would have been the one to stock his own cupboard normally, wouldn't he? We would expect to find his fingerprints on the bottles—not bottles that were suspiciously clean of *any* prints."

The others nodded, eyes gleaming with the thrill of having caught the scent of their quarry.

"My supposition is that Humble's killer entered the cottage while he was out having breakfast, and took the chance to substitute the bottles in his cupboard for some pre-contaminated alternatives," Ryan said. "I take it Humble recycled the same beer bottles each time?"

MacKenzie nodded.

"From what the team could find, he kept a quantity of washed bottles in his shed," she said. "There isn't any way of knowing how many he had in total, or to know if any are missing."

Ryan rose to his feet and walked to the window, where he looked out at the city lights while he tried to imagine walking in the footsteps of a killer.

"There wouldn't have been any time to wash out the contaminated bottles and return them to the shed," he murmured. "They only had half an hour to get in and out again, switching any remaining contaminated bottles for 'normal' ones, so they're the ones we would find. There were seven bottles in the cupboard, when I looked—"

He turned to MacKenzie, who checked the inventory Faulkner had taken and nodded the affirmative. "Seven."

"But this person would have brought more, in case they had to replace anywhere up to…say, ten bottles," he said, thinking of the cupboard space. "There was always a chance Fred would notice if some bottles were missing from his usual number."

The others nodded.

"Why not just bring one?" Yates asked, and then clicked a finger as the answer to her own question presented itself. "Because they couldn't be sure which bottle Humble would choose to drink, so they had to contaminate the whole selection in his cupboard."

"Exactly." Ryan nodded. "They must have entered by the back door or risk being seen on the main road at the front…but the back door was locked when we arrived."

He paced away from the window, then came to a standstill.

"How high is the fence separating Humble's back garden from his immediate neighbours, Christine and Paul Harvey?" he asked suddenly.

There was a rustle of papers while the others flipped through their binders to find the CSI photographs taken of the property.

"It's barely more than a picket fence," Lowerson said. "Why?"

Ryan glanced at the images and tapped his index finger against one of them. "Look," he said. "The Harveys keep their wheelie bins at their back door, which is just over the fence from Humble's back door, within easy reach. The Harveys must wheel their bins around to the main road on collection days. Which are—?"

Again, there was another scramble to check the council's waste and recycling collection schedule, which was published on its website.

"Monday was recycling collection," Yates said.

"How convenient." Ryan smiled. "If I was a killer in a hurry, I could just dump the bottles in the neighbours' recycling bin and wait for it to be taken away the next day. I'm surprised the CSIs missed it."

"They probably checked for weaponry or anything unusual in the neighbouring bins, but there was no reason for them to check for ordinary recycling on Sunday night—especially as there was no definitive case for murder, then."

Ryan acknowledged that was true. "Jack? Mel? First line of enquiry is to contact the recycling plant," he said. "I want those bottles found."

"They might not be there—"

"Maybe," Ryan said. "It's a long shot, but worth looking."

"Don't forget the bottle bank," MacKenzie said quietly. "And the recycling bins at the pub, where their used bottles are discarded."

"I don't recall seeing a bottle bank," Ryan said.

"It's on the outskirts of the village," she told him. "I noticed it when we were driving in the other day. That's worth checking, too, in case our killer left the cottage by the front door and dropped them off himself, either there or in the pub's bins, thinking they'd get lost amongst all the others."

"Ballsy," Lowerson said.

"Stupid," Ryan argued. "They're an amateur, but they've had a bit of good luck, probably because they're a regular face in the village. They blend in, so people don't notice somebody carrying a holdall or a backpack full of bottles—unless, for example, there happened to be a protester sitting outside Humble's house at all times. Zachary White may have seen more than he was supposed to."

"How did the killer get a key to enter Humble's cottage, anyway?" Lowerson wondered.

"They didn't need one," Yates supplied. "It was also common knowledge that Humble never locked his doors. He was old-fashioned that way, and Holystone has always been a very safe area. He probably isn't the only one who doesn't bother."

"Well, well," Ryan said. "If Fred Humble never locked his doors, perhaps his killer was the one to lock the back door before leaving by the front? He just couldn't help himself, again."

"I wonder if they realise they're doing it," Lowerson said. "You know, turning things off, locking doors…even when it'll be incriminating for them."

Ryan shook his head. "I don't know, but they'll certainly realise it when their compulsiveness leads us to *their* front door," he said, and then stifled a yawn. A quick glance at the clock on the wall told him it was almost six-thirty, and he would need to leave in the next ten minutes if he was going to make it home in time to read Emma's bedtime story. Aside from the obvious, not seeing his wife and daughter as much as he would have liked represented the biggest downside to the job, and navigating a balance between work and home life was one of the biggest challenges he faced.

"Almost time to wrap things up," he said. "Turning to the second line of urgent enquiry, we need to know where the killer sourced the pesticide, the remnants of which we found in two containers within the vicinity of Zach White's campervan."

He moved across to the whiteboard, where he scribbled a quick timeline for them all, as a visual aide.

"Now, as Mac has already told us, Pinter's team isolated the fatal compound that killed Humble," he said. "It was a pesticide containing *thiacloprid*, which isn't legal in the UK but is legal in other countries like the US, so it's possible some retail outlet or farmer managed to source a pesticide not usually manufactured or sold domestically. Of the two containers found near Zach White's body, the older one contained the thiacloprid, whereas the newer container didn't, despite having identical packaging. What do you make of it?"

There was a brief lull, before Lowerson took the first punt.

"Well, if we're right, and it was necessary for the killer to pre-fill a bunch of contaminated beer bottles, perhaps he laced them with pesticide from the older container before dipping into the shed to top them off with beer and plant them in Humble's cupboard?" he said. "We know that none of the residential cottages have CCTV cameras front or back, so it would have been very easy for someone to slip into the shed via Fred's back garden."

Ryan nodded. "What else?"

"The pesticide in the newer container must have been the one used to contaminate the main water supply,"

Lowerson continued. "It didn't contain thiacloprid, so that's consistent with the analysis of the pipework and other water samples that were taken at the time. In terms of where somebody could have got their hands on the pesticides, it's always possible they bought it from one of the agricultural shops? There are dozens across the county, so it wouldn't be hard."

"And risk having the sale traced back to them?" Yates queried. "It seems more likely they'd have stolen some from a nearby farm."

Jack thought about it, and was forced to agree it would have been the simpler approach. "Either way," he said, and folded his arms.

"In the absence of my better half, I feel obliged to represent his interests in your recent wager," MacKenzie said, and Ryan cast her an amused glance. "Therefore, I have to ask whether we can rule out the possibility of Zachary White having bought or stolen the containers of pesticide? His fingerprints were found on the edge of one of the containers, according to Faulkner's preliminary findings."

Ryan leaned back in his chair, and sighed deeply.

"No, we can't rule it out," he admitted. "Until we hear from Pinter's team with the autopsy report, we can't rule out the possibility of Zachary having done all of that before killing himself, just as it appeared when we attended the scene."

"But the ignition key," Lowerson reminded him.

"I haven't forgotten it," Ryan said. "Ignition keys don't turn themselves but, since there were no fingerprints on the key and Faulkner's still going through the DNA samples, it doesn't give us any clue as to the identity of that second person." Ryan rose from his chair and began shouldering into his jacket.

"That's a wrap for today, folks. Tomorrow, we'll look into possible outlets for the pesticide, and contact all the farms within a five-mile radius of Lady's Well to see if they're down a couple of containers," he said. "Let's hope our protesting friends decide to take the day off from blockading any major road networks."

"Don't shoot the messenger, but there was talk of them holding a candlelight vigil for Zachary," Yates said. "If it goes ahead, there'll be hundreds of them turning out."

Ryan scooped up his files under one arm and braced his other hand on the doorframe. "What I'd really like to know is, between road protests and candlelight vigils, when the hell do these students ever *study*?"

It was a mystery.

CHAPTER 26

In the small hours of the morning, two people lay awake in their beds.

One of them was Melanie Yates.

She listened to Jack's rhythmic breathing beside her and tried to take comfort from it, but all she felt was irritation. If not his breathing, heavy and slumberous beside her, then the sound of the old cast iron radiators churning away was enough to give her a headache; though, only a few months ago, it had brought her such joy to restore them and see them installed in their lovely new home. Now, they were a nuisance, their sound like a pin in her eye.

Trickle.

Whine.

Snore.

The noises circled her mind like a cyclone, whipping into a frenzy of anxiety so that her chest cavity tightened, the intercostal muscles spasming as she tried to remain calm, to practise the breathing techniques she'd been taught.

In...one, two, three...out...one, two three...

But the weight became unbearable, pressing against her chest so she felt pinned down by invisible hands, the force of it enough to bring tears to her eyes. She heard her own shallow breathing and began to feel light-headed, fear and panic warring with self-loathing.

Melanie rolled off the bed and sank to the carpeted floor, wrapping her arms around her knees as she sucked in enormous gulps of cool air. When she felt able, she crawled towards the en-suite bathroom and closed the door behind her while Jack continued to sleep, unaware of her struggle.

Was it thoughtful? she wondered, as she faced herself in the vanity mirror and began to hunt for the small box of tablets prescribed by her doctor for severe panic attacks. Was it thoughtful, or kind, to keep Jack so much in the dark, never confiding the extent of it all? Mostly, she told herself it was the right thing to do; she didn't want to burden him with the details of an internal battle she fought every day.

And yet...

She looked at herself again, at a woman who'd grown thin and pale, whose eyes betrayed the fear locked inside the casing of her skin.

It wasn't being kind, she realised.

Melanie was forced to accept that she no longer trusted Jack Lowerson, nor anybody else around her. She also accepted it wasn't their fault. They were, she knew, kind people she'd had the good fortune to befriend and, in the case of Jack, to contemplate building a life and a future with.

But, until her mind was sufficiently healed, there could be no future with Jack, or with any of them.

Melanie thought of the man asleep in the next room, and might have wept.

So close, she thought.

They'd been so close to happiness.

She sat on the edge of the bath and stared at her surroundings: the toothbrushes in a pretty bamboo cup; the plants on the window ledge; the bottles of shampoo and mint-scented shower gel Jack loved but she hated, because it stung her eyes. Two robes hung from pegs on the inside of the door, both white, both gifts to one another the previous Christmas.

He wanted to marry her.

Melanie knew that; she'd known it for some time, but hadn't encouraged him to ask because she'd known they weren't ready for it and there was still work to do—particularly from her side of the fence. She thought of MacKenzie's suggestion that she go back to the beach hut where she'd been held by Andrew Forbes, one of the country's most prolific serial killers with a career spanning almost twenty years without detection, and wondered if it would really help.

How many others? her mind whispered.

How many other killers were out there, right now, with families, friends, jobs…pretending to be human?

"Stop it," she whispered. "Stop torturing yourself."

But when she looked in the mirror again, she saw Andrew Forbes' face behind her, looking over her shoulder with dark eyes.

"That's *my* job," he said.

Melanie grabbed one of the bottles on the edge of the vanity and spun around, throwing it across the room before she could think about what she was doing.

Seconds later, Jack burst inside. "*Mel*! Mel? Are you all right?"

He took in the scene with one glance, then focused his attention on the woman who whimpered in the corner, hunched down into a ball to make herself small while her body shook all over and her eyes bore through him, as though she didn't recognise him.

"I—I saw him," she whispered. "Jack, he was right here, I *swear*. I'm telling you, he was standing right behind me… he was…he—" She raised a finger and pointed towards the spot where she thought she'd seen Forbes, and then let it fall again. "I—I'm sorry," she said, in a more controlled voice. "I realise how ridiculous it sounds. Andrew Forbes is dead. I *know* he's dead."

"Yes," Jack said softly, and crouched down beside her very slowly, so as not to startle her. "Mel, he's dead. He's never coming back."

She nodded, but her mind didn't fully believe it.

"Why not come back to bed?" Jack reached out a hand and, so that he wouldn't worry, she took it and allowed herself to be led back to the bed, to be tucked in and snuggled for a while.

But, when she heard him fall into another deep sleep, she crept from beneath the covers and left, walking on soundless footsteps to the living room. She dragged one of the dining chairs to the window, where she stationed herself and watched the empty street outside for long, long hours, noting times and changes, people and faces, until the first light of day.

Another person couldn't sleep that night.

They thought of the box hidden beneath a floorboard; just a tiny, nondescript little thing, but it contained their most prized possession—like the creature, Gollum, to them it was their *precious*.

They could *never* look inside the box, it was far too dangerous. It was a firm rule they'd made from the beginning; the only condition for having taken what they'd taken, and the only way in which they could keep their trophy without running the risk of discovery.

But, oh…*oh*, how they wished they could see its contents and feel the power of it, one more time.

Who would know?

Nobody knew it existed. Nobody at all.

The danger was not that others would discover its existence, but rather that their own backbone would weaken and the terrible *need*, the terrible *ecstasy* that came from remembering and reliving those final moments would be too much to bear, so their own foolish weakness would be the thing to betray them.

It could not happen.

They could not sacrifice everything, not *now*, when they were so close to the only other thing they'd ever wanted.

And so, the box remained where it was, dormant beneath the floorboards, but they could have sworn it spoke to them, barely more than a whisper as the clock continued to tick away seconds, minutes and hours.

Ryan woke suddenly, as though somebody had tapped him on the shoulder.

His eyes flew open in the semi-darkness of the room he and Anna shared, and he felt the rise and fall of her chest as she lay curled against his body.

Nobody else was there.

He raised himself to a seated position while his eyes tracked every corner of the bedroom, searching the shadows.

Something had woken him, he was sure of it.

With extreme care so as not to disturb his wife, he slipped out of bed and, in one fluid motion, dropped to the floor to check beneath it.

Nothing.

One by one, he searched their wardrobes, feeling more ridiculous by the second.

Again, nothing.

Moonlight bathed his body in silvery-white light as he entered their en-suite, but there were no figures lurking there, nothing to give him any cause for alarm.

Ryan caught himself in the bathroom mirror—a tall, raven-haired man whose eyes shone with the focused expression of one who hunted, and was used to being hunted in return.

Let it go, he thought.

Go back to sleep.

Ryan ignored the well-meaning advice of his own psyche and continued out into the hallway, where he made directly for his daughter's bedroom. Her night light cast a gentle aura around the nursery, and he saw the ghostly outline of a row of stuffed toys she'd lined up in a circle on the floor beside a plastic tea set. Harmless, imaginative fun during the day but, at night, without the comfort of a well-lit room, the toys looked as if they might animate and start walking towards him at any moment.

Teddy bear's picnic, he thought, with a shiver.

He unlocked the child gate and stepped inside, where he made his way across the room towards his daughter's little cot bed.

Emma was not there.

Ryan felt his heart slam against the wall of his chest, before falling to the pit of his stomach. He spun around, eyes wild with fear.

Emma—

He hurried back out into the hallway and gripped the wall for support, holding himself up so he could try to think clearly.

"Daddy?"

She emerged from the door leading to the family bathroom.

"I couldn't flush," she told him, and pulled a face that told him very clearly that she would be expecting him to do the honours. "The handle's too high."

He said nothing at first, then caught her up against him, holding her close against the bare skin of his chest, feeling his child safe and warm and alive. "Emma." He held her for a moment longer, then let out a tremulous breath. "How did you manage to go to the bathroom by yourself?" he asked of his toddler. "There's a safety gate—" It had been firmly shut when he entered the room, and he'd closed it again after leaving.

"Watch, Daddy. Watch." She wriggled from his arms and proceeded to climb over the safety gate with the kind of agility Bear Grylls would have been proud of. "See, Daddy? Easy-peasy." She looked up at him, her dark hair the same shade as his own, and her expression an almost perfect mirror of the determined look he wore so frequently, had he only known it.

Ryan looked back, pride and love mingling with relief and all manner of new fears. "Emma, this safety gate is there to keep you…well, *safe*," he said. "You're still very little, so we have to be careful."

"I'm careful," she repeated, and he had the funniest feeling she was trying to placate him.

Shaking his head at the absurdity of it all, Ryan scooped her up again and administered another loving cuddle before settling her back into bed.

"Time for sleep," he said. "Next time, Emma, give your old dad a bit of warning. I nearly lost my stomach, back there."

"How?" she wondered.

"Never mind," he muttered. "Sleep tight, darling."

Emma's footsteps must have woken him, Ryan told himself, as he waved her goodnight and stepped back into the hallway, intending to return to bed for some much-needed sleep.

Again, something stopped him.

He could not have said what it was; there was no other person there, but he felt the presence of one as if there had been a figure standing right beside him.

Careful, they seemed to say.

Be careful.

Shivering, but not from cold, Ryan moved swiftly through the rooms of his house, checking the doors and windows, then re-checking them again. The air was perfectly still, and no demons awaited him behind doorways.

He should go back to bed, he thought.

He was imagining things.

Instead, he stayed awake, guarding those he loved through the small hours of the morning until Anna found him shortly after six, tall and tired, but still blazingly alert as he patrolled the main rooms separating front and back doors.

He still could not explain it.

CHAPTER 27

The next morning

"Dad? *Dad!*"

Frank Phillips had been enjoying a *very* salubrious dream involving a red-haired siren with a liking for banana smoothies and ever-so-slightly overweight detectives, when he was rudely awakened by the high-pitched squeal of his pre-teen daughter at the crack of whichever Godforsaken hour of the morning it happened to be. He barely had time to force one eye open and see that it was still pitch dark outside, before Samantha came galloping into the room brandishing a rolled up newspaper.

"*Umfph,*" he said. "What time is it?"

Samantha checked the clock and perched herself on the edge of her parents' bed, bouncing excitedly while she waited for them to pull themselves together.

"Six-oh-three," she said. "Mum, Dad, you *have* to see this. The paper boy just dropped it through the letterbox."

Their adopted daughter, so perfect a fit for him and Denise as they could ever have dreamed of, had been calling them 'Mum' and 'Dad' for a while. Still, it warmed the cockles of his heart to hear it, even if it was an inhuman hour to be yelling it at the top of her blessed lungs.

"Right," Frank muttered. "I'm up, I'm up."

Phillips dragged himself into a seated position and propped himself against one of the many pillows and floral scatter cushions Denise insisted they have, presumably in the unlikely event of a worldwide shortage.

"What in the name of all that's holy—" Denise muttered, and emerged from beneath the bedclothes with extreme caution. "Samantha, what've I told you about coming to get us after six-thirty, unless there's an emergency?"

She, too, dragged herself into a half-seated position, and wished fervently for coffee; even just the *smell* of it would suffice.

"Sorry," Samantha said, not sounding in the least bit apologetic. "But you've gotta look at this! Dad's on the front cover!"

She waved the newspaper in front of them, hot off the early morning press. Thanks to a longstanding friendship with Nadim, the owner of their local newsagents, the MacKenzie-Phillips household was always the recipient of a timely delivery before either party left for work. They supposed it was the reciprocal kindness that came after Frank had, several years earlier, put his boxing skills to good use in defending his friend against a racially aggravated assault. Nadim had never forgotten it and, come to that, neither had Frank.

"*Frank*," MacKenzie said, staring at the front page. "What have you done?"

Phillips let out an indignant squeak, and clutched a hand to his wounded heart. "*Me*? I haven't done a thing!"

"Mm," she said, and unfolded the paper. "Oh, dear."

"What does, '*Oh, dear*', mean?"

MacKenzie didn't bother to respond, her attention focused entirely on the large, central image which showed her husband bending down while appearing to serve members of Northern Resistance a tray of coffee and cakes. Beside it, the headline read:

LET THEM EAT CAKE!

"Frank, why were you serving the protesters coffee and snacks?"

Phillips grabbed the newspaper, and made a series of increasingly frustrated noises as he read the piece that had been printed in one of the country's most circulated broadsheets.

"Aww...howay, man, that's not..." He skim-read the rest, and then threw the offending paper onto the bedspread. "That's not what happened! Whey, they're tryin' to make out that I was on the protesters' side—"

"Yes, but when you're seen to be laughing and hand-feeding those you're supposed to be moving along in the line of duty, it does rather *look* like you're on their side, doesn't it?"

Nine times out of ten, Phillips was delighted that his wife happened to be his direct senior in the police hierarchy. However, judging by the strong whiff of disapproval he detected in her voice, now was most definitely not one of those times.

"Sam, why don't you go and get yourself ready for school, pet?" he said. "We'll be down in a minute to sort out a bit o' breakfast."

"Okay," the girl said, and then leaned in for a spontaneous hug. "I think it's so cool you're on the front page!"

They waited until she'd trotted off again, then Frank turned to his wife.

"I think the thing to do here is to see the funny side," he said, with more hope than he felt.

MacKenzie sighed. "Frank, you don't need to convince me that this was just a case of unfortunate timing," she said, tapping the newspaper. "I know you wouldn't do anything to compromise an investigation or bring the department into disrepute. This has been blown out of proportion by the press, and naturally they haven't chosen to feature any of the images they must have of you and Jack moving the protesters off peacefully, without any need for unpleasant or forcible action. It isn't fair, Frank, but I can tell you the Chief won't be happy when she sees this, because it isn't only about *being* professional, it's about being *seen* to be professional."

He swore softly. "I bet some muppet from the *Daily Fail* writes a comment piece about how the police should take a firmer hand, or how we're all overpaid for doin' nowt… some such rubbish," he said, and she was sorry to hear the upset in his voice. "I've let people down."

She reached across to take his hand. "You haven't let anyone down, Frank. You acted with the best of intentions, and had Ryan's support, which you'll always have, I'm sure. Besides, your way was effective, wasn't it? Morrison wanted the road blockage removed, and you got the job done."

"Aye," he said. "But at what cost?"

Just then, his phone buzzed with an incoming call, and a quick glance told him it was Ryan at the other end of the line.

He took a deep breath, and held the receiver to his ear, ready to face the music. "Mornin'," he said.

"Well, if it isn't the local celebrity," Ryan said, with genuine amusement. "Look, I was just calling to ask if you need any special measures, now you're a VIP? What about a Frankmobile? You know, like the Popemobile, only more Geordie?"

Phillips couldn't have expressed the relief he felt at having his friend's unequivocal support, shown more clearly in the banter they shared than could ever have been conveyed in a simple message.

"You tell me, son," he said, leaning back against his mountain of pillows. "You're the one who's been fightin' off the lasses all these years. I swear, you fell in the river deliberately that time, knowin' there was folk about takin' pictures of you with a wet shirt plastered to your chest."

"It'll be *you* modelling the wet shirt look, once I prove Zachary White didn't kill himself," Ryan said, and Phillips could almost hear his friend smile. "In the meantime, c'mon, get your arse out of bed and stop feeling sorry for yourself. It'll be tomorrow's fish and chips, Frank."

"Have you heard anything from the Chief?"

Ryan smiled, and mouthed 'thank you' to Anna, who'd made coffee for them both.

"At this hour?" he said. "Of course I have. Morrison sleeps even less than I do, so she was the first to impart the good news. She wants to see us both at nine a.m. sharp."

"What for?" Phillips dared to ask.

"Well, I don't think it'll be for coffee and cake," Ryan said, and his smile grew wider when Phillips released a stream of colourful language in response.

"That lad's got no respect for his elders and betters," Phillips declared, good-naturedly, once the call ended.

"You taught him everything he knows," MacKenzie pointed out. "Has the pupil become the master?"

Phillips smiled. "There's a long way to go before that southerner masters my full repertoire of northern insults," he said, with pride. "And, that's not counting the ones we've borrowed from the Scots, o'er the border."

MacKenzie just shook her head, and then checked the time. "C'mon," she said. "Time to get ourselves washed up and ready for the world."

"You go first, love," he said. "Your hair'll take longer to dry than my lustrous mane." He patted his thinning patch on top.

"Or, we could save water and go together," she said, with a mischievous smile.

It took him a couple of seconds, and then Phillips almost leapt from the bed. "I'm nothing, if not environmentally friendly," he said, and made a comic show of sneaking after her into the shower room, which she played up to with an exaggerated shriek.

CHAPTER 28

At precisely the moment Ryan and Phillips entered Chief Constable Morrison's office, armed with the latter's 'gift of the gab' and very little else, Davie Hetherington and Nick Humble parked their slurry truck in the side road that ran along the outermost edge of the late Fred Humble's cottage. With permission granted by the authorities, they gathered the necessary equipment and let themselves through the gate to begin the long overdue process of emptying the waste in the septic tank.

It was an unpleasant job for many, but Davie was a man who garnered satisfaction from improvement; whether that be himself, his home, his farm, his village or the people around him, which included the younger man who walked beside him, lost in his own thoughts. He was methodical but, as a working farmer with employees, animals and machinery to think of, he told himself that it paid to be organised. His nature could, at times, be a bone of contention between him and Sabrina because, unlike himself, she was a carefree spirit who could live with a degree of clutter in her surrounding environment—it suited her personality and artistic temperament. Over the years, he'd come to accept the things he couldn't change, but that didn't remove the occasional niggle of irritation.

"Morning!"

Both men looked up from their task of unravelling a long, rubber pipe to find Christine Harvey waving to them over the tiny dividing fence that separated the two gardens. At a glance, it was obvious she and her husband had already begun the process of clearing and weeding their own patch of earth, whereas Humble's lawn had gone to seed and the borders were a graveyard of plants that might once have flowered a very long time ago.

That was Fred Humble, Davie thought bitterly. So adept at possessing things, so inept at caring for them until they withered and died.

He looked at Nick, with his blond hair and blue eyes, and found himself wishing he didn't look so much like his mother.

"Finally, the day has come," Christine was saying, excitedly. "I can't thank you enough for coming around at such short notice—" She stopped herself, blushing a bit. "I mean, I'm so sorry about what happened to your father," she said to Nick, as kindly as she could. "But, between him, the police and the forensics people, I'm just glad to be able to have this septic tank emptied, finally. The stench has definitely been worse these past few weeks, and I was beginning to think we'd be forced to live with the smell for all eternity."

She wasn't kidding, Davie thought. The tank smelled worse than a cow's arse.

"I'm sorry it's taken so long to sort it out," Nick replied, with the air of a man who'd tried numerous times to convince his late father to take the necessary steps. "Thank you for being so understanding."

Christine was a kind-hearted woman, as well as an astute one, and she saw in his eyes a world of pain.

"No need to thank me," she said, and reached across to give his hand a quick squeeze. "I didn't expect you to be getting around to this so soon after…well, you know."

"No point in waiting around," Nick said. "I've had an offer for the house which I'm planning to take, so it makes sense to get everything in good order ahead of probate and all that."

Christine wondered who her new neighbour might be, but was too polite to ask.

"Won't take long," Davie reassured her. "I've a sneakin' suspicion the tank is broken, which is why the thing hasn't overflowed in all this time. It's made of brick, put in over a hundred years ago, so the bottom has likely failed or the side walls have collapsed…"

He shrugged one broad, workman's shoulder.

"The waste has probably been seepin' into the ground."

Christine pulled a face as she cast an eye over her own lawn which, considering the time of year, looked remarkably green.

"Hmm," she said, and gave a discreet sniff.

"Either way, we'll get it sorted for you," Davie said.

"We're happy to contribute towards the maintenance or replacement of the tank," she said, and told herself not to worry about the cost of it all. "We're fifty per cent responsible."

Davie and Nick nodded, pleased with the new additions to their small community. They were even more pleased when she disappeared and came back shortly afterwards with cups of steaming tea and a small plate of biscuits.

"You might want these before you start getting your hands dirty," she said, with a smile.

Davie bit into what was, he had to admit, an excellent chocolate chip cookie.

"Don't tell Rina, or Karen Russell come to that, but these cookies are—" He made a 'chef's kiss' motion with his fingers.

Christine smiled happily.

"Likewise," Nick said, after he'd inhaled the first biscuit. "They remind me of the ones mum used to make."

Davie put a silent hand on the man's shoulder. "We best be gettin' on now."

They made their way back towards the site of the tank, which was covered with foliage and weeds that had grown over a long period of time and neglect. Clearing the ground to allow access to the tank cover took the best part of forty minutes, and, even then, it took all their strength to lever the concrete cover from its rusted seal.

Immediately, the stench hit them, and both men gagged.

"Bloody hell," Nick said, wiping a sleeve over his watering eyes. "That's got a kick to it."

"Worst I've seen or smelled in a good long while," Davie agreed. "Surprising, really, since it's lasted all this time."

"It's finally given up the ghost."

Davie looked at him for a long moment, wondering if Nick was referring to more than just the bricks and mortar, then turned away and busied himself feeding the rubber suction tubing down into the hole they had exposed.

"Start the engine," he said.

Nick made his way back to the truck and soon afterwards the machine began to whirr, before coming to an abrupt stop.

Nick popped his head around the gate. "What's the trouble?" he called out.

Davie sighed. "Must be a mechanical fault," he called back.

"It was working fine the other day," Nick argued. "Here, let me have a look."

He walked back towards Davie and, with younger and stronger biceps, crouched down, took a deep breath and heaved the cover further off the tank to reveal the dank cesspit below.

"Can't see much," he complained. "Got a torch?"

Davie shook his head. "Never mind, I'll use my phone torch," Nick said, but soon discovered the light wasn't powerful enough to penetrate the darkness.

Never one to be beaten, he looked around the vicinity and his eye fell on a long branch which must have fallen from one of the overhanging trees in recent winds.

"I'll have a poke about and see if there's anything blocking the pipe."

Davie watched him lever the branch down into the tank and begin to explore what lay beneath the layers of excrement.

"Seems to be something causing a blockage," Nick confirmed. "Here—let me just—"

With some nifty movements, he wriggled the branch and withdrew it again.

"I don't know if that's helped—" he began to say.

Hooked on the end of the branch he held was a woman's handbag. Stained and sodden but, as he tipped it onto the grass at their feet beneath the unforgiving light of day, Nick recognised it immediately.

The bag belonged to his mother, Diane Humble.

CHAPTER 29

"Nick—*no!*"

No force in that world or any other could have prevented Nick Humble from lowering himself into the festering depths of the septic tank, least of all the man who'd been a father to him in all the ways that mattered. He heard nothing but his own thundering heartbeat, thought of nothing but the desperate need to *know*.

Davie watched him with eyes that burned, his throat constricted by the weight of his own grief, for he knew what Nick was searching for and, as he looked at Diane's leather handbag, he also knew that he would find it.

A moment later, there came a sharp cry and then Nick's voice filtered upward, shaky and barely audible.

"There's—there's a skeleton in here—*Davie!*"

Hetherington drew himself in, banishing any feelings he might have had to the recesses of his mind before hurrying to the edge of the tank.

"Nick, you need to come out of there!"

There was a small hesitation, but the man acquiesced and Davie helped to heave him out, waders dripping with festering muck that neither man noticed.

"You're sure you saw a skeleton?" Davie asked, grasping the man's shoulders in a punishing grip. "You're *sure*?"

"Aye," Nick said, in a funny, faraway voice. "I'm sure."

A million thoughts swam through his mind, but there was no time for them now.

"My phone's back in the truck," Davie said. "C'mon, we'll call it in."

They made it halfway towards the gate when Christine intercepted them again.

"Ready for another cuppa?" she called over, before catching sight of their faces and the state of their apparel. "Hey, is everything all right?"

Nick continued to stare at the ground, while Davie tried to find the words.

"Do you have the number for that detective handy?" he asked. "The tall one, with the sergeant? I think he's called Ryan."

"I do, yes. But, why—? Have you found something?"

There was a question, Davie thought, and one that would need answering before long. "If you could just tell him to come as soon as he can," he replied, not wishing to alarm her and not quite knowing how much he should say. "It's important."

Christine must have seen something in his eyes or heard the tremble in his voice, for she asked no further questions and promptly spun around and rushed back inside her house, where she snatched up the mobile phone she'd left on the kitchen counter and hunted out the small white business card Ryan had left with the number of the Incident Room printed on the front.

While she was inside, Nick looked down at his hands, which were beginning to shake.

"It's *her*," he said, voice thick with unshed tears. "I know it's her."

Davie watched a flock of birds cruise overhead. "I know it, too," he said.

"She—she never left, after all," Nick managed, and then sank down onto the grass, his legs no longer able to support the emotion he carried.

"No," Davie murmured, still looking up at the sky, where a cloud formation was rapidly coming together to form the outline of a woman's face, or so it seemed.

All around them, the world continued to turn; birds chattered and insects hummed in the undergrowth while the people of Holystone carried on their daily lives, oblivious to an evil that had lain dormant, walking amongst them every day bearing the face of a friend.

Ninety minutes later, Tom Faulkner supervised the careful transfer of the remains of what had once been an adult female, judging by its torso, cranial diameter and length of femur. Her bones were laid carefully atop a plastic undersheet in pieces, beneath the protective cover of a large forensics tent that was set up over the tank and grassy area beside it, awaiting removal to the mortuary. The lack of airflow combined with an unseasonably warm day made for a stifling interior, and several junior members of staff had been driven outside rather than risk losing their breakfasts, not to mention their professional standing. More experienced members of staff remained, having already taken the precaution of dabbing a bit of Vicks VapoRub beneath their nostrils to provide a small barrier against the worst of the nasal assault.

"We're sifting through the rest of the tank," Faulkner told Ryan and Phillips, who stood beside him, bedecked in overalls and protective hairnets. "One of the less glamourous days on the job, I have to admit."

"Have you found anything of interest?" Ryan asked him.

Faulkner nodded, and pointed a gloved hand towards another area of the tent, where a pair of CSIs were photographing and cataloguing several smaller items laid out on plastic sheeting.

"There was a black leather handbag, which Nick Humble found, but we also recovered a large holdall—brown polyester, which might have started out being cream, for all we know. There were quite a few items relatively well preserved inside it, including clothing, toiletries, that sort of thing. All female, UK size eight, which gives some indication of the victim's build, presuming these articles belonged to her. The handbag must have been open when it was chucked inside, because we're still recovering its contents. So far, we've found a lipstick—Elizabeth Arden, mid-pink colour—a rollerball pen, some sort of paperback novel which is too damaged for us to decipher at the moment, and a few other bits and bobs."

"Any identifying objects?" Phillips wondered. "Purse, bank cards—?"

Anything to help them to confirm the woman's identity without having to wait for dental analysis to come back was always a bonus.

"We haven't found a purse *yet*," Faulkner replied. "But we did find something even better."

He led them to a trellis table where a small, rectangular object was being cleaned and photographed by a young woman in overalls and Perspex glasses.

"Her passport," Faulkner said, with satisfaction. "It's too damaged for us to read the page entries without a proper clean-up back at the lab, but the photograph was protected by a plastic cover which has survived remarkably well."

He nodded to his assistant, who prised open the brown-stained pages and flipped to the back of the passport. She gave the plastic shield a careful wipe to improve the photo, then held it aloft.

Upon seeing it, Ryan let out the breath he'd been holding.

"That's Diane Humble," he said. "Fred's wife, who was also the woman in the framed picture we found beside his body the other day."

Ryan looked at the miserable collection of bones lying a few feet away. "Everyone thought she left him," he said. "Perhaps she did, but not in the way they imagined. Look at the side of her skull, Frank."

Phillips turned and saw a huge fracture, nothing but a jagged, empty space where bone matter should have been.

"Aye, looks like she took a wallop to the head."

"Heavy blunt trauma," Faulkner agreed. "Of course, the process of decomposition will have made matters worse. I've called in a forensic anthropologist who's going to come down from Edinburgh to look at the bones with Pinter, so we should have more information for you in the next few days."

Ryan nodded, but didn't place too much hope on a fast turnaround. Specialists were in high demand, especially after the usual funding cutbacks, and they were yet to receive Pinter's autopsy report on Zachary White, for one thing.

"I know it isn't your area, Tom, but you've had enough experience to make an educated guess. How old d'you reckon the bones are?"

"Difficult to say, without the proper analysis," Faulkner reiterated. "The body is fully skeletonised, as you can see. That would take *years*, because it wasn't left at the mercy of scavengers in, say, a river environment, but would have been exposed to a lot of active bacteria. Frank? Are you doing okay, mate?"

In point of fact, Phillips was having a hard time controlling his diaphragm, which wanted to expel the malodourous air that swirled around them in the stuffy tent.

"Divn't worry about me," he said, while breathing audibly through his teeth. "I was just thinkin', y'nah, one of us should have a word with Fred's son, shouldn't we?"

Ryan decided to humour his friend, because sometimes they all needed a break.

Not before a bit of gentle fun, however.

"Good idea," he said. "Frank, you take over here, and I'll run along outside and have a word with Nick Humble and Davie Hetherington."

Phillips looked crestfallen. "Ah—well—"

"Unless, *you'd* rather take their statements?" Ryan suggested, after a couple of ticking seconds.

Phillips nodded vigorously. "Aye, well, you know I've got a way with witnesses," he said, and that was entirely true. "I'll see what I can find out, eh? You just…" He started backing out of the tent. "Just let me know, if…" He cast a final glance towards the gaping eyes of the skeleton, and nearly tripped over his own feet. "If you need me." With that, he dipped out of the tent and made his escape.

"Gets to the best of us, sometimes," Faulkner remarked, and Ryan nodded.

"It isn't the smell that bothers me so much as the cruelty," he said. "It takes a certain kind of mind to dump a body in a septic tank, doesn't it, Tom?"

When it came to cases of human destruction, Faulkner had arguably seen more than Ryan and Phillips combined.

"The psychology is something I prefer to leave to the experts," Faulkner said. "But it's fair to say you *can* tell a lot about the mentality of a person from just looking at the methods, the motives and the mess they leave behind. For instance, with gangland murders, the perps view the act of killing as part of their 'business'. Even for the ones who enjoy it, there's a kind of formulaic style to the injuries they inflict, and a definite sense of expediency." Ryan nodded his agreement, and Faulkner continued. "But, in this case, if we assume the lady was murdered—because, I think even without Pinter's opinion, you and I can see for ourselves it would have taken more than a nasty fall to cause that degree of head trauma—then, we can see her injuries were inflicted most likely in close proximity, and would have required some real force."

Ryan nodded. "Up close and personal," he muttered. "They weren't afraid to get their hands dirty."

Angry, he thought. *Her killer had been angry with her.*

"Then, as you say, there's the choice of the septic tank as her final resting place," Faulkner continued, and cast a brief glance over his shoulder to where his team operated a kind of large, sieving device to weed out any larger items of interest. "It seems to convey a sort of—" He rolled his finger in the air, searching for the right adjective.

"*Contempt,*" Ryan finished for him. "Their decision to dump her in the muck conveys a total lack of respect."

Faulkner nodded. "Whoever did this *wanted* her to suffer, and *wanted* to inflict a kind of final humiliation, judging by those factors alone. If this lady is Diane Humble, do you think it was the husband who killed her? Because, if it was, and she died in their house, the septic tank was a convenient dumping ground."

"Also a risky one," Ryan pointed out. "I'm surprised the police didn't do a thorough check for her whereabouts at the time, but then, apparently she sent some e-mails.

It might have been enough to prevent anyone from making a Missing Persons report."

He thought of all he knew about Fred Humble, which was very little despite having seen the man laid bare, all pride removed in death's final indignity, and wondered if he'd been capable of murder.

Everybody was, in the right circumstances.

"According to all who knew him, including his own son, Humble was disliked and generally thought of as disagreeable and prone to petty disputes," he said. "On top of that, he liked rigid routines, if not strict cleanliness, judging from the state of his house. As far as we've been told, his wife left him twenty years ago while Nick was a teenager, although, obviously, what we've discovered today calls that into serious question; it may still be true that Diane Humble left, but she certainly *returned* at some point and died here, or alternatively, she never left and was killed before she could go anywhere."

Ryan went to stick his hands in his pockets, remembered the polypropylene suit didn't have any pockets, and folded his arms instead.

"There might have been domestic abuse," he said. "I need to bottom that out when we speak to Nick and his aunt, Sabrina. It seems possible, at least, that Fred Humble's behaviour could have escalated beyond control, if he was in the habit of being violent. He could have killed her rather than allow her to leave him."

Faulkner nodded.

"Taking all of that into account, and bearing in mind the articles of clothing and other items we've found, should we treat the DB as having been identified as Diane?"

Ryan looked across to the sad jumble of bones and thought of the smiling blonde woman in the picture he'd seen. "Perhaps it was, once," he said, and experienced a surge of anger that was all for the dead woman and what had been taken from her. "We'll wait to have her identity confirmed through dental records or bone analysis, and run a trace to check she isn't living happily in Bognor Regis; but, on the face of it, everything points in her direction, Tom."

"The son will take it hard."

"He already is," Ryan said. "He's only just learning that he can let go of one hatred and transfer it to someone else on the very same day."

CHAPTER 30

"Is it her?"

Phillips took a chair opposite Nick Humble, who was seated at the table in his kitchen and bore the grey, exhausted look of a man who'd run a marathon rather than having walked a few hundred yards from one house to the next. With his slurry truck impounded for police inspection—just in case any smaller items had been suctioned from the tank in the brief time the pipe had been operational—Davie joined them at Nick's request, while his wife was at work and their child at school.

"You can say anything in front of Davie," he said.

Phillips thought that, as far as formal statements went, he would certainly be speaking to both men *separately*. However, for present purposes, a joint meeting would suffice and, in any event, they both looked shell-shocked and could use the additional support one provided to the other.

"Well?" Nick asked again. "Is it my mother?"

Phillips could have rattled off any number of responses, but fell back on the truth. "Your mother's passport was amongst the things we recovered," he said. "We also recovered a black leather handbag and a polyester holdall containing some clothes, toiletries and whatnot. The team are still dredging the tank, so there may be more things to find."

"The handbag was hers," Nick said, without hesitation. "She didn't have many to choose from, so I remember it distinctly. She used it almost every day."

Phillips looked at Davie, who had stationed himself by the window and stared out across the fields towards the River Coquet, where he'd paddled as a child and still did, on hot summer days. He thought of a time when he'd been young—perhaps sixteen or seventeen—and all the teenagers of the village, including Diane and Sabrina, Lynn and others had splashed about, without a care in the world. He remembered the way the light had bounced off the water, reflecting the golden fall of Diane's hair—

"—Mr Hetherington?"

He snapped to attention. "Sorry, I was miles away."

"It's all right," Phillips said, but watched him keenly. "Why not come and join us at the table?"

It was an instruction rather than an invitation, but delivered in such a friendly way that people rarely noticed the difference.

"There, now," he said, once Davie had taken him up on it. "I was just talking to Nick here about some of his mother's possessions which were found inside the septic tank. They include an overnight bag—"

Davie came to attention, fully alert even in the throes of shock. "Overnight bag?"

"Yes," Phillips said. "We found her passport and various other items of significance which would suggest she was planning to go away."

Nick's eyes were raw with tears he was yet to shed. "I know you can't say it for certain…" he whispered. "I know you need to wait until the—the body—can be tested. But—but—"

He couldn't get the rest of the sentence out, and Davie, whose own throat was working hard, put an arm around him, offering comfort as he'd done so many times before. He said nothing, could find nothing to say, simply held him as a united front.

In that moment, something struck Phillips which hadn't fully registered before.

How alike they were.

Both of a similar height and muscular build with broad shoulders, and there was a familiarity to the shape of the jawline…a certain bluntness to their hands that was more pronounced when seated side by side. Remembering the images he'd seen of Fred Humble as a younger man, there might have been a likeness in height between him and Nick, but that was where any obvious similarity between father and son ended.

It was something to think about.

"To answer your question, Mr Humble, I'd have to say that, regrettably, we do believe the body we found today belongs to your mother, Diane. I must caveat that by reminding you that we have yet to run our checks against other databases, as well as the forensic analyses you've already mentioned," he said, in his most professional tone. "However, given the personal effects recovered today, it's very likely to be her, so I'll offer you my sincere condolences. I'm very sorry for your loss."

Nick just nodded, his head bobbing up and down while he fought another rising tide of grief. "All this time—" he whispered. "All this time, I've despised her for abandoning me with *him*, hated her for not loving me as a mother should. But, all this time—"

His breath hitched, and he broke down.

"There, lad. There, now," Davie said, keeping an arm around his shoulders. "You weren't to know."

He looked across at Phillips, and there was a kind of desolation in his eyes that commanded attention. "He killed her, then?"

Phillips didn't pretend to misunderstand. "We don't know," he answered honestly. "We'll investigate but, I have to warn you, given the passage of time, most of the usable DNA and other evidence will have been lost. That'll make things all the harder."

"Hardly seems to be a great mystery, though, does it?" Nick said, swiping a hand over his eyes. "For years, the old bastard never wanted anybody to touch that bloody tank. Now, we know why."

His hands curled into fists against his lap, and he pushed up from the chair to pace around, anger overtaking grief.

"He took my mother from me, even while she was alive," he snarled. "I remember all the fights, the slaps, the kicks… he was a pathetic excuse for a man. She warned him, time and again, that she would leave, and we spoke about it. She said she had a plan, that we'd be going away."

"Did she tell you anything about her plan?" Phillips asked.

"No specifics but, in the days before she—she *left*—I could see she was lighter, somehow... she was excited. She hinted it wouldn't be long, and of course I'd be going with her." Nick braced both hands on the back of the chair he'd vacated, for support. When he looked up, his eyes were bleak. "Instead, she disappeared and left me with him, knowing what he was...except, she didn't leave me, after all, did she?"

There, shining through the eyes of the man, was the heart of a boy.

"She loved you," Davie said quietly. "She—" He fell silent, and scrubbed a hand over his face. "I need to tell Sabrina about this," he said, abruptly. "Do you know how much longer we'll be?"

Before Phillips could respond, there came a knock at the front door. Nick made as if to answer it, but Davie patted his shoulder to indicate he should stay where he was.

"I'll go," he said, and was grateful for the thirty seconds or so that it gave him to be alone with his thoughts. In those brief moments, he allowed himself to lean heavily against the door before social propriety compelled him to open it.

When he did, he found Ryan on the doorstep.

"Mr Hetherington," he said. "I understand my colleague, Sergeant Phillips, is already inside speaking with Mr Humble?"

"Aye, he is. Come in."

It had often been remarked upon that Ryan had eyes that missed very little and, in those few moments, Davie was left with the impression of having been stripped bare. It was disconcerting at best, and deeply troubling at worst. With a man like DCI Ryan, it would not be long before he found out all there was to know; the deepest and most shameful of all being the fact that, if Diane Humble had been murdered, then he, David Hetherington was to blame.

CHAPTER 31

Melanie Yates left Lowerson and MacKenzie happily employed in the task of investigating the possible sources of agricultural pesticides in the Holystone area, and took the stairs two at a time in an effort to catch the Chief Constable in her office on the executive floor. After a brief conversation with Morrison's fearsome personal assistant, she was told to knock and enter, but stay no more than ten minutes or face her wrath.

"Sorry," Morrison said, while she completed an e-mail she was typing to the Commissioner. "I'll only be a minute—have a seat."

"No rush, ma'am."

Morrison noted the formality, and the fact Melanie hadn't chosen to sit, but didn't bother to reiterate her offer. Some members of her staff preferred to keep the distinction of rank intact, and it seemed Yates was one of them. In her peripheral vision, she watched the younger woman fidget while she waited, obviously troubled.

"Right," she said, and gave the girl her full attention. "That's done. To what do I owe this pleasure?"

Throughout the morning and all the way up until she'd stepped inside Morrison's office, Melanie wondered if she was on the cusp of making an enormous mistake. However, when it came to it, she found she was calm, her heart no longer racing with anxiety but beating slowly and steadily.

"I understand from reading the Employee Handbook that I could be entitled to some sabbatical leave, in cases of long service or considerable trauma requiring an extended period of recovery," she said.

"That's correct," Morrison said, comprehension dawning. "Would you like to apply?"

Yates shifted her feet. "Yes. I'd like to make an application for six months' leave of service," she said. "I realise this may come as a shock—"

Morrison smiled, but not unkindly. "No, Mel," she said. "It isn't really a shock."

Yates looked down at the floor, then back up again. It was hardly a secret that she was struggling, although she'd hoped to hide the worst of it from those around her, and shield them from the darkness that lingered inside her soul; a terrible curse inflicted by a man who no longer lived except as a parasite inside her mind.

"I take it you've found the last day or so back at work difficult?"

Melanie could have used it as an excuse, but she was innately honest and her lips would not form the lie. "I've coped well enough," she said. "If you discount the general paranoia and feeling of impending doom. The problem goes deeper, ma—Sandra," she corrected herself. "I need to sort my head out after what happened. For some people, like Denise, it helped to have people around as a distraction. In my case, I'm afraid I come from the DCI Ryan School of Trauma Recovery."

"What's that, exactly?" Morrison asked. "'If in doubt, steal a boat and ride into a storm?'"

Yates had to laugh. "Not quite," she said, although perhaps, as a metaphor, it wasn't too far off the mark. "I do need time alone to heal, away from people and away from the memories. I need some space to think."

Morrison heard sadness, but also resolve. "The trauma counsellor—?"

"Tried their best," Melanie assured her. "But they can't perform miracles, can they?"

The Chief Constable shook her head, then rested it on her hand. "How soon do you want to go away?"

"As soon as possible."

"Do the others know?"

Melanie looked away. "No," she admitted. "I couldn't find the words."

"You have to," Morrison said gently. "They care."

"I know. I hope they'll understand."

Morrison thought of the circle of loyal men and women who would walk through ice and fire for one another, and sighed deeply. "They will, Melanie. Perhaps not at first, but they will."

"Thank you, ma'am."

"No, Melanie, thank you."

Unaware of how much was soon to change, Ryan and Phillips delved further into the life of Diane Humble, and those who had known her intimately.

"The questions I'm about to ask you are sensitive," Ryan told her son, Nick, and Davie, the tall, quiet guardian who stood beside him. "If you need to stop at any time, please let me know."

Nick thought of his daughter who would be finishing school in a few hours, and knew that he would need time to pull himself together before then.

"I want to get through as much of this as possible before Mia comes home," he said. "Ask whatever you need to ask."

Ryan sucked in a breath, and took his chance. "It would help us to know how things were, when your mother was still around."

He was careful not to say *alive*. Not until things were unequivocal.

Nick preferred never to think of those times, partly because he'd spent the intervening years trying to forget her face, which he'd loved so much, and partly because it served only to remind him of some of the darkest days of his life.

"It was hard," he said, with glorious understatement. "My father was all of the things you already know. He was also petty, jealous, unkind, mean-spirited and a regular drinker. He was made redundant when I was young, and never bothered to find a new job. We struggled, and he blamed that struggle on my mother and me."

"To what extent?" Phillips had to ask.

"He—um—" The words caught in Nick's throat.

"The lad was covered in bruises." Davie stepped in, turning to them with blazing eyes that were full of anger. "I had words with Fred, countless times, and—I don't mind tellin' you—I gave him a couple o' good thumps as a warnin' not to harm the boy or his mum."

"It worked for a while," Nick said. "Then he'd start up again."

"What about your mother?"

"She tried her best to shield me, but ended up taking the brunt of it herself," he said. "He always avoided her face."

Davie closed his eyes, remembering the bruises he'd seen so often on Diane's ribs or thighs.

"Bloody coward, that's all he was. If I'd only known sooner—"

"Don't blame yourself," Nick murmured.

He could have cried at the irony of that simple remark, but instead just shook his head.

"Can you tell us what happened, the day she went missing?" Ryan asked, deciding to change tack.

"It was a Friday, the day she went, and I was at a friend's house in Harbottle—the next village over—for a party with most of the kids from school," Nick said. "He happens to be my brother-in-law, now."

He gave the name and address of his wife's brother.

"I stayed overnight, so I didn't realise she was gone for good until much later the next day, which would have been Saturday 11th November, when…when *he* started asking questions about where she was, ranting and raving," he said, tiredly. "Probably all just for show, since he'd shoved her in the septic tank the day before."

"We don't know that for sure," Ryan warned him. "I think it's best to focus on the facts, for now. For instance, do you remember what time you returned home on Saturday 11th? I realise it's a long time ago, now, so take your time."

Nick rubbed his eyes, thinking carefully. "It must have been about five o'clock," he said. "In those days, I wasn't in any rush to get home, so I stayed overnight after the party and took my time walking back the next day. Mum usually made dinner for half past five, so I wanted to be home in time for that."

Ryan nodded. "Do you remember how your father seemed?"

"To be honest, he looked pale and exhausted," Nick remembered. "Far more tired than usual, which was surprising. He didn't do much with his days, except terrorize his family, drink beer and watch telly."

They all heard the bitterness, but there was nothing Ryan nor Davie could say to heal a wound that was too old and too deep to heal.

"It's like I told you before," Nick said, irritably. "Mum said she had a plan, and she'd let me know the details. I had the impression she was waiting for something…I don't know what. But she'd always made it clear I was *part* of the plan. That's why it came as such a shock when she left without me, when she went missing. I came home the next day to find she was just…gone." He remembered the gut-wrenching feeling of loss, the acute pain of abandonment that still lived inside him twenty years later.

"That's just it, she didn't just go 'missing,'" Davie put in softly. "Diane *must* have left and come back again, because she sent Sabrina an e-mail…and I got one, too. I don't think you had an e-mail account, back then, or I'm sure she'd have sent you a message as well."

Ryan frowned, and looked across to see the same expression mirrored on Phillips' face. Namely, that Davie Hetherington must have meant something special to Diane Humble, if she'd bothered to send him an e-mail when she left; that is, *if* she was the one to send the e-mail and not the person who killed her.

Food for thought.

"When did you receive the e-mail?" he asked. "Do you still have it?"

"I couldn't speak for Sabrina, but I've still got mine," Davie told him. "Diane sent it to me on 10th November, a few minutes after ten p.m."

"Do you remember what it said?"

Hetherington cast a sharp glance towards Nick's downturned head. "I—ah, I don't remember offhand," he lied. "It's been a long time. I can find it for you."

"That would be very helpful," Phillips said, making quick notes in his jotter. "Do you remember what you were doing, that day?"

"I'll try," Davie said, and looked down at his hands. He remembered it as if it were yesterday. "I was looking forward to new beginnings."

He turned to Ryan, who understood clearly the message he was trying to convey, and acted upon it immediately. "Frank? I think it's time we had a break to allow Mr Humble to shower off the day and have a strong cup of sugary tea," he said. "Would you mind seeing that he gets it?"

Phillips didn't need to be told twice. "Aye, good plan," he said. "Howay, let's see if you've got any jaffa cakes knockin' about, eh?"

Before he knew it, Nick Humble found himself ushered from the room and upstairs towards the bathroom where he could shower off the remnants of his experience, if not the memory of it. Once their voices receded down the passageway, Ryan shut the living room door and turned back to Davie.

"Well?" he said. "Do you have something you'd like to tell me, Mr Hetherington?"

Davie gripped the edge of one of the chairs. "Aye, I do," he said. "I need to tell you the lad's right. Diane *did* have a plan. I know that, because it was me who was plannin' it with her. We were...the two of us loved each other, Chief Inspector. I loved her all my life, since we were kids. She didn't feel that way, at first, but then, after she married Fred and saw how he really was, things changed."

Ryan took a step closer, so he could study his face for any traces of deception. "What was your plan?"

"She was goin' to leave him," he said. "I had a job lined up to manage the land on some big country pile near Jedburgh and, while I was doin' that, Diane was goin' to work as housekeeper up at the main house. It was perfect and, better yet, it came with a cottage so we'd have had a roof over our heads. There was even a nice school nearby for Nick...he wouldn't have liked leavin' his friends but he hated Fred, so he'd have come around to it. It would've been a new life for all of us."

"You would have been prepared to leave your family and give up the chance to run your own farm?"

Davie nodded. "I loved her," he said, and took a moment to swallow a fresh wave of grief. "It wasn't easy for her, though. She felt guilty...he *made* her feel that way, threatenin' to take Nick away from her and all that. It took a while for her to find the strength to break free. I s'pose that's hard for people to understand."

Hetherington looked at the tall, indomitable man standing before him, and couldn't imagine he'd have the slightest clue about coercive control.

Of course, he was quite wrong in that regard.

"Not at all," Ryan murmured. "Go on."

"In the early days, we all tried with Fred," Davie said, casting his memory all the way back. "But it wasn't just that he didn't like the countryside, or its people; he was rotten, right through to his core. Fred saw a pretty woman when he met Diane, who'd just inherited her parents' cottage—"

"She had?"

He nodded. "Diane and Sabrina's parents were killed in a car accident when the girls were twenty-one," he explained. "They left the shop to Sabrina—it used to be a newsagents, and it comes with a flat above it—and they left the cottage to Diane, so both girls would have a start."

"So it was never Fred's," Ryan surmised.

Davie shook his head. "He brought *nowt* to the relationship except good looks, which soon faded, and a bit of charm Diane would've seen through if she hadn't been so distracted at the time," he said. "She was a loving person, Chief Inspector. Gentle, kind, and she always believed the best in people. She made you want to *be* the best, so as not to let her down. If Diane had a fault, it was that she always believed people were better than they were."

Ryan heard the echo of lost love in the other man's voice, and wondered if it was real.

"In any event, you can't make a silk purse out of a sow's ear," Davie continued. "Fred Humble died the same man he'd always been, and that was a bloody wash-out."

Ryan began moving around the room while his mind pieced together the timeline of the last day Diane Humble was seen alive.

"How did you and she turn from friends to lovers?"

Davie barely remembered; it had been so natural. "Over the years, we grew close," he said, thinking back. "Diane used to pop over to the farm and help out during lambing season, or to exercise the horses when she wasn't workin' in the pub."

"I didn't know she worked in the pub," Ryan said.

"Aye, she and Lynn were friends, and she offered Diane a job when they were strugglin'," Davie said. "It's a tight-knit community, Chief Inspector."

He'd seen a few of those before, Ryan thought.

"Anyhow, with everyone knowin' everythin' about your business, when we started feelin' more for each other, we decided to keep things quiet," he said. "If Fred ever found out, she was worried he'd hurt Nick, and I was worried he might hurt *her*." Davie thought of the skeleton they'd exhumed that very day, and shivered. "We used to leave notes for each other," he said, so quietly Ryan strained to hear. "Old-fashioned, I s'pose."

"Where did you leave the notes?" Ryan asked him.

"Hm?" Davie's eyes were unfocused, still glassy with shock. "Oh. Most people don't know, but there's a little priest hole in the pub, behind a panel. It's never used and, with Diane workin' there, it was the perfect spot. Secret, but right under people's noses."

"You're sure nobody found the notes?"

"Well, there was never any sign they had," Davie replied, but the seed of doubt was planted. "Nothin' was ever missin' or tampered with."

And yet…

"It's always possible."

"Where did you and she usually meet?" Ryan asked.

"Back then, my Mam and Dad were still around, so Diane couldn't come around to the farm without being seen," he explained. "We used to meet up at Lady's Well or we'd book a hotel room, if we could get away."

"Sabrina couldn't help out?" Ryan wondered. "I assumed the sisters were close."

"Oh, they were," Davie said. "Although, I think Sabrina found it frustrating when Diane refused to leave Fred; I felt a bit of that, myself." He sighed, thinking of Sabrina…not knowing what to think, anymore. "In any event, Diane decided not to tell her or anybody else, including Nick," he said. "She didn't want anybody to have to lie for us—lying didn't come easily to her, at the best of times."

Ryan wondered if it came naturally to Davie, but set the thought aside.

"Where were you on the night she went?"

"With my parents," he said. "They were havin' a 'do' and half the village was there. I was expectin' to see Diane and Fred, but they never turned up. I assumed they'd had a row and she'd had to stay at home. I was furious, just thinkin' about it."

Plenty of witnesses at a party to corroborate his alibi, Ryan thought. *On the other hand, it was easy to slip away unnoticed in a crowd.*

He'd known plenty of cases when lovers had become enemies, often where obsession was involved.

"How long had you and she been…intimate?"

"Since about two years after she was married," he said, and turned his back to stare out of the window again.

Ryan did the maths, and understood even more. "Did Fred know?"

"Know what?" Davie asked. "You mean, about me and Diane?"

"No," Ryan said quietly. "About Nick."

Davie rested his forehead against the glass of the French windows in his son's home, bone weary from living a lie.

"You see a lot, don't you?" he said, and the question was rhetorical. "I don't know. I assume not. I *hope* not, because that might just have been the thing to push Fred over the edge."

"Does Nick know you're his real father?"

Something twisted in Davie's heart. "He knows I've been all that Fred never was," he replied. "That's all he really *needs* to know, and I can live with that."

Ryan wondered.

"I gave her a ring, you know," Davie said, mostly to himself. "My grandmother's ring, which she left to me when she died. She told me, 'Give that to the girl you love', and so I did. Diane kept it in its little red box, since she couldn't wear it openly."

He closed his eyes, remembering a crisp day in Spring, when they'd walked beside the riverbank and he'd gone down on bended knee.

"Did you find it?" he asked, urgently. "Did you find a gold diamond ring, opal-cut, surrounded by smaller diamonds?"

Ryan checked the rough inventory list he'd taken of what had been recovered from the sewage.

"I'm sorry," he said. "As far as I know, no jewellery has been recovered, but the forensic team are still sifting through the tank. It's a small but durable item, so there's a chance it could be recovered if it was with her when she died."

Davie nodded, and turned to look out of the window again. "If I hadn't loved her so much, none of this would have happened."

"What do you mean?"

A muscle clenched in Davie's jaw. "If Fred killed Diane, it's because he found out about us, or Nick, or that we were plannin' to leave," he said. "If I'd kept my distance and left well alone…if I'd only been a *friend* to her, things might've rubbed along."

Ryan hadn't intended to reply, but the words came out anyway.

"Nobody is to blame except the person who killed her," he said. "As for Fred Humble, we can't say whether he was responsible, but we'll be investigating all possibilities to discover what we can. Violent people tend to escalate."

Davie looked over his shoulder at Ryan. "You've got a determined way about you," he remarked. "The kind who never gives up."

Ryan's lips curved into a smile that was all predator. "No, Mr Hetherington. I never give up."

CHAPTER 32

"Can we go home yet?"

Lowerson's plaintive voice filtered from behind a computer monitor at Police Headquarters, where he'd been wading through an influx of new data retrieved by the intelligence analysts.

"Nope," MacKenzie called back, from her own desk. "Besides, who *wouldn't* want to know all about the different types of agricultural pesticide, and where to find them in Northumberland?"

"I was wondering about it myself, just the other day," Lowerson replied.

"Not to mention popular brands of sheep dye," she added. "You know, it's not too late for you, Jack. You're young enough to pack it all in and become a social media influencer, instead."

Lowerson played along. "Oh, yeah? What would I promote to my enormous fan base?"

MacKenzie grinned. "Aside from cleaning products and cat food? With style like yours, I could see you opening new clubs and restaurants instead of spending your days pulling bodies out of the river. It's something to think about."

Jack fell down the fantasy rabbit hole for a second, then shook himself out of it. "Don't be daft," he said. "For one thing, I'd need to be a lot more buff than I am, dance a lot better than I do and who's got the time to cultivate a six pack?"

"Not Frank, that's for sure," MacKenzie said, with affection. "You could probably get away with posting cute videos of Sir Pawsalot wearing a mini Newcastle United football shirt, and you'd be an overnight sensation." She referred, of course, to Jack and Mel's beloved cat.

"Do people really sit around watching cat videos?"

MacKenzie stole a glance around the side of her computer screen and pointed a knowing finger at him. "Don't pretend you haven't scrolled through a few of those yourself," she said.

Jack held up his hands. "Maybe a couple," he admitted. "Blame insomnia." He checked the time on the large, industrial clock on the wall. "Hey, d'you think Mel's okay? She's been gone a while."

"Must've been held up," MacKenzie said, keeping her voice carefully neutral. "Probably ran into someone and got chatting."

Lowerson accepted it, and turned his mind back to the business in hand. "Did you know that Nick Humble was given a police caution for joyriding when he was eighteen, and another for common assault outside a bar in Newcastle?"

MacKenzie spun around in her desk chair. "That's surprising," she said. "On the other hand, Humble thought he'd been abandoned by his mother and was living in a deeply unhappy household with his father. He was probably acting out, which is why the police only handed him a caution. Sometimes, we're both sword and shield, y'know."

Lowerson nodded. "Still, looking at the mug shot of a young Nicholas Humble, I've gotta say, he was built like a brick shithouse—pardon my language—even at that age."

"What are you driving at?"

Lowerson shrugged. "Nothing much, really, just an observation that some teens are more developed than others. It looks like Nick Humble could have held his own in most situations."

"You mean against his father?"

"Yeah, or anybody else."

MacKenzie nodded, and filed away the information.

"How's the pesticide search coming along?" he asked.

"*Ugh.*"

Lowerson chuckled. "That good?"

"Let me put it to you this way," she said. "If I was a contestant on *Mastermind* my specialist subject would now be, 'Agricultural Pesticides of the North East and Where to Find Them.'"

"You're in the hot seat," Lowerson said, affecting his best game show voice. "Let's start with an easy one: can you buy pesticide containing thiacloprid within a fifty-mile radius of Holystone?"

MacKenzie pretended to think about it. "No," she said.

"N—" Lowerson dropped the voice and rolled his chair a bit closer. "Really?"

"Mm hm," she said, taking a sip from a can of Irn Bru she'd found squirreled away in one of Frank's desk drawers. He'd go mad when he found it missing, but he'd never suspect her as the culprit—not with her clean-eating, clean-drinking ways—and Jack knew better than to squeal. "Pinter was right. You can't get hold of pesticide containing that compound here in the UK, not legally, anyway."

"Somebody managed to."

"Exactly," she said. "Which brings me on to my next line of enquiry: possible suppliers. I compiled a list of seven major agricultural outlets selling that brand of pesticide in the region, all within fifty miles of Holystone and, d'you know what, Jack?"

He smiled, and shook his head. "What?"

"One of them closed last year, after a scandal involving widespread mis-selling and repackaging of goods, including pesticides. Apparently, one of the staff who worked there tipped off Environmental Health and they did a raid on the warehouse, only to find they were buying in considerably cheaper produce from overseas in bulk, shipping it over illegally, repackaging it and selling for a higher price in UK."

"Hard to see how they could make a profit," Lowerson said.

"It's marginal if you're selling small-scale, but this shop delivered nationwide so it adds up," she said. "In any case, my money's on that place having been the source of the dodgy pesticide."

"Yeah, but you said it closed down last year...it would have taken a hell of a lot of pre-planning to go out and find that particular—"

MacKenzie shook her head. "Remember, we found one container with the illegal compound and one without," she said. "I'm betting Fred's killer had absolutely no idea there was any difference between the two containers, because any type of pesticide in sufficient quantity would have killed him, and the packaging looked identical—albeit one appeared older than the other."

"So, do you think they purchased the pesticide in advance?"

Again, MacKenzie shook her head. "No, all things considered, I don't think our killer purchased anything at all," she said. "Which makes him a tight-arse as well as a sociopath, but let's not split hairs."

Lowerson laughed, as she'd intended.

"Aside from agricultural stores, the most simple and obvious place to acquire some pesticide would be to steal it from a farm," she said. "Now, there are four farms within striking distance of Holystone—bearing in mind, our pesticide thief only needed two containers and he or she is unlikely to have used transportation because it's too risky, that means they probably made the grab on foot."

"Which means they needed to live close enough to the farm to lift the containers without being seen or heard, and without running too great a risk of being discovered."

"Exactly," she said, and gestured him forward to look at the map she'd brought up on her screen. "Look here,

Jack. The red dots are the farm locations, the yellow dot represents Zach's campervan and the other green dots are key sites in the village."

"One of the four farms belongs to Davie Hetherington," Jack said to himself. "It's close, but the closest to Zach and to Lady's Well is that one."

He pointed to one of the dots on the screen.

"Maple Farm?" she said. "Yes, the owner, John Maple, has been abroad on holiday with his wife and family. He got back yesterday, as it happens."

"You've already spoken to him, haven't you?"

"You bet I have," she said. "Maple says he can't be sure if any containers have been stolen, because he keeps a pretty big stockpile and hasn't taken a recent inventory. However, when I mentioned thiacloprid, and described an old-looking container, he knew exactly what I was talking about. He said he had one old container set aside from the rest which he'd been meaning to get rid of, because it was part of a job-lot he'd bought a while ago from a particular agricultural store, which—"

"Was closed down for mis-selling?" Jack guessed.

"Exactly right," she said. "Now, call me a cynic, but that's a mighty big coincidence to me. Unfortunately, the only CCTV cameras he has on the farm work more as a deterrent, and the active ones are trained on the barn where he keeps the heavy machinery because it's worth far more to any potential thief than a bit of pesticide."

"That's a pity. Mind you, it looks like we've found our source," he said. "It still doesn't answer the question of whether Zach could've been the thief, or whether someone else set him up as Ryan seems to think."

MacKenzie reached for the computer mouse and brought up her e-mail inbox on the screen.

"I have something here which could answer a few questions regarding that young man, not to mention the long-term future of the Police Benevolent Fund."

"Eh?"

"Never mind," she muttered. "Pinter's sent through his post-mortem report on Zachary White, so let's see what light it can shed."

There was a brief lull, during which MacKenzie began to read Pinter's report and Jack returned to his desk where he tried unsuccessfully to focus on the facts and figures in front of him.

"Denise?" he said, after a few minutes had passed.

"Mm?"

"Where's Mel?"

MacKenzie's fingers stilled on the keyboard, and she turned to face her friend. "I don't know for certain, Jack, but my guess would be that she's speaking to Morrison."

Just as he'd thought.

"Maybe she's reporting in, after her first day or so back on the job," he said.

"That could be it."

"But—"

"Leave her to tell you in her own words, Jack. You know that, in our line of work, it never pays to make assumptions."

Lowerson said nothing, but wheeled his chair back around to her desk where he reached across to snaffle the last of her Irn Bru. "I needed that."

"Any other time, I'd have written you up for a disciplinary, but I'll let you off this once."

"That's only because you don't want me ratting you out to Frank."

"About what?"

"The Irn Bru, of course."

"What Irn Bru?"

"Wh—" He turned to point to the spot where he'd set it down, and found instead an empty space. "Where did it go?"

He looked all around, under the desk and even in her handbag, which sat open on the floor beside them.

"That's seriously impressive," he declared.

"What is?"

"Talk about a Poker Face," he said. "You're good."

"It's often been said. You know what else has been said?"

He shook his head, full of admiration.

"The hand's quicker than the eye, and Samantha's quicker than both. She taught me a thing or two she picked up during her early years."

"I think I need her to teach me."

MacKenzie smiled, and gave his arm a friendly squeeze in solidarity, because she knew he was no longer talking about fizzy drinks. "You know the greatest lesson my adoptive daughter taught me, Jack?"

He shook his head.

"To have patience," she said, softly. "You have to be patient, and remember the dove."

"The dove?"

She nodded. "You have to set the dove free, to know whether it loves you enough to come back."

Tears sprang to his eyes and, perhaps with anyone else, he might have been embarrassed. Not with Denise.

"I don't know if I can," he admitted.

"You'll do what's right, when the moment comes."

But he wasn't Ryan, Jack thought to himself. He didn't always know what was the right thing to do.

"None of us really know, in the moment," she continued, as if she'd read his mind. "You have to act according to your own conscience and hope it's giving you good advice."

"What if it's telling me to keep hold of her, and not let her go?"

MacKenzie shook her head. "That isn't your conscience, or your mind, Jack. That's your heart."

CHAPTER 33

One woman who knew the true meaning of letting her loved one go was Sabrina Graham.

She caught sight of Davie and the two detectives crossing the road towards her little shop through the bay window, where the early afternoon light shone through its display of colourful trinkets like a rainbow. Music by Enya played softly in the background, something from *The Lord of the Rings* that was both soothing and rousing, and a reed diffuser filled the air with a scent she described to her customers as, 'woodsy with a hint of spice'. There was a quality to their solemn march which told her there would be no glad tidings, and she was reminded of a time twenty years earlier when Davie had come to tell her that Diane had left. There'd been no police with him, that time, but his face had worn the same broken expression as she saw now, marring his strong features and making him appear years older than he was.

Luckily, there was nobody else in the shop, so she had a moment to compose herself before opening the door.

"Davie, Chief Inspector…Sergeant," she said. "Come in."

She gestured them inside and, without needing to be told, swiftly locked the door and tipped the sign to 'CLOSED'.

"Can I offer you some herbal tea or water?"

"Rina, it's bad news," Davie said, unable to wait any longer. "When Nick and I went over to empty Fred's tank, we found somethin' inside."

She waited, looking between them. "What was it?"

Davie could hardly bring himself to say the words, but held up a hand when Ryan would have stepped in to help.

"It's Diane," he said, hoarsely. "We found a skeleton, along with a load of her things…her handbag, overnight bag, clothes and all that. They're going to do the proper tests, but it's looking like it's her. I'm so sorry, love."

Sabrina gave a small shake of her head. "I don't understand," she said, in a funny high-pitched voice she hardly recognised as her own. "How can it be Diane? She's living away, somewhere. She told me she was leaving—"

"No, Rina," Davie said. "She never left."

Sabrina's mouth fell open to form an 'o', and Phillips intervened just before her knees buckled.

"There now, easy lass, easy," he said.

Davie moved forward to take her other arm, and they settled her on the chair behind her little counter.

"Would you like some water?"

Sabrina raised a shaking hand to her head, and let it fall again to her knees.

"No…no, thank you," she mumbled. "Sorry, I was a bit…overcome. I can't seem to get my head around what you're telling me. You're saying Diane was in the *septic tank*?" Tears sprang to her eyes, and she looked between the three of them.

"We believe your sister was murdered, Ms Graham. I'm very sorry."

This came from Ryan, who had never and would never shy away from saying what needed to be said, no matter how painful the truth could be.

Davie came down to a crouched position beside her chair, and placed a warm hand over her cold one.

"I'm so sorry, Rina. I don't know what else to say."

"I can't believe it," she whispered. "Who'd want to kill her? Fred. It must have been Fred."

"You seem very certain," Ryan said.

"It's obvious," she said, and knuckled tears from her eyes. "He was violent, we know that much already. He had means and opportunity, you would say."

"What about motive?" Ryan prompted her.

"Obviously, he must have gone too far one day, to have cracked her skull like that," she said. "The man was deranged." She began to cry again, tears falling in rivulets down her rounded cheeks. "To think, all these years, I've been so angry at Diane," she said. "I feel terrible."

"You didn't know," Davie said. "None of us did."

"Somebody did," Ryan remarked, and three pairs of eyes looked at him. "Somebody knew, all this time, and they've been living with the knowledge for twenty years. They probably thought nobody would find out, so long as Fred continued to prevent the septic tank from being emptied."

"That's why it makes sense for it to have been Fred to have done this terrible thing," Davie said. "Why else be so obstructive, unless he knew there was something to hide? If he wasn't already dead, I could kill the man for doing what he's done."

"He took my sister," Sabrina said, wretchedly. "Diane was all I had in the world, apart from Nick…and *you*."

She looked at Davie, who set aside whatever feelings might have been churning around his belly to focus on the woman who needed his help.

In that moment, Ryan saw several things very clearly.

The first was that Davie was, indeed, a man who liked to fix things if he could.

The second was that he had no idea his fiancée had been the one to murder her sister.

The third was his suspicion that Davie was, by his own earlier admission, the reason Diane Humble had died.

"We'll come back another time," he said, having learned the best approach with intelligent criminals was often a soft and careful one.

Phillips was surprised at the sudden turn, but made no comment and followed Ryan back through the jingling door of Love and Light out onto the main square. The sun was already slipping towards the horizon but not before casting a wide arc of fiery light across the Coquet Valley.

"Thought you'd want to ask a few more questions," Phillips remarked, after he'd given his friend a minute or so to stand there looking tall and brooding.

"She told us the single most important thing we needed to know, Frank."

Phillips' eyebrows flew up. "She did?"

Ryan began to walk back towards the forensics team with slow, measured footsteps rather than his usual striding gait. "Let me ask you a question, Frank. Did either you or I, or Davie Hetherington, mention the fact that Diane Humble's skull displayed the hallmarks of blunt force trauma?"

Phillips replayed the conversation they'd just held, and shook his head. "Not that I recall."

"And yet, Sabrina Graham knew all about it. How, Frank? How did she know there'd been a fracture to the skull?"

Phillips considered it, and swore softly. "I'll be damned," he said. It'll be hard to pin that one, mind. Can't rely on that little snippet of conversation; nothing was recorded and her legal team would laugh us out of court. We need evidence, but she's been clever, all these years. Not a single slip-up. Then, there's the e-mails she must've sent."

"I think we'll find her loving sister—the one who was so trusting and kind—probably shared things like passwords with her, as well as a key to her home for emergencies. Sabrina could have let herself in and packed a bag for her unfortunate sister, before dumping everything in the septic tank. It's accessible from the road, even if she couldn't access it from the house, or even from the field at the bottom of the garden."

"It would've been heavy graft," Phillips said.

"She was younger then, and her sister was slight," Ryan argued. "She could have dragged her easily enough, under cover of darkness."

"Fred would have seen something, surely."

"I'm interested to know more about Fred," he said. "Especially his financial situation, and his whereabouts on the night his wife went missing. I agree with you, it seems unusual that he wouldn't have seen any of this."

"Jack's pulling all the details he can find, but nobody made a Missing Persons report at the time," Phillips said. "Everyone believed she'd left of her own volition, so they didn't bother."

"A clever device," Ryan said, and paused to look back over his shoulder.

Love and light, he thought.

"There's another small matter, Frank. When we were interviewing Davie, earlier, he was adamant Fred knew nothing about his relationship with Diane."

"I remember. What about it?"

"Killer psychology," Ryan said. "If Fred Humble killed his wife, but for some reason other than finding out about her affair with Davie, how would he have known to e-mail Davie as well as Sabrina? The logical step to cover his tracks would have been to e-mail Sabrina, perhaps, because she's Diane's sister, but there was no need to include Davie, was there?"

"Aye, I see what you mean," Phillips said, and tried to imagine the killer's mindset, which was something he found difficult. "Whereas, if Sabrina's our killer, she's done it precisely because she'd found out about her sister and Davie, therefore she'd have known it would have been important from Diane's perspective to have sent him a bogus e-mail. The thing to do is read those e-mails and see what they say."

Ryan nodded.

"You could be wrong, y'nah," Phillips said, after a minute or two. "Sabrina could have made a guess at the cause of death, and happened to be right."

"Have I been wrong about these things before?"

Phillips made a face at him. "Nobody likes a know-it-all," he said, pointing a stubby finger at his friend. "Besides, you still haven't proven your theory about Zach White, have you?"

"Only a matter of time," Ryan said. "I hope you've been thinking about your outfits for this calendar shoot, Frank. I hear 'Sexy Sergeant Santa' is popular."

Phillips thought of the little red number he had in his bottom drawer at home, which had proven a hit with his good lady, but he wasn't about to splash that about the town.

"Aye, that'll be the day," he said, to cover his tracks. "Here, I've got a question."

"Shoot."

"If Sabrina's the one we're lookin' for, how did she find out about Diane and Davie?"

"I imagine she took a keen interest in his comings and goings," Ryan said. "However, I'm also thinking of something Hetherington told us earlier. He said this was a tight-knit community, and that Lynn and Diane had been friends since school."

His eye fell on The Watering Hole.

"Let's have a word with the landlady and see if she can't tell us a bit more about that priest's hole."

"Sounds a bit dodgy, when you say it like that," Phillips remarked.

"It only sounds dodgy to a dodgy mind, Frank."

"Exactly."

CHAPTER 34

The Watering Hole bustled with life.

Around a dozen members of Northern Resistance enjoyed a liquid lunch after the exertion of a morning's peaceful picketing, and gathered in one of the comfortable 'snug' areas of the old pub to put their heads together to discuss the plans for their next round of principled misadventures. Ryan spotted several other tables occupied by reporters grouped by channel or paper and, when several of them jumped to their feet to pounce upon the new arrivals, he shot them a look which had them promptly sitting their arses back down again.

"That's a skill, that is," Phillips said. "In fact, they should teach that manoeuvre to new recruits—'How to Make a Journo Cack Their Pants in Under Ten Seconds.'"

"I should patent it," Ryan agreed. "The only people who seems impervious are the women in my life."

Phillips laughed and gave him a manly slap on the back. "You and me both, son," he said, cheerfully. "They're our kryptonite, but I wouldn't have it any other way. Right!

I'm off to drain the radiator," he declared, having spotted the gents toilets. "Grab us a couple of packets o' pork cracklin' and whatever you want." He started to fish out some money.

"And have Denise hunt me down like a dog?" Ryan swept a hand through the air. "You must be crackers. I could get a couple of packets of trail mix, though?"

Phillips looked like a man who'd lost a pound and found a penny. "If that's how you treat your best mate, I s'pose I should be grateful."

Ryan rolled his eyes. "Emotional blackmail won't work on me," he said. "I'm impervious to it. Remember, I've dealt with the worst of humanity, some of the most devious and depraved minds, so don't think you can sway me with that textbook reverse psychology, Frank, because you can't."

Phillips could smell more than an all-day breakfast. He could smell the sweet aroma of *victory*. He put a hand on Ryan's shoulder. "I know you'll do the right thing," he said.

With one last soulful look, he trundled off to the toilets, leaving Ryan weighing up the balance of two evils. On the one hand, there was his best friend; a man who'd been there for him through thick and thin, who'd probably walk through fire, if he asked him to. All *he* asked was the occasional bit of crackling and a bacon stottie—or two. On the other hand, there was the prospect of imminent heart failure: Frank's, by excess fried meat, and his own, by Denise MacKenzie's fair hand.

Friendship always won out.

Ryan knew when he'd been played like a cheap fiddle, but that didn't remove the simple fact that he, too, fancied a packet of pork crackling, and was as human as the next carnivorous male.

"DCI Ryan! I was hoping I'd see you." Lynn Gibbins, who'd been pulling pints steadily since late morning, greeted him at the bar. "Can I get you anything?"

Ryan placed the order, and sent up a prayer to a God he didn't believe in.

"Comin' up," she said, and handed him the sachets which he held in one sweaty palm. "I saw the police cars outside Fred's cottage again. Have you found some new evidence?"

Even if it wasn't good practice, Ryan was naturally disposed to be discreet. However, he was also a realist, and knew that the rumour mill in Holystone would churn wildly unless the residents of the village were given some basic information to set them at ease, or at least stem any further speculation.

"I'm afraid a new body has been discovered," he said, and watched her eyes widen in shock, followed by dismay.

"Who—who is it?"

"That's yet to be confirmed," he said.

Further questions were forestalled by the arrival of another man at the bar.

"Pint of bitter, Lynn," Ian Bell said, plopping himself onto one of the bar stools after emerging from the gents. "Hello, Chief Inspector. How's the investigation coming along?"

"We're making progress," Ryan said, and took a sip of dandelion and burdock.

On duty.

"I saw the forensics van was back outside Fred's place, earlier," Ian continued, while his hand smoothed the crinkles from a thick cotton bar mat. "Does that mean you're having to go over things again?"

"They've found another body," Lynn said, in a theatrical whisper.

Ian was surprised, as they all were. "*Another* one?" he repeated, dumbly. "Who is it?"

"Just what I asked," Lynn said, tucking a towel into her back pocket. "They can't tell us yet."

Ryan took another sip of his drink, since he wasn't required to contribute.

"I don't understand who it could be," Ian said, frowning into his pint while he polished the edges of his glass with a paper napkin. "Fred lived alone, didn't he?"

"Well—"

"That's better," Phillips said, joining them after his ablutions. "I think one of your bulbs might have gone in there, pet. The lights went out right as I—well, let's just say, at an awkward moment."

Lynn chuckled. "Thanks for letting me know," she said, and called to the young man who was her bartender. "Tom! Go and check the light in the gents would you?"

Phillips' eye fell immediately on two packets of crackling on the counter, and he turned to Ryan with pride. "I knew you'd do the right thing."

"Eat it quickly, before I start to regret my poor judgment," Ryan muttered, and reached for his own packet.

Moments after the first morsel met their lips, both men were disappointed.

"What the hell is this?" Ryan demanded, and snatched up the packet again.

"Tastes like sawdust, if I'd ever tasted sawdust," Phillips said, while still shovelling it into his mouth with the gusto of a starving man.

Watching them, Bell laughed. "That'll be Lynn's vegan pork crackling," he told them, keeping his voice low, in case the lady herself should overhear. "I went through the same heartache when I first moved into the village."

"Who'd do such a thing?" Phillips couldn't have been more upset than if they'd discovered a mass grave.

Ryan caught sight of one of the students, who had obviously heard their vocal objection to vegan foodstuff and was whispering to one of their comrades.

Things could escalate quicky…

"Keep it down, Frank, we're not at the Toby Carvery now," he said.

"Can I get you another packet?" Lynn asked, bustling back over to them.

"Aye, that'd be lovely!" Phillips said, loudly.

Ryan and Ian Bell looked at him in surprise.

"I panicked…" he said, when she moved off again.

Ian laughed, and scooped crumbs from the counter. "Do you have a timeframe for when the police work will be completed at Fred's cottage?" he asked again.

Ryan gave him an empty smile. "Not at present," he said. "Why do you ask?"

"Oh, it doesn't matter, really," Ian said. "It's only that I've made an offer to Nick for the property and I was trying to gauge how soon things could progress."

"I see," Ryan murmured. "I imagine things will be tied up in probate for a while, anyway. What's brought on the sudden rush to move house?"

"*Well*," Ian said, looking around them. "I was thinking of refurbishing the place and letting it out, you know, for holidaymakers. Holystone's a quiet place, but it's well situated for walkers and lovers of history, like myself. Homes don't often come up, so I thought it was worth making my interest known from the outset."

"Take a fair bit o' work to bring it up to scratch," Phillips remarked, thinking of Fred's brown-stained décor and the general air of death. "The place has more land that you'd think, n'all. There's a long garden out the back which'll need a bit of TLC."

"Some other land too, I think," Ryan said, and watched Ian over the rim of his glass. "Not worth very much, just a bit of scrubland, but probably fine for grazing horses. In fact, Frank, didn't you say you were looking for somewhere new to graze Samantha's horse? I'm sure one of the nearby farms could stand in and provide livery, and that bit of land would be perfect. Since Ian's only interested in the house, I'm sure something could be worked out between you, couldn't it?"

Phillips was at a loss, since it was the first he'd heard of any of it. "Er...aye, aye, it would."

"*Well*," Ian said, quickly. "I have to say, I was thinking of using the extra land, myself."

"Really? What for?"

"Same reason, funnily enough."

Ryan smiled again. "We'll have to see how it all pans out, won't we? Incidentally, how's the dig? Found anything interesting?"

"Oh, we're always finding plenty of interesting Roman pieces," he said. "You should come by, sometime."

"Perhaps I will."

Again, Phillips looked at his friend as if he'd sprouted three heads. Despite having a historian-cum-writer for a wife, Ryan wasn't known to be a great lover of history when given the choice between it and almost anything else.

"I'll look forward to showing you some of the finds," Bell said. "Now, I must be going."

They watched him leave and, soon after, Lynn wandered over to join them again.

"We were hoping you could tell us about the priest hole you have here in the pub," Ryan said.

"*Goodness*, who told you about that?" she said. "I often forget about it myself. It hasn't been used in years and, even then, only by the kids as a hiding place."

"Or as a post box, for private messages?" Ryan suggested, and caught a flicker of recognition.

"I couldn't say."

He remembered again what Davie had told him about theirs being a tight community, and that Lynn had been at school with himself, Diane, Sabrina and others still living in the village. Never mind blood being thicker than water; he'd often found the ties of friendship could be just as binding.

"I think you might know what I'm talking about," he said. "If so, it's important that you're honest with me. We're investigating three murders in the village, and nobody can afford to keep secrets. Not anymore."

He must have struck a chord, because her lips suddenly loosened.

"All right," she said, leaning across the bar. "*Yes*, people might have used it as a way to exchange messages from time to time, if there was a reason to avoid using their phones."

"Who might those people have been?" Ryan asked, and leaned forward himself, so that his face was close to hers.

Her heart rate quickened, and her faculty for speech seemed to evaporate. "Well—um—"

"Take deep breaths," Phillips advised, in a deadpan tone, as he polished off his second packet of vegan pork crackling. "This happens all the time."

Lynn turned an even deeper shade of pink, if that was possible. "You were going to tell me about who exchanged notes using the priest hole?" Ryan said gently.

"Yes, but I don't want to speak out of turn," she said.

"You're doing the right thing," Ryan assured her.

"In that case, I'd have to say that Davie used to exchange notes with Diane, when she was still here," Lynn confessed. "But that was a long time ago—"

"How do you know? Did Diane tell you?"

"Diane was a good friend of mine but, no, she kept it secret. I found out by accident, while I was doing a deep clean one weekend, as I recall."

"Did you tell anyone?"

Lynn's eyes slid away from him. "No—o," she said, uncertainly.

"Not even Sabrina?" Ryan said casually. "I mean, she was Diane's sister, after all."

"I might have…sort of, mentioned it," she admitted. "I assumed Sabrina would know about the two of them already, what with her being Diane's sister, so we had a bit of a natter. I know Diane was married to Fred, but she deserved a bit of happiness, if you ask me."

"What about Sabrina?" Phillips asked, keeping his voice light. "Was she happy for her sister?"

"Of *course* she was," Lynn replied, although, to tell the truth, she couldn't remember for certain. "Sabrina knew what a devil Fred Humble turned out to be, so I'm sure she wouldn't have begrudged Diane some happiness, back then. Mind you, it must feel so strange for them both now."

"For who, Mrs Gibbins?"

"For Sabrina and Davie," she replied. "Perhaps it's all for the best, though. Davie was smitten with Diane, judging by his letters, but he's obviously got over her now, hasn't he? Besides, without Diane being around, he and Sabrina are free to love one another, aren't they? If Diane was still around, Davie might never have looked twice at her sister."

And there, Ryan thought, *was the crux of the matter.* "Some people, you don't get over," he said quietly.

Tom the bartender rounded the corner at that moment, forestalling further comment. "Nowt wrong with the bulb in the gents," he said, cheerfully. "It was just turned off, mate!"

Something tugged at the fringes of Ryan's mind, something he felt was important.

"I must be goin' barmy, in me old age," Phillips said, cheerfully.

Outside, Ryan stood on the kerb watching his staff deal with the general public, who had swelled in number since the news reports over the past few days. He saw Ian Bell exchanging a friendly word with some of the protesters, including the young man named 'Rain', and caught sight of Councillor Russell giving another interview about her custodianship of the village and its people and her determination to ensure the 'farce' was not allowed to continue wreaking havoc with ordinary people's lives and livelihoods—which was rich, considering her tearoom had never been busier. Even as Ryan's stomach turned, he was presented with a new problem that was far worse than Russell's 'gobshitery', as Phillips so eloquently put it.

Tik-Tok Sleuths.

Following the initial wave of reports following the discovery of Fred Humble's body, and the frenzy that followed the discovery of Zachary White, dozens of conspiracy theorists had sprung up, spouting theories about the deaths of both men. They consisted of social media 'influencers' who were hungry for online engagement from people scrolling through the void. The more likes and shares, the more views—the more views, the greater their capacity to monetise the persona they'd created. In this case, Ryan spotted a young man and woman kitted out with selfie sticks and mobile ring-lights, reporting without being reporters, telling thousands of people "facts" that were not facts at all.

"*Idiots*," Ryan ground out. "I'm going to shove that selfie stick right—"

"Up their priest's hole?" Phillips put in.

Ryan gave a reluctant smile, but his eyes remained flat and hard. "These wannabes are impeding the work we're trying to do," he said. "They're the reason I've had to draft in more staff to protect the village from all the rubberneckers turning up in their droves, camping out all over the place trying to 'discover the real truth' behind Fred and Zach's deaths because, apparently, years of working as murder detectives doesn't qualify us to know best how to handle things. On the other hand, 'Fran from Accounting' can tell us all about it, because she's seen a couple of Tik-Tok videos made by these chumps. For pity's sake."

"You're forgettin' somethin' important," Phillips interrupted him.

"What?"

"Not all of them realise they're bein' malicious or obstructive," he said. "Some of them are just gannin' on daft because they're numpties. You're not dealin' with a class act like Kate Adie here, lad. You're dealin' with some bloke who fancies the sound of his own voice and, on TikTok, he's King o' the World. It makes 'im feel important, like he's doin' a public service and all that."

"If he wants to do a public service, he can go home," Ryan said, and, without further ado, made a beeline for the amateur sleuth who was, at that very moment, discussing the possibility of ghostly nuns having risen from the dead to wreak revenge for the dissolution of their abbey, which stood in ruins nearby.

Phillips hurried to keep up, and regretted his decision when the two TikTokers turned to film their approach.

"I'm capturing everything on film!" the first one cried, obviously hoping against hope that Ryan would throw the first punch and elevate his viewing statistics for the week.

"Really? That's good, because I'd like to make a statement—" Ryan said, darkly.

But before he could begin, Phillips interjected with a stroke of pure genius. "What we want to say is that, ever since the water turned red, it's had magical, healing powers," he said, in a tone that never faltered. "Take me! I used to be completely bald, but look at me now. My hair's growin' back in since I splashed a bit of well water on it."

To prove his point, Phillips drew out his phone and pulled up an image of himself taken by Samantha the other night, dressed in his bald skullcap while imitating Uncle Fester. It had been taken close-up, at their kitchen table, so there was no real view of the rest of his costume.

"See? This was taken the other day and, already, me mane is growin' back in."

"Wow," they said, and turned back to their followers.

"Aye, but it only works if you do something important," Phillips tagged on.

"What?" they demanded. "What do we need to do, to cure baldness? It's a miracle…"

"Bugger off home and stop bein' so credulous," Phillips told them. "Your ma'd be ashamed o' you! While you're on, get a proper job and let us do ours!"

CHAPTER 35

Davie watched Ryan and Phillips in action, from Sabrina's shop window.

"They seem dedicated," he said, and smiled at the sight of Ryan moving along a group of tourists by strength of character alone.

While he watched the police, Sabrina watched him.

She sat atop a wooden stool she kept behind the counter, and clutched a brightly-coloured mug between her hands but didn't drink from the liquid which had, by now, gone stone cold.

She waited.

"Come and sit by me," she said. "There's another stool in the back—"

Another time, perhaps he would have done, but he had things to say. "I need to talk to you, Rina."

Again, she waited. She was good at that.

"You can talk to me about anything, Davie. You know that. There's been an awful lot of upset, these past few days."

Davie thought of how patient she was, and hated himself all the more for not having told her the truth from the very beginning.

Cowardice, he supposed.

"It's about Diane," he said quietly. "There are some things I never told you."

Even hearing her name on his lips was enough to turn the acid in her stomach to bile, Sabrina thought, and looked away in case he should suddenly turn and see the hatred which must surely be visible on her face.

"What's that, my love?" She was proud of how sane she managed to sound.

"This is…difficult." He sighed, and ran a hand over his head, feeling every one of his years in that moment. "Before Diane left—" He broke off, and swallowed a fresh surge of pain. "No," he said huskily. "Before she was *killed*, she and I—well, I might as well tell you, Rina; I loved your sister."

If she'd had a dagger within reach, Sabrina thought she might honestly have plunged it into his belly for having the temerity to say those words aloud, and to *her*, of all people. It was one thing to have thought about them being together, to have *seen* them, when she'd followed them over the fields and beneath the canopy of trees, but…*love*? She would not accept it. Like any man, he'd been tempted by a damsel in distress, and that was all.

She'd put a stop to it, for Davie's own good.

"We *all* loved Diane," she lied. "It's terrible to think that Fred killed her and dumped her body, that way. Wicked, wicked man."

Davie shook his head, and turned to face her. "No, Rina. I mean, I *loved* her. We were going to be married, as soon as she got a divorce from Fred."

Her fingers turned white and, very carefully, she lowered the mug to the counter. "I see."

"I know I should have told you," he said quickly. "But, when she left us all, I felt…God, I felt so hurt, so rejected, but there was no time for self-pity. I put everything I had into the boy."

He smiled at the thought of Nick, who'd been a teenager then and badly in need of a guiding hand.

"So did I," she lied, and thought of all the times she'd poured poison into the child's ears, reminding him daily of his mother's faults.

A little here…a little there.

That was all it took.

And yet, they *still* mourned Diane. *Still* missed her. *Still* worshipped at the altar of her dead sister, as though she was a saint.

"You've been wonderful with Nick," Davie said, with genuine admiration. "No boy could have wished for a better aunt. He treats you more like his mother."

"It's what Diane would have wanted," she cooed.

But it had been a penance, she thought, having to see Nick grow to look more and more like her sister each day, and less like—

She looked at Davie just as a shaft of afternoon light fell upon his profile and, for a moment, it made him look younger, the spitting double of his son.

Sabrina wondered how she'd never seen it before.

She hadn't wanted to.

Rage burned then, white hot and venomous. "You should have told me…about you and Diane."

Davie nodded, and crossed the room to come beside her, reaching for one of the hands lying limply in her lap.

"Twenty years have passed," he said quietly. "I might have harboured some hope she'd write to me again, or come back for Nick and me, but she never did. You remember, I was going to make a Missing Persons report?"

"Knowing what we know now, I should never have talked you out of it," she said, with a wobble to her voice she hoped was convincing. "I blame myself."

"No, sweetheart. None of this is your fault," he rushed to say, and clasped her hand in his own warm, calloused ones. "What I'm trying to say is that all of this was a very long time ago. I won't lie to you: finding her body today has shaken me up. It's raked over some very old ground and brought up some old feelings, but that's just what they are…old. I can't bring Diane back or resurrect the life we'd planned."

The life we'd planned, Sabrina thought.

What a joke.

"I'm so sorry for you both," she said, magnanimously. "Diane never told me about the two of you."

"We agreed not to tell anyone," he explained. "You know how volatile Fred could be."

Sabrina nodded.

"You should have told me," she said again, but wished he hadn't. She wished Davie had never so much as spoken the words 'Diane' and 'love' in the same sentence.

"I know," he said. "It was the coward's way. I should have told you from the beginning, when things started to change between us. You had a right to know. But, I s'pose, I couldn't believe my luck in having found you, Rina. I didn't want anything to spoil things between us and I worried that, if I told you about Diane, it would put you off trying for a bit of happiness with me."

If only he knew, she thought, that fifty years of bitterness weighed heavily in her stomach.

"Nothing could have put me off you," she said, and meant it. He was the reason for everything.

Davie frowned slightly at her tone, which had a note to it he hadn't heard before, but ignored his own ears which were likely clogged with the stress of the day.

"Do you think you can still love me, still marry me, knowin' what I've told you today?"

Sabrina looked up at him with shining eyes.

Cat eyes.

"Of course, my love. Of course, I can. There isn't anything or anyone who could stop me from loving you, Davie Hetherington."

Not even the man himself.

Relieved, shaken, in need of comfort, he fell to his knees and wrapped his arms around her waist, counting his lucky stars to have such a warm and understanding woman. She held him, one hand stroking his head, and glanced up to the ceiling where, somewhere beneath the floorboards of the room above, the ring he'd once given her sister lay hidden inside its velvet box.

Bitch, she thought angrily.

Even in death, Diane still wouldn't *die*.

Her eye fell on the window, and the police who gathered across the street. Davie was right; they were dedicated people, the kind who'd never rest until they had all the answers.

She hoped that wouldn't be a problem.

CHAPTER 36

"I think I've found something."

Melanie Yates gestured towards her colleagues, who'd greeted her return to the office with studied nonchalance an hour before. There would come a time to have a serious conversation, but, before then, there was work to be done and she'd stumbled on a breakthrough.

"Jack! Denise!"

Lowerson wheeled his chair across to where she sat—so close, and yet, it seemed to him, so very far away. "What've you got?"

MacKenzie joined them, packet of *Frazzles* in hand. "Found something?"

"I've been wading through Fred Humble's old medical records," she said. "Good God, the man could moan about anything and everything…but that's not the issue. Look at this."

They peered over her shoulder at a series of entries, which were GP notes dated Friday 17th November twenty years ago, discussing Fred's knee surgery, which had taken place a week before then, on Friday 10th November. Additional notes detailed post-operative progress, which had been good, 'especially in the circumstances'.

"I'm sorry, I don't understand the significance," Lowerson said. "He had knee surgery twenty years ago. So what?" There was a sharpness to his tone he couldn't prevent, his verbal defences snapping into place like iron shutters to cushion whatever blows Melanie would later inflict, whether she intended to or not.

"Look at the dates," MacKenzie said, and put a steadying hand on his shoulder that was part-comfort, part-warning.

Go gently, she told him, without uttering a word.

He looked at the screen again and, this time, he saw it.

"Bloody hell," he muttered. "Fred couldn't have killed his wife, could he?"

"Not if he was in hospital overnight recovering from knee surgery," Melanie said. "Which he was, on 10th November. According to the statements we have, that's the date Diane Humble disappeared, isn't it?"

MacKenzie nodded. "We'll need to check the hospital records, just to be sure," she said. "But, assuming there's no discrepancy, we can be pretty certain that Nick Humble was at a party in the neighbouring village all day and overnight, while Fred Humble was in hospital during the same timeframe. That means neither of the people who lived with Diane could have been responsible for her death, assuming of course that she died on that date."

"I can't think why she'd have left on 10th and come back at any later stage," Melanie said.

"Unless she realised she'd made a mistake in leaving, and wanted to come home," Lowerson said, and a short, heavy silence followed.

"There's always that possibility," MacKenzie said. "For now, let's assume it's Option A, and Diane Humble was killed sometime on 10th November. Who does that leave?"

"We'd need to go back and interview everyone who was resident in the village at that time," Jack said. "Even if they *could* remember their movements on that date twenty years ago, which is doubtful, we'd have to cross-check every story to see who didn't have an alibi. It's a mammoth task."

"Let's focus on one person at a time," MacKenzie said. "Ryan's just sent a message. He and Frank are heading back now, and he wants a twenty-four hour watch put on Sabrina Graham and Davie Hetherington."

They looked amongst themselves.

"For safety reasons, or surveillance?" Lowerson asked, because it made a world of difference.

"He's given instructions that they should be detained if either one looks like they're about to fly the nest, so I'd say it's surveillance."

"Must be one of them, in that case," Melanie said.

"Or both of them," Jack pointed out. "But why would either of them want to kill Diane Humble?"

MacKenzie shook her head slowly, while her mind whirred with possibilities.

"Both of them *could* have killed for love," she said. "But only one of them had a reason to."

"Ryan's forwarded the e-mails that were supposedly sent from Diane, on the same day she went missing," Melanie said, and opened the files so they could read them.

The first was written from Diane to her sister, Sabrina:

My dearest Sabrina,

I'm sorry to be writing to you like this, but Fred's left me no choice—I have to leave.

I wanted to tell you how much I love you, and how I think you're so much smarter and more beautiful than I ever could be. I've always felt in your shadow, and it's been hard to watch you shine every day without feeling my own inferiority. But then, you're so kind and understanding. Nick loves you, sometimes I think more than he loves me, and so I'm begging you to look after him, to protect him and bring him up as best you can, as though he was your own son. I should have listened to you about Fred. I should have listened to you about many things, but I didn't because I'm stubborn. If I am unhappy, it's my own fault. Everything is my fault.

I hope everything good comes to you, and that you can go on and continue to shine brightly without me there to spoil things.

Blessings,
Diane.
X

P.S. Please don't ever try to contact me. I want to make a clean break of it and start afresh. I know this might hurt people, but it's the best thing in the long-run.

"Wow," Jack said. "She sounds miserable, for one thing, but, at least she loved her sister—"

"Ryan thinks Diane didn't write it," Mel reminded him. "Read it again through the prism of Sabrina or Davie having written it, and it sounds very different, doesn't it?"

He followed her advice, and read it again while imagining one of those people had written it.

"It's most interesting from Sabrina's perspective," MacKenzie said, and both heads turned towards her. "She had a bit of a field day, didn't she? "Smarter and more beautiful'," she quoted. "Quite an opinion of herself."

"Yeah, not to mention the transference," Jack said. "She's placing the blame squarely on Diane's shoulders, saying she "spoils" things and that everything is her fault."

"Which tells us something interesting about her character," MacKenzie said. "Namely, that, if she was responsible for Diane's death, she takes no responsibility for it, whatsoever."

"What d'you make of the sign-off?" Mel queried. "Isn't 'love from' or 'all my love' more appropriate for a letter like this? Why say, 'blessings'?"

MacKenzie remembered the shop Sabrina Graham ran in the village, and her belief system.

"She considers herself Pagan," she said. "A lot of the rituals contain forms of words that are a bit similar to that."

"Could equally have been said by anyone of any faith," Lowerson said, fairly. "But I can't imagine Davie Hetherington signing off like that, for one thing, and, for another, there's no mention anywhere of Diane Humble having the same beliefs as her sister."

"She didn't," Melanie confirmed, reading back over a statement given by one of the other members of the village. "She used to be involved with the local Anglican church."

"There you go," MacKenzie said, and then leaned across to scroll down to the second letter, which was supposedly written by Diane Humble to Davie Hetherington. "This should be interesting, if it was written by the same hand."

Dear Davie,

By the time you receive this e-mail, I will be gone. Please don't look for me, or try to find me; I've made my decision and it's final. I've been a poor mother to Nick, and he's better off with you and Sabrina to watch over him—my sister is a far better woman than I could ever hope to be, and I think it's only right that you and she should parent him together.

As for our association, I trust you understand this was a fleeting mistake on both our parts, and I apologise for ever having put upon you in such a way. I am ashamed of how I behaved, as a married woman, and want to make a fresh start.

I wish you all the very best and know you will be far happier, this way.

Blessings,
Diane.

"Couldn't help herself, could she?" MacKenzie said, and leaned back against the edge of the desk. "If Sabrina Graham wrote that, she's passing off her sister's romance with Davie as a kind of aberration; something they should feel ashamed of."

"She's twisting the knife in, all right," Lowerson remarked, and his eyes slid across to the woman seated beside him, just for a second. "Not only is she telling Davie that she's a far better prospect, Sabrina is telling him she'd be a better mother, and, by writing as Diane, it's as though she's approving all of it. Manipulative, eh?"

MacKenzie nodded. "She signed off with "blessings" again."

"It just doesn't carry the ring of Davie Hetherington," Melanie said, after reading and re-reading the e-mail. "If he wrote this to himself, as if from Diane, he'd have focused on different motivators, wouldn't he? It would be all about how she'd played him for a fool, wasted his time, how he was too good for her and so on."

Jack felt another caustic remark rise to the surface, but held his tongue.

It would do nothing, and help nothing.

"I think you're right," he said. "There's just one problem, which is that we haven't got a single shred of evidence about all of this, not even enough to execute a search warrant. Instinct won't convince a magistrate, more's the pity."

"So what do we do?" Mel wondered aloud. "We can't sit around *knowing* who her killer is, and not do anything about it."

"As Ryan says, we'll watch her closely and see if she trips up," MacKenzie said. "We'll do the legwork, continue digging…do what we always do to catch a killer."

"If it is Sabrina Graham, do you think she killed Fred and Zach, too?" Jack asked. "I can't see why she'd need to off the old man, unless he was making noises about emptying the septic tank—?"

"If anything, he was doing the opposite," Melanie said. "And isn't that interesting?"

"Are you thinking what I'm thinking?" MacKenzie asked. "That there could have been some sort of business relationship between Sabrina and her late brother-in-law?"

"I'm wondering about it," Melanie said.

They brought up the records recently sent through by the late Fred Humble's bank. Aside from a check to see if there were any regular amounts being deposited, they hadn't yet gone through the figures with a fine-toothed comb.

"Fred had particular habits, didn't he?" Jack said thoughtfully. "I mean, there was the tearoom on Fridays, the newsagents…"

"Yes, he liked things to run to schedule," MacKenzie agreed.

"Karen Russell says he mostly paid in cash," Jack remembered, from the statement she'd made. "Here, we can see regular amounts going in, specifically his state pension and whatnot. Bills are paid via direct debit or standing order, and they're coming out regularly, too. But, when you look at the columns, I can't see anything coming out as petty cash to spend down at the tearoom. Barely any cash withdrawals and, when any were made, they were tiny amounts—barely enough to cover his Full English."

They checked, and found he was right.

"Again, we can't prove this until we're able to cross-check with Sabrina Graham's bank account and find any corresponding dates and amounts being debited in cash, but I bet Frank knew something, or *suspected* something at least. There has to be a reason why he was so dead set against having the septic tank emptied, all these years. It must have been in his interests for it to remain untouched."

"So, Fred Humble was complicit," Melanie confirmed.

"It seems that way to me," Jack said. "I don't know how he found out; perhaps he found something incriminating or saw something. It would explain a lot."

The broader truth hit them like a deadweight.

"If all this supposition is right, and Fred Humble knew his wife lay in the tank at the bottom of his garden, then we have to conclude it wasn't in Sabrina's interests to kill him," Melanie said.

Jack shrugged. "If he was blackmailing her, perhaps she'd had enough?"

"Possibly, but after twenty years of toeing the line, why would she suddenly crack? It seems more likely they'd reached a certain understanding."

"She's still a 'maybe' in my book," Jack said, obtusely.

"But, why would she kill Zach?" Mel argued, and both of them knew it was no longer about the case. "Have you thought about that?"

"Of course I have," he muttered. "Same logic applies. She set him up as the fall guy, after killing Fred. Her plan was always to have us believe it was about the fracking, and it was the polluted water to blame."

"But think about it, Jack. Sabrina Graham could have killed Fred at any time," Melanie argued again. "There was no need to concoct an elaborate cover story, to dye the water red, or any of it. She could have just knocked him off any old day of the week, rather than waiting all this time to do it. Besides, she's in good shape, but she's still a woman in her sixties; how do you imagine she was hulking canisters of sheep dye and pesticide over hill and vale?"

"I don't know, Mel!" he almost shouted. "I don't have all the answers! I don't seem to have the answers for very much, these days!"

They stared at one another, eyes burning, and MacKenzie made a 'T' sign with her hands.

"Okay, kids. Timeout. I think it's a good idea if you two call it a day," she said.

"I don't need to—"

"It wasn't a request," MacKenzie said. "As your senior officer, I'm instructing you both to go home and cool down. You have some things to discuss, I think."

There was no argument to that, so they gathered their things and bade her a sulky farewell.

"Breaks my heart," MacKenzie said, to her empty crisp packet.

A short while later, she was packing up her own things to leave for the school run, when a call came through to her desk phone.

She reached across to make a grab for it, one eye on the time. "DI MacKenzie."

"Detective Inspector, this is John Maple, from Maple Farm in Holystone?"

"Oh, yes, hello. How can I help you?"

"Ah, well, I don't want to waste your time," he began, in a manner she had heard a hundred times before.

"I'm sure you won't," she said. "Have you remembered something?"

"Not exactly," he replied. "But you said to let you know if we came across anything here at the farm? Well, my son was swilling things out, clearing the drains and all that near the barn where we keep those canisters of pesticide."

MacKenzie told herself to be patient. "Mm?"

"Well, he *found* something, you see. A funny looking sort of tool, not quite a hammer, but looks a bit like it."

MacKenzie let her bag fall to the floor. She had time to hear this. "Can you describe the hammer, or take a photo of it and send it to me, please?"

She told him her mobile number and waited for the image to come through. At first glance, she could see why he'd thought it was a hammer, but the metal had been forged in such a way that one side was flat edged, the metal perpendicular to its wooden handle, while on the other side the metal had been twisted the other way, to allow for a kind of jabbing rather than a scooping motion.

A mattock, she recognised immediately, from previous investigations. It was a tool most frequently used by archaeologists while digging.

In any event, it had no place on an arable farm that she could think of.

"Have you been visited by anyone from the archaeology dig?" she asked him.

"No, not at all," he said. "Not for a good long while, anyway. They shut it down, you know."

MacKenzie's ears pricked up. No, she hadn't known, nor had anybody else. "Really? Do you know why?"

"I've no idea," he replied. "It was odd, come to think of it. My youngest, Terri, quite fancied doing a bit of work experience with the team but, when she asked about it, Ian told her the funding had been withdrawn and the team had disbanded. It's just him left there now, tinkering away."

'That's a pity," she said.

"It would be, if it was *true*," the farmer shot back. "Turns out, Ian didn't renew his application in time, so he missed the funding deadline. Probably feels like a right plonker, now."

"I bet," she said, but her mind was already thinking ahead.

No CCTV in that area, she remembered. Even if they could pin it to Ian, or someone else from the dig team, she supposed, it was circumstantial and nothing more.

"Are you at home now, Mr Maple?"

"Yes, I—"

"Stay there," she urged him. "I'll send someone over to you."

Before she put an urgent call through to Ryan and Phillips, she brought up the map of Holystone again, her eyes searching for the location of Ian Bell's home.

Look at that, she thought, a moment later.

He and John Maple were practically neighbours, and a mere stone's throw from both Lady's Well and the site of Zachary White's campervan.

Which was all very interesting, but not enough to bring a prosecution.

They needed proof, and they needed it fast.

CHAPTER 37

"Mr Bell!"

Ryan and Phillips caught up with Ian Bell as he was about to open the front door to his smart, stone-built bungalow on the outskirts of the village. It was a secluded spot, perfect for individuals who preferred their privacy and the freedom to come and go as they pleased.

He turned, a pleasant smile already firmly in place.

"Chief Inspector, Sergeant. I didn't realise you were so keen for that archaeology tour," he said.

They smiled like Cheshire cats. "Perhaps another time," Ryan said. "Actually, I wonder if I could grab a glass of water?"

Ian seemed to hesitate, the silence growing heavy, but he knew there was no choice but to admit them. "Well, you'd better come in, if you're prepared to risk it," he joked, and they managed to force a laugh in return.

Some jokes were a little *too* close to home.

Inside, they entered a plain, white-washed hallway with wood veneer flooring underfoot. There was no staircase since the property was all on one level, and there were no trinkets or photograph frames lying around; the only personal items on display were a couple of pairs of well-worn boots laid out neatly beside the door, an overcoat which hung from a row of wooden pegs fixed to the wall, and a large, grey-black rucksack which looked as though it could take some considerable weight propped in the corner.

Ian positioned his body in front of it.

"Hey, that's a canny lookin' rucksack," Phillips exclaimed. "Me and Denise were thinkin' of goin' walkin' round the Lakes next summer and I could use somethin' like that. D'you mind if I have a look?"

Phillips' manner was so open, so unassuming, it was impossible to refuse.

"Sure," Ian muttered, and turned around as if only then remembering the item was there. "I should really get rid of this old thing. I haven't used it in a very long time."

Phillips, who still wore his woollen winter gloves, took hold of the rucksack and made a show of inspecting its stitching.

"Solid bit of craftsmanship, this," he chattered, and stuck his nose into the main compartment, ostensibly to see how much capacity it had.

He reared back out again, having seen—and smelled—all he needed to.

The faintest aroma of beer.

"Oh, aye, this'd do just fine," he said, handing it back to the owner. "I've made a note of the brand. Thanks for that, mate."

"The kitchen's straight through there," Ian said, motioning them ahead of him. "I'll just hang up my coat."

Ryan and Phillips moved towards the kitchen and, seconds later, the hallway light went off behind them and the kitchen light was turned on, instead.

"Right, gentlemen," Ian said, closing the door behind him. "Was it just the water, or can I offer you some tea?"

"Water is fine, thank you."

While they watched him look out some glasses, they inspected the kitchen, from its sparkling clean work surfaces to the glossy, white-painted doors. Not a single thing out of place, no dirty dishes in the sink, not even a banana past its prime lying in the fruit bowl.

"Here you go," Ian said, and handed them both a glass.

"Thanks," Ryan said, and raised it to his lips, but didn't drink. "Before I forget, the reason we're here is because you mentioned you were interested in knowing how long it might be, before the police and forensic teams vacate Fred Humble's cottage?"

"That's right," Ian said, trying not to focus on the way Phillips set his untouched glass on the kitchen counter without using one of the coasters he'd laid out.

"Well, I'm sorry to be the bearer of bad tidings, but I'm afraid it'll be a while, yet," Ryan said. "I shouldn't be telling you this but, since you're on the Parish Council—"

"I won't repeat it," Ian said quickly.

Ryan smiled. "As you know, we found another body earlier today, and, all things considered, we're worried there could be a lot more. It turns out Fred Humble was quite a dark horse, and we all remember what was found in Fred and Rose West's garden, not so very long ago."

"Awful business," Phillips intoned. "A lesson to all of us in the police, to be thorough in our investigations."

"Oh," Ian said, catching on quickly. "Well, obviously, Fred wasn't well liked, but I'd hardly put him in the same category as the serial killer *Fred West*—"

Ryan and Phillips looked at one another, made serious faces, and then looked back at him.

"Unfortunately, we can't be sure at this stage," Ryan said. "The point is, I've ordered a full ground search to begin first thing tomorrow. They'll scan the entire garden, plus any other land he owned, including that bit of scrubland you were talking about, to be sure it hasn't been used as a burial ground over the years."

Ian could hardly believe his ears. "Honestly, it seems so unlike Fred," he said again, working hard to keep the desperation from his voice. "I'm sure somebody in the village would have seen or heard something over the years."

"That may be true, and we hope it is," Ryan said. "But, with the Force coming under more and more scrutiny—"

"All those TikTokers," Phillips chimed in.

"Exactly," Ryan said, and tried to keep the smile from his face. "Against that backdrop, we have to be seen to be following every line of enquiry and doing all we should be. We thought you'd want to know, in case you might have wanted to find another renovation project with a swifter turnaround."

"Ren—? Oh!" Ian laughed. "Yes. It's certainly something I'll think about, thank you." He began drumming his fingers against the countertop. "You're starting excavation work tomorrow morning?" he said, as casually as he could. "That's fast."

"Better to get on with things sooner rather than later," Ryan said. "There isn't a moment to lose."

Ian nodded, thinking the same thing himself.

"Incidentally, I know Karen will want to know whether your investigation has turned up any suspects—are you any closer to finding out what happened to Fred? And, it's about time Zach's family understood why he felt compelled to end his own life."

Ryan merely smiled. "Don't worry, Mr Bell. When we bring somebody into custody, you'll be the first to know."

CHAPTER 38

The silence throughout the journey home was deafening.

Jack and Mel both thought this as they pulled up outside the house they shared, but neither of them was willing to interrupt the calm before the storm; they knew it could be the last quiet, peaceful moments they might share before words were said that could not be unsaid.

But the storm was inevitable, and they knew that too.

They discarded their jackets and fed the cat, then faced one another across the kitchen island, where so many small, inconsequential battles had been fought but none so important as the one they now faced.

"You went to see Morrison today, didn't you?" Jack blurted out. The words were accusatory, but it was not his intention to accuse.

Melanie forced herself to face it—and him. "Yes," she said simply. "Yes, I did. I asked her for a period of sabbatical leave."

He swallowed the pain of knowing she hadn't discussed it with him first, and tried to see things from her perspective. "If you need time, you should take it," he said.

Melanie nodded. "I hoped you'd understand," she said. "I wasn't sure that you would."

Outraged by the implication, Jack took a step forward but stopped immediately when he saw her whole body shudder in reaction. "You're breaking my heart," he whispered, all the anger draining from him. "Did you think I was going to *hurt* you, Mel?"

Tears started to fall silently down her face. "I—I know you wouldn't," she managed to say. "My mind isn't my own at the moment, Jack. I'm not myself. I don't know if I ever will be again."

He brushed tears from his own eyes, and wished she would let him hold her. "How can I help you, if you look at me as though I'm the enemy?" he threw at her. "I'm not *him*!"

"No, but you're the one who's here!" she admitted, brokenly. "Andrew Forbes died, and I can't punish him. He robbed me of that."

"You killed him in self-defence, Mel. Isn't that punishment enough?"

"*No!*" she roared, running frustrated hands through her hair. "He should have faced the parents of every victim he ever took; he should have spent a lifetime in the bowels of prison, caged like the animal he was. By dying, they were robbed of that justice."

I robbed them of it, she thought.

"You saved yourself," he reminded her. "There wasn't a choice and, if there was, it was his life or your own. You avenged your sister and you survived. There isn't any better outcome, in the circumstances."

She wished she could see and feel things so clearly.

"We can work on this," he tried again. "Let me help you, Mel—"

"No, Jack," she said softly. "You've tried your best, everybody has, and I'm grateful to you—to all of you. I haven't been easy to live with—"

"Don't say that."

"It's true," she said, because it was. "It must have been so hard for you to love someone and not be able to help them. It's the worst kind of feeling. But I realised something these past few days. I need to stop expecting anybody else to help me and start helping myself. I need to rediscover who Melanie Yates is now, after all that's gone before."

It was the most positive thing he'd heard from her in a while, and it gave him hope.

"I'll support you however you want me to," he promised.

It was his kindness that almost broke her resolve, and tears began to fall again.

"You're a wonderful man, Jack," she said. "But what I need you to do is *let me go*—at least, for a while."

He said nothing at first, while he tried to understand what she was asking of him. "You—you want some time away?"

She nodded.

"Where?" he asked. "For how long?"

"I don't know," she answered, honestly. "I've asked for six months, to begin with. Whether I come back to the Force after that will depend on whether I've managed to heal myself enough to be of service to others."

She was so hard on herself, he thought. She didn't know that she was of service to so many people, without even trying.

"Can I come with you?" He knew the answer already, but had to ask.

"No," she said. "You can't come with me, Jack. I need to do this myself, to stand on my own two feet again. I need to see if I can manage that much, or else I'll be a slave to fear for the rest of my days."

He looked away, at the living space they'd created together, and wished he could find the energy to shout or scream.

That required anger, and he wasn't angry.

He was merely heartbroken.

"Do you still love me?" he asked.

Her chest tightened painfully, and she forced herself to speak the truth.

"To love someone, you have to love yourself first, and I don't. I don't like this person I've become, and that needs to change. Until I'm whole again, I don't think I'm capable of loving anyone—not as they deserve to be loved, anyway."

Even in his despair, Jack understood that only too well. After his experience with Jennifer Lucas, he'd become a stranger to himself and others and, like Melanie, had needed time to rediscover himself. MacKenzie's words came back to him then, especially her advice about letting the dove fly away. He hadn't understood what she'd meant by the metaphor at the time, but he did now.

"You should find Melanie again," he said, drawing himself together. "We'll be waiting for you when you do."

She reached her hand across the counter to touch his, and he held her fingers in his own.

"Don't wait for me, Jack. Don't waste your life waiting for me."

"It wouldn't be a waste—"

In a great show of trust, she bridged the gap between them and rested her head against his chest, feeling only peace when his arms came to circle around her in the gentlest embrace.

"Thank you," she whispered, as the cat curled around her ankles.

CHAPTER 39

The villagers of Holystone slept beneath a moonless sky.

All except one.

Ian Bell cut a solitary figure as he made his way across the fields separating his bungalow and the bit of rough scrubland owned by the late Fred Humble, which appeared so worthless and yet, he was quite certain, was worth a King's ransom in gold.

Old, Anglo-Saxon gold.

During the 7th Century AD, the Kingdom of Northumbria had been the most powerful of the seven Anglo-Saxon kingdoms in Britain, yet no 'major' archaeological hoard had ever been uncovered in the area; nothing to rival the glory of finding an undisturbed ship burial at Sutton Hoo in the 1930—nor the Staffordshire Hoard of 2009, which was the largest discovery of Anglo-Saxon gold and silver metalwork to date, with thousands of items having been discovered by a bloke using a metal detector he'd bought at a car boot sale for a couple of quid. That find had been worth almost three and a half million pounds and, in Ian Bell's conservative estimation, represented only a fraction of what might be waiting for *him* beneath that bit of disused scrubland.

For more than a year he'd concealed his suspicions, never hinting at what lay beneath the surface. It had all begun with the discovery of a stash of pottery in the course of his routine excavation at the Holystone site. The pottery should have been a celebrated find, something to shout about in the field of archaeology, but he'd held off making any announcement when he'd cleaned up and pieced together the broken shards to discover they told a story, like the Lindisfarne Gospels but in miniature.

The earthenware had been highly decorated, more so than anything he'd ever seen before, to commemorate the date of what had been a summer celebration led by the mighty Anglo-Saxon King Edwin, in celebration of his marriage to the queen consort, Æthelburga. From what he'd been able to decipher from the faded text, the celebration had drawn hundreds of people to a place further north of Holystone, at Yeavering, or *Ad Gefrin* as it was known at that time. Little more than an idyllic rural landscape now but, back then, Ad Gefrin had been the site of a royal summer palace, as well as the site of numerous Christian baptisms in the nearby River Glen. The pottery told the story of St Paulinus of York, a seventh century monk sent by Pope Gregory I to convert the Anglo-Saxon people to Christianity. He lived in Kent until 625 AD, when Paulinus accompanied Æthelburga, the sister of King Eadbald of Kent, to Northumbria to marry King Edwin.

According to the commemorative pottery, undoubtedly made after the event, Paulinus and Æthelburga stopped at the ancient watering hole of St Ninian's, located on the Roman road between Bremenium, which was modern-day 'Rochester', and the River Aln. There, it is said that the monk took the opportunity to baptise "thousands" of people in the clear waters of the well—*most likely in a single afternoon*, Ian thought cynically. Paulinus knelt upon a flat stone at the eastern end of the pool to undertake the baptisms, which became known as the 'holy stone' from which the village took its name. Unfortunately for Paulinus and Æthelburga, while the monk was doing God's work, it seems that thieves made off with a large chest of gold and silver belonging to the bride and constituting her dowry, which was never seen again, and only through superior diplomacy was the marriage able to proceed without it.

Even in mediaeval times, the disappearance of the gold and silver had become something of an urban legend, drawing travellers to the area who were, he supposed, the equivalent of the modern-day TikTok sleuth. They took it upon themselves to pester local residents and dig up farmland without consent in their quest to find the treasure and keep it for themselves, or else present it to the King to curry favour.

Quite separately, a short outbreak of plague had been documented in the area around that time, which ended only shortly before the arrival of Paulinus and Æthelburga, if the dates were to be believed. Given Ian's experience of previous digs and his knowledge of Anglo-Saxon burial practices, he'd devoted himself to studying the geology of the village in order to pinpoint the most likely gravesite. Pagan cremation practices had been outlawed by that time in favour of Christian burial, but he was counting on the locals having adhered to the King's religious edicts, which was a debateable matter. Considering the prevailing number of Pagan followers even hundreds of years later, it was very possible the people of Holystone had cremated their dead in the old tradition, after all.

Which would rather spoil his theory, because it was Ian's firm belief that Æthelburga's marriage dowry had found its way into one of the open gravesites, or a grave only recently filled, which would have presented a perfect hiding place for a stash of gold and silver to a thief on the run. It would have been sacrilegious to turn over the ground, so their ill-gotten gains would have been safe from detection, leaving the thieves to return and recover the chest at a later date. Unless, of course, they'd succumbed to plague themselves and the treasure had lain in wait for generations, until he, Ian Bell, claimed it for his own.

And he was determined to claim it.

A few exploratory outings at night with his own metal detector had confirmed the existence of a large quantity of metal in several areas of Humble's scrubland, roughly mapped out at even intervals to correspond with gravesites wherein the dead would have been buried with some of their worldly possessions at the time. With enough time and patience, he knew he would find the main hoard; the one that would change his life and make him a household name.

They'd name museums after him, he thought.

And, the money…

The money.

His mouth watered at the prospect of all that delicious cash, which would set him up for life.

The plan had been so flawless, so *fool proof*, he couldn't understand what had gone so badly wrong. The first step had been to make sure the university lost interest in the Holystone dig, which had been achieved through a combination of false reporting and shoddy record-keeping, not to mention a failure to re-apply for that year's grant, which meant a lack of funds to pay the dig staff, forcing them to walk off the job. It had been the perfect way to regain the place to himself, without prying eyes watching his every move.

That only left Fred Humble.

God knows, he'd tried to convince the old man to sell him the land, but none of his attempts to persuade him had worked. Ian had offered Fred double, triple, even *quadruple* the going rate for agricultural land, but the old goat had consistently knocked him back. He didn't know why; perhaps the old man had been a chancer once, and could spot another one from a mile away. Or perhaps the chief inspector was right, and Fred was reluctant to give up his own share of secrets.

Ian supposed he could have declared his archaeological discovery while Fred was alive, and without owning the land, but there was one major drawback to that approach. Namely that, by law, he'd have been forced to share the spoils. Ian wasn't a man who liked to share, and never had been.

It was far better to own the land outright, and reap the full reward.

Since Fred wouldn't sell, he'd been forced to press the issue. When Fred *still* refused to sell, he'd been left with very little choice but to remove him altogether, following which he planned to buy the land from his son, whom he'd been buttering up for some time.

Simple.

He hadn't *liked* killing, Ian reassured himself. It had merely been the most efficient and expedient way to bring about the correct outcome, that was all. In any event, the villagers should be thanking him because, now that Fred was gone, they were free of his surly, obstinate presence in their lives.

As for Zachary White...

Zachary troubled him, a bit.

Ian hadn't really wanted to kill him, truth be told, but it was a case of acting in the interests of 'the greater good'. Besides, he'd been a downright *nuisance*, poking his nose into things that were none of his concern, drawing attention to the village and, more importantly, the land around it.

He had to go.

With hindsight, using one of the protesters as cover for Fred's death might have been a little shortsighted. He should have accounted for the possibility of sparking further protests, but Ian had never really understood emotion, not as other people did. He saw them sometimes, crying or laughing, and tried to emulate them, but the emotions simply weren't there. He felt very little reaction to the things that upset others, which was why he hadn't anticipated such a visceral response to the loss of a single person.

He supposed he was a psychopath, or a sociopath, or something like that.

Funny how the labels didn't bother him, Ian thought.

Fred was an obstacle that had to be removed.

Zachary provided the perfect cover.

That was all there was to it.

His mind racing with such thoughts, Ian picked up the pace and hurried onward, shovel in one hand and metal detector in the other. It wasn't the way he'd planned to excavate and, were it not for the interference of the police, he'd have been able to proceed at his leisure. The news that they planned to scan the land for bodies from the very next morning had come as a considerable shock, and the hours between then and now had been a torturous wait for night to fall. They'd left him only one remaining opportunity to dig before his discovery—*his,* mind you—was stolen right from under him, and all his efforts would have been in vain.

He would not allow that to happen.

The thought spurred him on, and Ian moved quickly across the terrain, casting frequent glances back towards the sleeping village until he came to the old wooden fence separating the land from a single-track access road leading back down to the village. Within walking distance but not close enough to encroach upon the residents, the nondescript field would have been the perfect spot to bury the dead and, he suspected, there might have been an Anglo-Saxon church somewhere nearby, before it was lost to the passage of time.

Not that he cared about history, now.

Fuelled by a cocktail of greed and ego, Ian Bell made for the far corner of the field, which was one of the areas he hadn't yet scanned. Stumbling in his haste, he struggled back up, encumbered by the backpack he'd brought with him for transporting his loot. With any luck, he'd have to make several trips during the course of the evening.

He was actually salivating at the prospect.

He spent thirty minutes scanning the earth with his metal detector, illuminated only by the light from a headlamp which was strapped to his forehead. Here and there brought a little *beep* from the machine, which told him there was something metal beneath his feet, but it did not bring the incessant whine he needed to hear that would signal he'd found what he knew, deep in his heart, was waiting for him.

Until…

The metal detector began to shriek, its tinny wail echoing across the quiet hillside as he moved the sensor over a patch of ground measuring a few feet wide either way.

Consistent with a gravesite, but unlike anything he'd detected before.

This was it.

This was it!

Sweating and shaking with excitement, Ian fumbled to turn off the detector and ran back to where he'd left his shovel, laughing like a maniac as he went.

"Come on," he muttered, tugging on workman's gloves. "Come on."

His shovel had barely touched the earth when he heard the sound of an engine approaching—not a car, but some sort of land vehicle.

Desperate, exposed, he looked around but there was nowhere to hide, no trees or other shaded areas to provide cover.

Twin beams of white light fell upon him, spotlighting a man who was hunched over the shovel like a gravedigger from a Gothic novel, and then a disembodied voice rang out into the night.

"Ian Bell! Set down your shovel and raise your hands in the air!"

He recognised the voice immediately.

It belonged to DCI Ryan.

Ryan exited Davie Hetherington's battered jeep and watched Bell hesitate, twenty or thirty yards up ahead. There was an edginess to the man, and he sensed there was very little stopping him from rabbiting away into the night.

He raised the loudspeaker to his lips once again. "Lay down the shovel, Bell, and walk slowly towards us!" He stood perfectly still, mirroring Bell's actions.

"He doesn't want to leave whatever's on the other end of that shovel," Phillips muttered, from his position inside the jeep. "He's found what he was lookin' for, and can't part with it."

Davie's sheepdog, who'd accompanied them for the journey, gave a kind of growling yap which might have signalled agreement.

"Quiet, Lassie."

"Lassie?" Phillips queried.

"Aye, what else would I name a respectable sheepdog?" Davie asked.

Phillips gave an approving nod, and both men turned back to the drama unfolding through the windscreen.

"He's got nowhere to go," Davie muttered.

But Ryan caught the shift in mood and in physical stance, and knew seconds before it happened that Ian Bell was going to try and make a run for it.

"*Bell*!" he warned him, and then swore as the dark figure sprang into life, thrusting aside the shovel to sprint off into the darkness.

Ryan yanked open the car door and hurled himself back inside.

"Quick!" he barked. "I've lost sight of him in the dark, but he's heading west so I can radio the team to head him off—"

"No need for all that," Davie said and, with what Ryan and Phillips considered to be supremely unhurried movements, heaved himself from the driver's seat. He gave a low whistle and, the next thing, Lassie leapt from the back of the open vehicle and stood quivering beside him.

"We don't have time—"

Phillips made a *shushing* sound, which elicited a raised eyebrow from his friend, but all fears were allayed when, in a flash of black and white, Lassie took off at full pelt across the field, legs pumping harder and faster than Ian Bell's could ever hope to, and with the kind of blind loyalty he would never hope to understand.

"Right then," Davie said, re-starting the engine finally. "Saves us wanderin' round in the dark, doesn't it?"

Turning the vehicle, Davie trained his headlights on the rear end of the sprinting dog, who covered the ground ahead of them. After a few seconds, they heard a couple of loud barks to signal she'd found the wayward 'sheep'.

"Good dog, that one," Davie said, conversationally.

When they eventually caught up, they could see what he meant. Lassie sat a few feet away from where Ian Bell had run blindly into the snare of a barbed wire fence, his limbs and backpack now tangled in its metallic grip as he writhed and screamed to be cut loose. The dog had seated herself and was watching him with an enigmatic smile on her furry face, tail wagging happily after a job well done.

"I think I need to put her on the payroll," Ryan said, before making his way across to where Ian was now blubbering, the sound of his self-pitying tears filling the empty night.

It seemed he *could* cry, after all.

"Mr Bell," Ryan said, cheerfully. "Fancy meeting you, here. Measuring up the space for that new pony you were on about?"

Bell hurled a couple of choice insults, but Ryan only smiled. "No need to thank me—all part of the service."

"I can't believe it."

Sabrina Graham rubbed moisturiser in slow circles across her arms as she and Davie prepared for bed after a very long day.

"Aye, it's a turn up," he agreed, and shook his head in disbelief. "Always thought the bloke was a bit of a priggish sort, but I never imagined he had it in him to kill anybody."

Davie looked across at her. "Just goes to show how people can surprise you," he said, buttoning the shirt on his pyjamas. "You never really know what anyone's capable of—I s'pose I felt a bit murderous, myself, after they found Diane. I'd happily wring the neck of whoever killed and dumped her that way."

Sabrina kept her eyes averted. "So they think Ian did it all because he was after Fred's land, and Fred wouldn't sell?"

Davie nodded, and she felt the bed dip beside her as he settled himself next to her.

"That's the long and short of it," he replied, with a yawn. "You should have seen him, Rina, as they took him away. Never seen a sorrier sight of a man. Wailing and crying, shouting the odds about being robbed of what was rightfully his…what a load of rubbish. He reckons there's some sort of big gold hoard lying down there beneath the surface, waitin' to be found. He was shoutin' all about how the credit belonged to him." He sighed, and yawned again. "Terrible what people will do for money, isn't it?"

Sabrina reached across to turn out the bedside light. "Or love," she whispered.

"What's that?"

"Nothing," she said. "Sleep well, my love."

Long after she heard his breathing deepen and the rumble of his gentle snore, Sabrina lay awake, consumed by jealousy. Even now, after she was dead and gone, she saw her sister reflected in his eyes; the love he'd felt for her still there, rooted in his heart. It felt like a betrayal, a knife in her back from both of them. Her sister, for taking him from her—Diane might not have known how she felt about Davie, but she should have. She *should* have!

As for him…

She looked across and watched his chest rise and fall, and wondered if he was dreaming of Diane because, no matter what he said about things being in the past, it had always been Diane for him. She knew that, and had always known it, ever since they were children. Even then, her sister had found a way to muscle into her life, and Diane was always accepted because she'd been born beautiful and gregarious whereas she…

Sabrina lifted her chin.

She had other qualities.

Other skills.

Davie should remember that.

CHAPTER 40

The next morning

"I heard the post-mortem report came back from Pinter—what's the headline?"

Ryan asked this of MacKenzie, who spun around in her chair.

"Aye, there's a lot ridin' on it," Phillips said, taking a slurp of his tea and gesturing towards Ryan with the crook of his thumb. "Wor lad's gotta start gettin' into shape for his photo shoot, hasn't he?"

Ryan cast him a long, sideways glance. "I think you're mistaking me for yourself, Frank. It's obvious, even without the postmortem, that Ian Bell killed Zachary White; it's the only thing that makes sense. Give me ten minutes with him in the interview suite and we'll have him singing like a canary."

"Aye, but there's been no confession yet, and we need a decider because we're not gettin' any younger. The post-mortem should do it so—howay lass, don't keep us in suspense."

MacKenzie cleared her throat and said a prayer for the lie she was about to tell.

"Um, yes, he did send it through," she said. "I'm afraid it's bad news for both of you boys, because the result came back inconclusive. He says Zachary could've died from hitting his head after falling unconscious from the carbon monoxide, or he could've been bludgeoned beforehand. Without the results of the Low Copy Number DNA testing, he can't be definitive."

She focused on a spot above their heads, and hoped they wouldn't look too closely at her shifty face.

"Maybe I should have a word with Pinter," Ryan said, with a tinge of desperation. "That can't be his final word on it—"

"Mm hm, well, it is," she said, with authority. "And that means both of you'll be gettin' your kit off for Christmas, because neither of you were right."

Phillips ran his tongue around his teeth, thinking it over. "Y'nah, so long as the room's heated, it might not be too bad—"

"Shut it, Frank."

"I'm thinkin' of you, lad. My nickname was 'The Tripod' at school—"

"For the love of God!" MacKenzie rolled her eyes.

"That's another consideration," Phillips said. "When the calendar comes out, I'm gonna be gettin' a lot of unwanted attention from the lasses round here, and I don't want you to be jealous, pet."

MacKenzie gave him a long, considering look from narrowed green eyes. "I'll struggle through it," she said, between gritted teeth. "As for the two of you, I've taken the liberty of booking the photographer—she'll be expecting you on Friday afternoon, so there's time for the calendars to be printed before December."

"*She*—?" Phillips squeaked.

"Ah—" Ryan was lost for words.

"She's seen it all before, I'm sure," MacKenzie drawled. "Besides, I'll be there with Anna to cheer you both on."

And take some snaps from the sidelines, for the office newsletter, she thought, with a wicked laugh.

"This constitutes an emergency," Phillips muttered to himself, and reached for his desk drawer to grasp the can of Irn Bru he kept there for times such as those.

And found an empty spot where it should have been.

"Wha—?"

"Everything all right, Frank?" his wife enquired, sweetly.

"Oh, aye, aye, just…lookin' for me stapler…"

"Since when do you staple things?" Ryan asked.

"Since *now*," Phillips replied, a bit testily.

He lowered his voice, and grasped Ryan's sleeve. "It was you, wasn't it?"

"Wasn't what?"

"The Irn Bru, man—the can I had in here! You've snaffled it, haven't you?"

Ryan patted his friend on the shoulder. "You're letting the pressure get to you, already, mate. Nobody's taken your Irn Bru."

"It was *here*—"

"Lost something?" MacKenzie called out.

"Eh—no, no! Just that stapler—"

"Borrow mine, if you like," she replied, and, a moment later, wandered over to drop it on his desk.

"Thanks," Phillips said, and then looked at his wife closely.

Her face bore an open, trustworthy smile and her eyes were clear and kind. But there was something nipping at the edges of his mind…

He took a sharp intake of breath.

Frazzles.

He was sure he'd smelled bacon-flavoured crisps on her breath, the previous day. At first, he'd thought it was his imagination playing tricks on him, owing to a general deficit of meat in his diet these days. The mind was a dangerous place, for a hungry man.

But now, he wasn't so sure…

He cocked his head at her, and she mirrored the action.

"Everything all right, Frank?" she asked him, with the hint of a challenge.

"Aye, only I'm missin' somethin' from my drawer…you wouldn't know anythin' about that?"

"What are you missing?"

This was tricky, because to tell her would be tantamount to confessing his secret stash.

She smiled at him, knowingly, and that's when he knew she was the pop-quaffing thief.

"Ah, it doesn't matter now," he said, leaning back to link his hands over his belly. "Probably bad for my health, anyhow."

"We wouldn't want that now," MacKenzie agreed, and then nodded towards his drawer. "I'm surprised you keep a can of Irn Bru in there."

He leaned forward, eyes widening in shock.

There, sitting in the spot that had been empty only moments before, was a can of Irn Bru.

"Hand's quicker than the eye, Frank," she winked, and sashayed back to her own desk.

"What a woman," he breathed.

After making her farewells to the team, who'd hugged and wished her well, Melanie Yates made her way down to the foyer of Police Headquarters, where Jack was waiting for her beneath the canopy outside. A light drizzle had begun to fall, and it matched the general mood.

"Frank made me promise to call in, every week."

Jack managed a small smile. "And will you?"

She looked away. "I'll try."

He nodded, understanding she was already somewhere else, her mind checked out of the physical space she occupied and the people she was speaking to.

"Where are you going, first?"

"There's a retreat centre, in Austria," she said. "I've got a bit saved up, so I thought I'd try a week beside a lake with low-calorie meals and massages, with plenty of walking. After that, I don't know."

There was a brief silence.

"I—"

"You—"

They spoke together, and Jack indicated she should go first.

"I want to thank you again," she said softly. "You've been my best friend, Jack, apart from everything else."

"I'll always be your friend," he said.

She nodded, and tried to hold back the tears. "I have to go now," she said. *Or she never would.*

"Good luck, Melanie."

She moved into his arms and he held her close, breathed her scent one last time, felt the shape of her against him, and told himself to make the memories last.

"You'll be fine," he assured her. "You can do anything, Mel. Absolutely anything."

Very gently, she reached up to brush her lips against his. "Be happy," she told him. "Live your life."

With that, she turned and ran across the car park, head bent through the light fall of rain which mingled with her tears.

They found him leaning against the wall beside the service entrance, watching the rain.

"Cuppa?"

Phillips pressed a cup of sugary tea into Jack's numb hands, and leaned back against the wall beside him. Ryan took up a position on his other side, so their young friend was flanked by friendship.

"MacKenzie's dealin' with Ian Bell," Phillips said, after a moment had passed. "He's got himself some flash solicitor from London."

"It won't help him," Ryan said, with satisfaction.

There was another prolonged silence, until he spoke again.

"Frank and I have been hoodwinked into posing for this charity calendar," he said, conversationally. "We were thinking, it seems a shame to deprive the masses of the full complement at Major Crimes, so why don't you join us? I'm sure Frank's got a spare pair of Union Jack boxers you can borrow."

Jack laughed, despite himself. "I thought the post-mortem—" He pulled himself up, as it occurred to him that MacKenzie might very well have pulled a fast one.

"What about the post-mortem?" Phillips asked, suspiciously.

"Oh, nothing," Jack said quickly. "I just thought we were still waiting for it to come through."

"Results are in," Ryan said. "So, what do you say?"

Both men looked at him, and Jack felt the force of their eyes burning into the sides of his head.

"Oh, all right, fine. *Fine*! I'll do it."

"Good lad," Phillips said.

Ryan exchanged a glance, and folded his arms. "So, how're you holding up?"

Jack sighed, and leaned his head back against the wall.

"That good, eh?" Phillips said, and put a comforting hand on his shoulder. "You know what they say. What doesn't kill you makes you—"

"An invalid?"

"Stronger," Phillips corrected him. "It makes you stronger, son."

"I couldn't help her," Jack said. "I'm not good enough—"

"You're more than good enough," Ryan interjected. "This has nothing to do with you, and everything to do with her wellbeing. I should know; I needed that time on Holy Island, I needed to watch the waves and feel the peace and solitude of the tide washing in, closing me off from the mainland each day. It was an escape, a cushion for my soul, so that I could come back from it. Melanie needs the same thing."

Jack listened to him and started to really understand. "Mel said to carry on with my own life," he said. "She doesn't know how long she'll be gone, and she said I shouldn't wait around for her. How can I think of anyone else, when I'm in love with her?"

"Take each day as it comes," Phillips advised him. "Don't think too far ahead."

They fell into a comfortable silence, and then Jack roused himself again.

"I saw that the new government has done a U-turn on the fracking issue," he said. "All applications have been cancelled indefinitely."

Ryan thought of Hector Farquhar's obtuse remark about events at Holystone being a moot point, and now understood what he meant; he must have already known the government was about to change its position, which was why Bernicia Energy cancelled its meeting with the Parish Council.

"Karen Russell won't be happy," he remarked.

"Everybody else will," Phillips said, and the three men nodded.

"What's the latest with the body you found in the septic tank?" he asked them. "Any new leads?"

Ryan blew out a long breath. "D' you want the good news, or the bad news?"

"I'll take the good news," Jack replied. "I could use a bit."

"All right. The good news is the body has been identified from dental records, and it's definitely Diane Humble. Further good news is that I'm almost certain I know who killed her."

Jack's head whipped around. "That's bloody fast! How—?"

"He's got a nose like a bloodhound, that's how," Phillips intoned.

"The sister," Ryan said simply. "She wanted what Diane had, but couldn't make it happen, so she took it from her—the man, and the boy."

Jack was disgusted. "And none of them know? She's wandering around playing the Good Aunt and the Loving Fiancée, and nobody knows about what she's really done?"

"Nope, and, without evidence, we can't cast any aspersions," Ryan muttered.

"You said, 'without evidence.'"

Ryan nodded. "That's the bad news," he said. "Forensics haven't found a single usable bit of third party DNA that could point towards Diane's killer. We have no idea where she died, specifically, so it's impossible to search for DNA there."

"So much time has passed," Phillips tutted. "It turns my stomach to think that woman will walk off, scot-free, after what she's done."

"We won't give up," Ryan said. "We'll keep searching for the answers, and perhaps the best way is to keep applying pressure. Sabrina Graham will be thinking it's all over, and life can go back to normal. She'll be patting herself on the back, congratulating herself on the 'perfect murder' but, as we all know, there's no such thing. She'll have made a mistake somewhere, some little error she should never have allowed, and it'll trip her up in the end."

"Let's make sure we're there, when it does," Phillips said. "In the meantime, we caught another one."

Ryan turned to him with a raised eyebrow.

"What's that?"

"Control just sent it through," Phillips replied, waggling his phone. "Male, forty-one, already identified as…oh, bugger. We know this feller."

They waited.

"It's Marcus Atherton," he said, with a catch to his voice. "The reporter, from the other day. He's been found dead at home."

Ryan read the report for himself and frowned deeply, remembering his last interaction with the journalist.

Does this have anything to do with The Circle?

He asked himself the same question.

EPILOGUE

Two months later

Holystone was bedecked in Christmas lights, which hung between the cottages and around a tall, central pine tree on the village green. It looked beautiful, and was a fitting backdrop for the celebration of two of their most beloved residents, who were to be married in an evening ceremony in the Pagan tradition. Friends and neighbours turned out for the 'handfasting', scattering petals at the feet of Sabrina and Davie as they made the short journey from the village centre to Lady's Well, where the ceremony would take place. As High Priestess in the village, Sabrina couldn't perform the rites herself, and so another Priestess had been drafted in from a different part of the county, a woman by the name of Jacqui.

The bride wore a long gown of multi-coloured silk beneath a warm red woollen coat, with a matching scarf woven through her curly hair. Layers of necklaces, earrings, bangles and rings completed her signature style but, as they all agreed, today, Sabrina glowed with the kind of happiness that was almost Otherworldly.

"Ready, lass?" Davie asked her.

They stood facing one another on St Paulinus' holy stone, surrounded by a crowd of well-wishers. Fairy lights had been strung between the trees and even those who didn't believe as she did could all agree there was a kind of magic on the air.

"I'm ready, if you are."

He smiled at her, and thought of how strong she'd been over the past couple of months, putting up with all the police badgering over Diane's death. He couldn't understand why they kept asking her the same questions…

It didn't matter now.

All that mattered was that they would spend the rest of their lives making one another happy.

The High Priestess began to speak, and a long woven cord of different coloured ribbon was bound around their hands as they agreed to love, honour and respect one another "until their love ends" which was, he hoped, a very long way off.

"Nicholas? Do you have the silver cord?"

It was a tradition for a member of the family to knot each cord and present some kind of 'gift', for example the gift of wisdom. In this case, Nick thought he had found the best possible gift, which would be a surprise to both of them.

"Yes, I have it here."

Davie and Sabrina exchanged a happy smile, not having realised Nick had colluded with the High Priestess to offer such a meaningful addition to their ceremony.

He stepped forward and presented a slim gold chain, from which dangled a band of yellow gold topped in diamonds.

Davie recognised it immediately.

So did Sabrina.

"I remember you said you'd lost a ring that was important to you," Nick said to his friend. "Well, you'll never guess, but our Mia found this just the other day when we were round for dinner. It had fallen beneath the floorboards in your apartment," he said, turning to Sabrina, whose face was deathly pale. "I don't know how it found its way under there, but, anyway, Mia was jumping around and thought she'd broken the floor—bless her. It turns out the floorboard was loose. Remind me to tighten that up, for you," he added, with a smile.

"Show me," Davie said, in an odd voice. "Show me the ring, Nick."

The younger man looked between them and felt a creeping sense of unease.

"I—I'm sorry," he said. "Isn't this the ring you meant? You described it so well so, when we found it, we thought it was the same one and that you'd want to give it to Sabrina. I thought it would be a nice surprise—"

Davie, whose hands were still bound to the woman standing before him, stared as the chain was lifted high enough for him to see the intricate detail on the antique ring that had once belonged to his grandmother.

His eyes slid over to look deep, deep into Sabrina's, and he saw what he'd missed before.

They were black, and hard.

"What does the inscription say on the underside, Nick?" he said softly.

"Should I carry on?" the High Priestess asked.

"What does it *say*?" Davie shouted, and a hush came upon the crowd.

"I—it says—"

Nick stumbled to a halt, and raised his eyes to stare at Sabrina, as if seeing her for the first time.

"*For my only love*," she spat. "That's what it says."

Her nails turned into claws and she tore herself free of the cords, no longer the woman they'd known but a stranger.

"Well?" she challenged them both. "Isn't that what it says?"

"You know it is," Davie said. "My grandfather gave it to my grandmother, and I gave it to Diane. She kept it on that chain around her neck at all times. How did you come upon it, Sabrina?"

There was only one answer to that.

She could have come up with some lie, something he'd accept for the sake of his own sanity, but she simply didn't have the energy. Twenty years was long enough to hide her true feelings, and she was certain the police knew or suspected something, anyway. They'd visited her every week since the body was discovered, always unannounced, and she wasn't fool enough not to know it was a shakedown tactic.

They'd find something, sometime, and she didn't want to wait around never knowing when that sometime might be.

She raised her eyes and looked around the villagers, then threw back her head and laughed.

"None of you knew a thing," she declared. "You're all so bloody nosy, but none of you suspected a thing, did you?" She raked venomous eyes over the man she'd almost married. "Especially not *you*," she cackled. "What a joke."

"You killed my mother." Nick's voice trembled, and his hands curled into tight fists.

Sabrina looked around her at the mossy floor before answering.

"Yes," she said simply. "Not far from where you're standing, as it happens."

Nick looked at his feet, imagining his mother's final moments, the fear, the horror...

"*Evil*," he whispered. "You're *evil*! I thought you loved us! I thought you were—were—"

"What?" she taunted him. "Mother to my sister's bastard son? Grandmother to your meddling little—"

Davie caught him before Nick could land the first blow, while others rushed forward to help.

"Get her out of here," Davie told them. "Call the police."

The two men stood there as the petals were swept away on the cold night breeze, and then Nick crouched down to touch his fingertips to the soil.

"Here," he whispered. "She said it happened here."

Davie couldn't speak, not yet, but allowed the tears to fall down his weathered cheeks as he thought of a girl who'd splashed in the waters there, and then walked with him and lain with him as a woman beneath the stars.

"She'll never be alone," he managed to choke out. "Not any more. Not now that we know—we know what happened. This was always a special place for us."

"For us, too," Nick remembered, thinking of the times he'd walked with his mother collecting pine cones or holly for a wreath.

He stood up and faced his friend, and the truth he should have realised long before.

"Sabrina said 'bastard son'. What did she mean by that?"

Davie turned to look at him, at the tall, decent man he'd had the privilege to create with the woman he'd loved.

"You're mine," he said simply. "You were always mine and hers, never his. Never any part of him."

Nick stumbled forward and was caught in his father's arms, which had held him many times before but now felt like the first time.

"I used to pretend it was true," he admitted. "I used to pretend you were my dad, not Fred Humble."

"Neither of us need to pretend any more."

"What now?" Nick asked, knuckling tears from his eyes. "Where do we go from here?"

Davie smiled. "I could use a pint."

"*Watering Hole*?"

"Aye, lead on."

AUTHOR'S NOTE

Thank you very much to my wonderful family and friends for their unstinting support during the writing of this book, which was much interrupted by illness but nonetheless managed to become my twenty-fourth consecutive Amazon UK number one bestseller. Many thanks to all the readers who have offered kind messages of goodwill and who were so patient in waiting a couple of months longer than expected; your thoughtfulness has been much appreciated.

Thanks must go to three special people, all of whom have characters named after them in this book. They are: Lynn Gibbins, a recipient of one of my big Christmas giveaways, who bagged a named character as her prize last year; Christine Harvey, whose husband donated a very kind sum to benefit Shelter UK, the homelessness charity we supported with the release of a charity anthology, *Everyday Kindness*, as well as a charity auction, which included a named character in one of my books; and, last but by no means least, Karen Russell, whose family likewise donated a kind sum to benefit Shelter UK and who is, I'm told, a very lovely person in real life and whose permission was kindly received to be written as a 'bit of a baddie' by contrast on these fictional pages! I am grateful to all of you for lending your names, and I hope it has brought a smile to see yourselves immortalised on the pages.

Special thanks to Emily Harris, who helped me to research the history surrounding Lady's Well—it was much appreciated! If you ever need any caramelised nuts, you know where to go (if you know, you know).

The real village of Holystone in Northumberland is indeed as beautiful and quaint as I have tried to describe it. Lady's Well is also a very real place looked after by the National Trust, which you can visit if you are in the area. However, it should be noted that, for the purposes of this fictional story, some small changes were made to the 'feel' of the village—for instance, various small businesses and a pub have been added which do not exist.

Likewise, on the topic of 'fracking', please be assured there is no fracking in the Coquet Valley, nor will there be, not only owing to its geological status but because fracking has been paused indefinitely under the most recent government shake-up. It is true, however, that fracking policy has changed back and forth under successive premierships in the UK and this is one aspect I have reflected in my fictional storyline.

Regarding the history Ian Bell's character relies upon, much of this was inspired by 'true' events; it is generally accepted that St. Paulinus did accompany Princess

Æthelburga to Northumberland for her marriage to Edwin in 625A.D., but the thousands of baptisms are recorded as happening two years later, in 627A.D. during Easter Week, so there is no explicit mention of Paulinus and Æthelburga stopping off at St. Ninian's Well, or the 'Holy Well' when they made their journey north. Likewise, the story of the stolen dowry is fictional, although the Staffordshire Hoard and, of course, the discoveries made at Sutton Hoo are quite real. Finally, there was a summer palace at Ad Gefrin (Yeavering) as well as an Iron Age fort at the summit of Yeavering Bell. According to my research, gatherings did happen at Yeavering, including baptisms in the River Glen, although there is no specific mention of a marriage celebration having occurred in the manner I've suggested. Yeavering and Yeavering Bell, both near Wooller, should definitely be added to any visit you plan to make to that part of North Northumberland, because both are beautiful landscapes and well worth seeing for yourself.

I hope you've enjoyed this instalment of Ryan & Co…

Until the next time.

LJ ROSS
FEBRUARY 2023

DCI Ryan will return in

DEATH ROCKS

A DCI RYAN MYSTERY

Turn the page for an exclusive sneak peek . . .

DEATH ROCKS – CHAPTER 1

Saturday, 23rd March

Northumberland

Of all the ruined castles of Northumberland, Dunstanburgh reigned supreme.

In the seven centuries since its foundations were first laid, walls had crumbled and wood rotted away with the winds that swept in with the relentless tide of the North Sea, but the fortress remained; rugged and magnificent atop its craggy headland, an imposing reminder that it would endure, long after the people who trampled over its remains were dead and gone.

Roger Aitken thought of this, and of his own mortality, as he approached the thirteenth tee of the Dunstanburgh Castle Golf Course. The course was situated to the north of the castle complex, and ran parallel to the sea, affording a beautiful view of Gull Crag—a sheer, vertical rockface that had once been a natural defence for the castle's northern perimeter, but was now a protected heritage site for birds and other sea life.

He paused, resting lightly against the club he carried, and lifted his head to the salty breeze that rolled in from the sea, which glimmered in the morning sunshine.

"It's a pretty sight, isn't it?" He nodded to another club member, Pete, who caught him up after a successful putt on the twelfth.

"Aye, it never gets old," he said, smiling proudly at the towering edifice that rose up like a mythical Camelot. "Makes you wonder what medieval soldiers thought, when they first caught sight of those walls."

"Probably wet themselves," the other man said, and wheezed a hearty laugh. "That's if they made it halfway up those rocks, or the hill on the other side, without gettin' an arrow between the eyes first."

The two men chatted for a while longer, exchanging mild gossip about who would be the next Men's Team Captain after old Kev's retirement. Naturally, both denied any interest whatsoever in taking up the role themselves, before Roger declared it was time he was getting along, while thinking privately that it was also high time he started canvassing for votes back at the clubhouse.

"Watch the crosswind on the thirteenth," Pete advised. "It's unlucky for some!"

Roger narrowed his eyes against the glare of the sun, breathed in the crisp air, and took a shot that landed within a foot of the hole.

"Not for me," he winked. Laughing at Pete's good-natured expletive, he sauntered towards the green, swinging the putter lightly in one hand while he looked out across the bay immediately to his left. It was known locally as 'Death Rocks', or 'Boulder Bay', on account of its large basalt rocks, which were dangerously slippery and had been the cause of many an unfortunate mishap over the years.

As he neared the green, he positioned himself and wiggled his hips for good measure, preparing to tap the ball into the hole. Before he could, there came a piercing shriek from one of the gulls circling the skies overhead, loud enough to break his concentration.

"Stupid birds," he muttered, and looked up to find an unusual number of them circling a spot near the edge of the course, where the long grass met the rocky shoreline.

Thinking it was likely to be a dead fish or some other carrion, Roger turned his attention back to the ball sitting neatly on the grass in front of him.

But the sound of the gulls continued, their cacophony only seeming to grow louder.

Unable to focus, he abandoned his putter on the ground and stomped towards the edge of the course, intending to chuck something to clear the flock and send them flapping elsewhere. He held up a hand to shield his eyes and peered across the dinosaur egg-shaped rocks to a spot a hundred yards away, where at least twenty gulls formed a cluster of excited, greedy chatter. It was impossible to see what they feasted upon, but, given their number, he assumed it was something larger than the usual wayward crab.

He cupped his hands and gave a loud shout.

It startled the birds for a moment, sending a few of them flapping up into the sky with an indignant cry, only to settle again within a matter of seconds.

Seconds was all he needed to catch sight of something colourful—and distinctly human.

A jacket? Trousers?

His skin prickled, a slow feeling of dread that crept along his spine.

Then, the gulls shifted, and he saw something else; something that could not be mistaken.

A hand.

The remains of a face.

"Everythin' all right, Roger? You look as if you've seen a ghost!"

Pete's voice called to him across the green, and with slow, careful steps, Roger backed away from the edge of the course, swallowing hard against the bile that lodged in his throat.

"Whatsamatter, man?" his friend puffed, having jogged the short distance between them. "You're not havin' a stroke, are you?"

Roger shook his head. "No," he muttered. "No…it's—it's over there, on the rocks. I think there's a body."

Pete's face registered comical shock. "A *body*? Are you sure?"

Roger nodded, and passed a shaking hand over his face as he tried to dispel the image.

"Maybe someone just turned their ankle, or banged their head and can't get up again?"

Pete started to move towards the rocks, but Roger put a staying hand on his arm.

"I'm telling you, the bloke's long gone. We need to call the police, that's what we need to do."

While the two men hurried back towards the clubhouse, the castle looked on, a silent sentinel keeping the secrets of all who passed beneath its shadow.

Available to buy now!

LOVE READING?

JOIN THE CLUB...

Join the LJ Ross Book Club to connect with a thriving community of fellow book lovers! To receive a free monthly newsletter with exclusive author interviews and giveaways, sign up at www.ljrossauthor.com or follow the LJ Ross Book Club on social media:

 @LJRossAuthor

 @ljross_author

ABOUT THE AUTHOR

LJ Ross is an international bestselling author known for her atmospheric mystery and thriller novels, including the DCI Ryan series which has sold over 12 million copies worldwide. Her debut novel *Holy Island* published in 2015 and reached number one in the Amazon UK and Australian digital charts. Louise has since released over thirty novels, most of which have been UK number one digital bestsellers. She is also the creator of the bestselling Dr Alexander Gregory series and the Summer Suspense series. Louise is a keen philanthropist and proud to support numerous non-profit programmes in addition to founding the Lindisfarne Prize for Crime Fiction, the Northern Photography Prize and the Northern Film Prize.

Born in Northumberland, England, she studied Law at King's College, University of London, then abroad in Florence and Paris, and worked as a lawyer before pursuing her dream to write. She lives with her family in Northumberland.

If you would like to get in touch with LJ Ross on social media, please scan the QR code below – she would love to hear from you!

Discover the international bestselling DCI Ryan series from LJ Ross

Atmospheric mysteries set amidst the spectacular landscape of the north east of England.

Discover the 24th novel in the DCI Ryan series...

New for 2026

If you enjoyed this book, why not try the bestselling Alexander Gregory Thrillers by LJ Ross?

Atmospheric thrillers featuring forensic psychiatrist and criminal profiler Dr Alexander Gregory. Loved by readers for the fast-moving and page-turning plots, international locations and shocking twists, with psychology adding fascinating depth to the stories.

Discover now the bestselling Summer Suspense series from LJ Ross

Suspense and mystery are peppered with romance and humour in these fast-paced thrillers set amidst the beautiful landscapes of Cornwall.